WHAT ARE YOU LOOKING AT?

AN ANTHOLOGY OF FAT FICTION

WHAT ARE YOU LOOKING AT?

AN ANTHOLOGY OF FAT FICTION

Edited by Donna Jarrell and Ira Sukrungruang

BLOOMSBURY

First published in 2003 by Harcourt, Inc.
This paperback edition first published in Great Britain 2004

Copyright © 2003 by Donna Jarrell and Ira Sukrungruang

The permissions acknowledged on p 265-7 constitute an extension
of this copyright page

The moral right of the authors has been asserted

Bloomsbury Publishing Plc, 38 Soho Square, London W1D 3HB

A CIP catalogue record for this book is available from the British Library

ISBN 0 7475 7341 7

10 9 8 7 6 5 4 3 2 1

All paper used by Bloomsbury Publishing is a natural, recyclable product made
from wood grown in well-managed forests. The manufacturing processes
conform to the environmental regulations of the country of origin

Printed in Great Britain by Clays Ltd, St Ives plc

www.bloomsbury.com

Contents

Acknowledgments

We'd like to acknowledge our mentors and friends who, from conception, provided invaluable feedback and support for this project: Brenda Jo Brueggemann, E. J. Levy, Stephen Kuusisto, and Bill Roorbach. Special thanks to Bob Mecoy and Ann Patty, whose faith in fat as a viable issue has delivered this book to the public. We'd also like to express our appreciation to Julian Haynes, whose gentle prodding kept us on schedule. And last but not least, we acknowledge our inspiration—the large people whose pain and joy are represented on the pages within: this one's for you.

Introduction

fat ('fat) n. **1a.** The ester of glycerol and one, two, or three fatty acids ... **2.** Obesity; corpulence. **3.** The best or richest part: *living off the fat of the land.* **4.** Unnecessary excess: *"would drain the appropriation's fat without cutting into education's muscle"* (*New York Times*).

adj: Inflected forms: **fat·ter, fat·test 1.** Having much or too much fat or flesh; plump or obese. **2.** Full of fat or oil; greasy. **3.** Abounding in desirable elements. **4.** Fertile or productive; rich· *"It was a fine, green, fat landscape"* (Robert Louis Stevenson). **5.** Having an abundance or amplitude; well-stocked: *a fat larder.* **6a.** Yielding profit or plenty; lucrative or rewarding: *a fat promotion.* **b.** Prosperous; wealthy: *grew fat on illegal profits.* **7a.** Thick; large: *a fat book.* **b.** Puffed up; swollen: *a fat lip.*
        —*American Heritage Dictionary of the English Language,* Fourth Edition

We each, Donna and Ira, had one—a day of reckoning, a *voilà* moment, of looking into a mirror and realizing we were big, large, oversized; not just a little overweight like we'd been telling ourselves for years. No. We were **fat**. Of course, we had known we were **fat**—"puffed up; swollen." We had known we were corpulent, encumbered with excess flesh; we had known we were outcasts, the butt of jokes. We had known we were lovers of food. We had known we weren't attractive in the capitalistic, commercial all-American way of our sports heroes and movie stars. What we didn't know was that we were *fat*!

We were "abounding in desirable elements...[the] best or richest part...prosperous...[and] having an abundance." And oh, the disbelief. We returned to the mirror. Touched the sag under our chins. Lifted up our bellies. Watched them squiggle and wiggle. Poked them. "I am fat," we each said. Fat had become a mere fact about us, one of our characteristics, like blond hair or brown eyes, like Thai or American.

Before long we were remarking on body size aloud, indeed in front of others. We felt less encumbered, free from the power of the humor at our expense, content to be, in the bodies that belonged to us:

MOM: [careful not to use the word fat] Donna! That dress makes you look so large.

DONNA: Mother! I am large!

Or in a crowded office space:

IRA: Careful now, you're about to have an encounter with this belly.

Nothing about our bodies had changed. We still carried excess pounds, but we had lost "weight," head weight. We were lighter. We felt the lightness—in our artery-clogged hearts, coursing through our sugar-infested veins. We had shed the mentality that had given fat the power to determine our identities; the power to make us feel less than and ashamed, as if fat itself was a character deficiency that diminished our ability to engage in meaningful relationships or participate in sports and recreation. As fat persons, we were required to be invisible, to be seen and not heard.

We met in grad school, and our mutual fatness drew us into a friendship. We shared fat experiences, talked about seat belts that wouldn't fasten and clothes that wouldn't fit, scales that wouldn't move no matter how little we ate, and the shame of our parents and children over our size. As writers, we became interested in how fat people—the fat experience—was portrayed in literature. After two years of research, guess what we found? Skinny people writing about fat (at least skinny by our scales)! Fat people writing about fat! Lots of people writing about fat! "Fat" has earned its way into the realm of human conditions that concern literary artists.

In selecting fat fiction and poetry from the sweeping work available, we searched for works of notable literary merit—structurally, intellectually, poetically, and emotionally complex—but more importantly, works that illustrate the range of "fat" experience.

Frederick Busch opens with a story about two brothers and their battle with life and their stomachs; Junot Díaz's "The Brief Wondrous Life of Oscar Wao" is a heartbreaking and hilarious tale of an overweight Dominican from New Jersey; the poet Wesley McNair imagines a fat heaven; Andre Dubus tells the story of a woman more comfortable in a fat body than in her new skinny one. In Jill McCorkle's story, Lydia copes with losing her husband and her body; Rhoda B. Stamell writes about a fat man's obsession with a peculiar woman; Allison Joseph speaks of how other women react to a "Full Figure"; Erin McGraw unfolds the story of Father Murray who eats candy bar after candy bar to sustain a higher hunger; Conrad Hilberry gives us a little girl who imagines her fat as something forced on her in a dark car; Stephen Dunn muses on the political base of a fat dwarf; Peter Carey imagines a fat man revolution in his surrealistic tale, "The Fat Man in History"; Katherine Riegel's alter ego, Katya, dreams about being a sumo; the speaker in Jack Coulehan's poem finds sympathy for "The Six Hundred Pound Man"; Rebecca Curtis writes about a waitress and her overweight therapist; Dorothy Allison connects food and love in her poem "Dumpling Child"; Vern Rutsala inverts the cultural condemnation of fat; and George Saunders writes about the sad life of "The 400-pound CEO." In S. L. Wisenberg's short story, "Big Ruthie Imagines Sex without Pain." Pam Houston's characters literally stuff their cat with love; Terrance Hayes explores the metaphors of hugeness; Denise Duhamel finds someone who can love her thighs; J. L. Haddaway gives us what fat girls really dream about; Sharon Solwitz explores the life of a ballerina. Donna Jarrell provides readers with "The Displaced Overweight Homemaker's Guide to Finding a Man." In Patricia Goedicke's poem, "Weight Bearing," an obese Kiowa Native American is starving for inspiration on the reservation. Tobias Wolff's "Hunters in the Snow" end up bonding over pancakes; Cathy Smith-Bowers writes about a traveling fat lady; in Rawdon Tomlinson's story, "Fat People at the Amusement Park" defy gravity; Monica Wood's character swims down to nothing; and Raymond Carver writes of a "puffing" fat man, who speaks of himself in the plural.

Literature is in a unique position to narrate the fat life. The authors we have selected bring you fatness in defeat and glory. This anthology is not intended to celebrate size but to celebrate self-acceptance; to acknowledge, matter-of-factly, our human value in spite of our human condition.

—DONNA JARRELL AND IRA SUKRUNGRUANG

Extra Extra Large

What the hell, try it once or twice. Lust after everyone. Live in a sexual lather awhile. Dine on the double veal rib, the lobster fricassee, the quail. Drink Latour. And order *dessert*. Baby: order anything you want. Baby: order everything.

Bernie and I look like nearly identical twins, from time to time. He's the one with the more attractively broken-looking nose. He has a strong bald head, sloping shoulders, long arms and wide hands. His legs, if you were fitting them into designer jeans, aren't quite as long as fashion might require. He cocks his bearded chin (more chestnut, less gray, than mine) and raises his slightly more peaky brows, and he sights at you down his nose—like a boxer, calculating when to duck his chin, when to pop you with the jab.

If you took my brother for a fading, spreading middleweight, you'd think of me as a heavyweight working to drop down a class. Bernie insisted I was reducing because of happiness in love.

"Believe me," I told him, "it might be love, but it isn't any pleasure."

Bernie was under stress of his own, but it made him expand. He looked swollen with vitality, pink and broad and fit for coping. He wasn't vital, coping, or fit. As his waist widened and mine declined, as his face broadened and mine diminished, our heavy heads and thick whiskers, large nose, small eyes mounted by brows that look like accent marks in a foreign language, matched each other's as our bodies did.

I thought this as we sat in Bernie's living room, in his little house in the bright countryside that rings suburban Philadelphia. We were part of the litter of the night before, I thought, two lightly sweating, pale, hungover men who rubbed our brows, took our glasses off and wiped them on the tails of our shirts—to no avail: the spots were in, not on, our vision—and nursed at light beer, waiting to feel better. The beer tasted thin and fizzy, and I kept thinking, while I watched him considering me, We'll both be *fifty* one of these days!

Bernie nodded judiciously. His lips frowned in evaluation and then turned up in approval. He said, "Bill, you're looking good."

I said, "For a dead person."

"You keep up the regimen," he said, "and you'll be svelte. Does Joanne make sandwiches for you, with bean sprouts in them, on homemade whole-wheat bread? You're so *lucky*. Does she nag you to drink mineral water and kiss your earlobes when you push your plate away?"

"This is a professional woman, Bernie," I said. "This is a lawyer. Instead of a pacemaker, she'll get an egg timer installed. I call her up because I have a sudden need to croon vapid remarks about passion, and she tells me, 'Bill, I don't have *time*.'"

"Well," he said, "it's tough for women in the law. The guys are waiting for them to make a mistake. They call it the Affirmative Action Grace Period—usually it's about five minutes long, I hear."

"No, she's good. They wanted her. They use her for the tough cases. Felony drug stuff. She's mean. She can be."

"And this is the person you're making a physical comeback for?"

I said, "How do *you* pick the women you love?"

"Right," he said. "Pow. You're right."

"I'm sorry, kid."

"No," he said, "you're right. There's Rhonda checking me out—long distance, of course—for one more open wound to lay the salt in, and I'm telling you how to pick lovers."

"You realize something? I'm forty-four years old. You're forty."

"Possibly," he said.

"And we're sitting around here in boxer shorts, talking about the dangers of *dating*. We— Bern: we ought to maybe grow *up*."

He closed his eyes above the soft, dark skin of their sockets, and he slowly nodded his head.

"You'll get through this, Bern," I said.

"Oh, of course," he said. He opened his eyes, and I couldn't meet them. "And you," he said, "you'll get through your— your—"

"—happiness," I said.

Showered and changed, I sat in the car as Bernie made the ritual inspection. Our father had always done this when one of us drove off—the pausing to prod with a toe, but not kick, each tire; the squinting at belts and pipes and filters under the hood. Bernie even checked my oil by wiping the dipstick on his fingers, his fingers on his pants. Then he gently lowered the hood and latched it, smiling his assurances with our father's expression of grave pleasure.

"Looks like everything's under there," he said, coming to my window. He leaned in, and we kissed each other's bearded cheek. Bernie patted my face as he withdrew. I made for I-95, climbing north and east, leaving Bernie to his heat, his solitude, his turn-of-the-century woodwork, his turn-of-this-century's architecture software and computer. I thought of how you aren't supposed to die of, starve for, fatten on behalf of, or mime Linda Ronstadt songs about, love. Yet I was consuming too few calories for comfort and strength, I was groaning situps on the clammy floor of my apartment, because of what I thought of as love.

And Bernie was going the other way, and because of a dark, intense and brilliant woman named Rhonda, who, with real sadness, I think, and with a regret that hurt Bernie as much as her determination, had left. Someone hugs a middle-aged man, or suffers him to seize at her, while someone else gives him back the house keys, and hundreds of pounds of American flesh begin to shift.

I stopped on the road at one of those joints that tried to look like another of those joints. I ordered the garden salad under plastic, and a diet soda. I ate in the car so I wouldn't smell the hamburgers frying. I sighed, like a man full of salted potatoes. What I wanted to do was go back inside and call Bernie up and ask him if he remembered the time that our father's heart, swollen and beating unreliably, and independent of our father's needs, had first been diagnosed. Bernie, from his high school's public phone, had called me at college.

He'd said Dr. Lencz's name, and that occasioned a long and difficult silence into which we breathed wordless telephone noises for relief. He'd been the doctor who attended our mother. He'd helped us be born, visited our school-day sickbeds, torn out our tonsils, lectured us on sexually communicated diseases, eased our mother—mercy-killed her, Bernie once said he suspected—and now he was fingering our father's flawed heart.

In the silence and static, I in New Hampshire and he in New York each knew what we thought: things could look up awhile, with doctors, but then they always come down. I'd traveled home by bus, I'd met him secretly at the Port Authority—he'd liked it, I remembered, that we were both playing hooky—and then, taking turns with my overnight bag, we'd stalked our father.

What can you do when you fear the man you know you can't protect, and whom you seek to shelter from his own internal organs? We needed to be underneath his skin, yet we sought to avoid his mildest displeasure. I usually called him sir. Bernie still called him Daddy. And we followed him.

Since he was at his office, we ended up standing on lower Broadway, or pacing in front of Trinity Church's wrought iron fence. At the lunch hour, we trailed him to a Savarin and watched him prod what seems now to have been poached fish. We trailed him back to his office building and watched him into his elevator car. I was broad and strong, pimple-faced, with a head of dark hair. Bernie was only slightly shorter than I, but very lean, his face full of shadows. We talked little, looked at everything, and waited until half past five, when our father emerged, one of hundreds of men there in dark blue Brooks Brothers suits and gleaming black wingtips. "Never wear brown shoes with blue," he'd warned me when I left for college, "and treat every woman with reverence." We watched his dark fedora as it rode on the large bald head that was fringed in the same pattern, I thought while I drove, as Bernie's and mine.

We pushed and pulled at each other on the rush hour subway, we instructed each other in the tradecraft of spies, his learned from TV shows, mine from the Geoffrey Household novel I'd read on the bus. At home, once we let him enter, then made our announcement of intentions, he seemed pale, weak, thin, pleased, and unsurprised. He sat in his shirt and tie while I fried the liver I'd instructed Bernie to buy. Somebody's mother, maybe even mine, had said that liver gave you strength. We sat, then, not eating, to watch our father try to chew what amounted to everything we could offer him. The sum of our courage and ability, all we could assay, was on that thistle-pattern platter from Stengl of Flemington, New Jersey—gristly, charred, oily, raw. And what he gave us in return, I wanted to say to Bernie, was his serious attention to the inedible. He let us, in our fright, push him around a little, as he pushed the liver around on his plate, bending his identical head to what we had served.

Bernie's Rhonda was tired, she had said. She was in her thirties, and too young to be so tired, she had said. She was afraid that Bernie tuckered her out by *needing* so much. "What else do you love people for?" Bernie had asked me during our weekend. We'd been walking into an art theater to watch the Truffaut film made from the Henry James story where Truffaut rants for about two hours. Good ranting, by the way: I could still remember the rhythms, and the splendid woman who loved him unrequited. "*Need,*" Bernie had said as he bought our tickets. "*Love* is need."

That made sense. I thought of my daughter, Brenda, and her distant mother, removed once by divorce, then twice by remarriage. We'd been a case of need overstated, and surely our child (whose specialty these days was *under*stating need) had chosen Columbia for college because of something like a requirement for me, since I and Columbia lived in the same city. Or so I insisted. And then there was Joanne, just this side of structural steel, but happy with me, at least often, I often thought. And surely you had to *need* somehow to hang around an older man if you were young and trim and flourishing among the other assistants in the office of the Manhattan district attorney. If Joanne's schedule and attention sometimes implied other needs, I forgave them, in light of my lack of any choice. Kissing my *earlobes*, Bernie?

On the other hand, I thought, picturing him as poised in mid-chew to answer me, eating too much is need, and drinking too much, driving too quickly on Route 95, overcharging on the American Express card, or simply saying her name in despair as you reach, in the early morning, on the living room floor—your hands clasped, like a prisoner of war's, behind your head—to touch your straining elbows to your knees. Actually, Truffaut did requite her love. But it was awfully close to the end, and I thought she'd deserved far better.

Postcard, in early autumn, from Bernie to me:

B—
Am currently designing condos for the erotically deficient—no bedrooms, but two kitchens. All of course is well.

B

All wasn't, of course. I wanted to call. I also didn't. Two nights later, while Joanne worked late, I telephoned. I held the Arshile Gorky postcard—*The Betrothed,* this serious incomprehensibility was called—when I punched out his number; I looked at the painting, and not Bernie's words, when I spoke.

"Bern, how's it going?"

"*Ça va*. Lots of *va*. Except, it seems I apparently called up Rhonda one night. On the phone."

"And she didn't tell you she was pleased."

"No."

"You didn't expect her to."

"No."

"She hung up on you?"

"Worse," he said. "She let her breath out very, very, very slowly. It was like listening to the Goodyear Blimp deflate. On and on and on and on, and then she said in that control voice of hers, the I'm-trying-to-land-all-these-jumbo-jets-at-one-*time* voice, she says, 'What, Bernie?' You know what I mean? Just 'What' and just 'Bernie.' I mean, what in hell am I supposed to *say*?"

"What *did* you say?"

"I puled."

"Well, you picked the right phone call for it."

"This is true. I was on target."

"What'd you say, Bern?"

"I believe I said. 'Oh, Rhonda.'"

"Damn."

"Yeah. I wanted, see, to make sure I didn't have any pride or anything sloshing around in the tank."

"No, I think you got it all."

"Any honor or pride or anything," he said.

"Did she answer you?"

"She waited a very long time, and then she whispered. Like a mother."

I said, "Like you were young and she was extremely old."

"You got the one," he said. "You ever do this before?"

"I wrote the lyrics and the music for it."

"Yeah," he said, "I guess we all do some supplicating now and then."

"But what'd she whisper to you?"

"'Please,'" he whispered.

"And then she hung up."

"Really gently. No rattle or bang, just the little click. I kept listening to the phone. She sounded *good* to me, Billy."

"You know—"

"You have the solution," he said. "You're on the verge of giving me the solution, aren't you?"

"No, kid."

"No."

I said, "You want to come up to New York for a while?"

"Later. One of these days I'll come in, maybe you can get tickets for something. We can take Joanne to the Stadium, she can watch a team play ball without being distracted by winning. You believe this, Billy? A couple of middle-aged guys who *go* through this?"

"We're late bloomers," I said, "it's not our fault."

"You're still starving yourself?"

"I'm being pretty good," I said. "I don't mean anything smug."

"*Be* smug. Listen: I am almost out of the Lands' End catalogue for pants. They don't believe in creatures of my proportion."

"You talk about guys like us, Bern," I said, "you're talking *about* proportion. Come on. You think Captain Marvel was sized Medium? Samson?"

"Even Delilah," he said.

"Atta boy."

I usually called Brenda's mother Susan Hayward because she made me feel and probably look like Victor Mature as Samson, pulling down the temple of the Philistines. Joanne and I were taking Susan Hayward's child and mine to an opening at a gallery on Greene Street. The artist was a man who had left off practicing law to get a degree in painting, and who taught around where he could—Sarah Lawrence, Cooper Union, NYU—and who, according to Joanne, had fallen in love with his life.

"Shouldn't you love someone else's?" I asked her. I was changing into a sport coat and long-sleeved shirt and tie because Joanne had cabbed down from Yorkville not in her jeans but in her longish black skirt, gray rayon shirt, long black silk scarf, smoky stockings and black half boots. I was angry not with the artist, and not about my clothes or hers, and not even with Joanne. I had simply been reminded once more that it took twenty minutes' cab time for me to see what she wore.

I did not again tonight raise the issue of her moving in. We were scattered all over the place, I thought: Bernie outside Philadelphia, Susan Hayward and her new husband in Maine, Brenda on the Upper West Side at school, Joanne up and east, and I, in no-man's-land, on 16th and Sixth, pulling a necktie tight and thinking that, for all our lighthearted fun, Joanne and I knew a lot about grimness.

She was ignoring me—ignoring my petulance, she'd have said. She sat on my coffee table, a big wooden crate used seventy-five years ago for shipping an Underwood typewriter, and she read the show's announcement.

I said, "I said shouldn't you love other people's lives as well as your own?"

"Well, your own isn't a bad place to start," she said. "Then you can expand the franchise. Being maladjusted's pretty overrated, don't you think, Bill?"

"Of whom do we speak, Jo?"

"Oh," she said, "*I* get it. We're having a fight." She came into the bedroom, smelling of Liz Claiborne's scent, looking (quite correctly) twelve years younger than I. "We're in a huff," she said. She pecked me on the lips, yanked on my necktie, and said, like a stiff, wary man, "Of *whom* do we speak?"

"Successful young artists make me insecure."

"Meeting your daughter makes you insecure."

"You make me insecure."

She cocked her head, considering my fear, or me, or both.

Brenda came into the gallery shortly after Joanne introduced me to the artist. He was in his early thirties, craggy, with thick, copper-colored hair, and he was possibly in love with

Joanne. He looked somehow elegant in his clay-colored cotton pants (and they were well within the parameters of the Land's End catalogue) and a thick dark corduroy sport coat the color of wet stones; he hastened to find us drinks, he sought to somehow be of service, he was cordial and reticent at once.

I said to Joanne, "You call *that* well adjusted?"

She stared up from under her ample eyebrows with large, dark eyes. "I call him Nicholas," she said.

I took a sip of Perrier.

"And sometimes I call him Nick."

I watched Brenda, long-legged in a metallic-silver miniskirt over silver tights, her hair a color of yellow I couldn't name and fluffed as if someone had rubbed it the wrong way so often that static electricity held it erect. The makeup under her eyes made her face look bruised. "My former child," I said, watching her stalk to us.

Brenda said, "Hi, Joanne. Hi, Bill."

"What would it take for you to call me Daddy?" I asked. But I hugged her hard, and she did hug back. "Baby," I said.

"A low level of sophistication," she answered.

"I *have* that."

Joanne said, "Ah, but your daughter doesn't." They kissed and then left me, Brenda pulling Joanne as if Joanne were her guest. Over her shoulder, Brenda said, "See you soon, Daddy," then laughed to Joanne as if they both knew the joke.

Nicholas returned with a little sandwich on a napkin. "Smoked salmon," he said, "capers, lemon juice—good food. The bread's from Dean and Deluca." As he gently laid the napkin and sandwich on the palm of my hand, bending his head to the chore as if performing minor surgery, I was filled with resistance. I felt like an elder being shown good care by a child. But I also, still, thought of surgery: what, I wondered, were we going to cut out.

"Nice," I agreed, not eating. "And a nice show, by the way. Congratulations. The idea of spraying through the wire forms, the patterns on top of the stained canvas—really interesting."

"You really like it," he said.

"Well, yes. I really do."

He nodded and beamed. His teeth were even and white, of course. "Jo told me you were a really fair guy. A really decent guy, she said."

"Decent?"

His big handsome head bobbed quickly with relief. *Relief,* god dammit.

"About what, Nick?"

"What?"

"About what things am I said to be decent? The refusal of the Yankees to be patient with young pitching? The city's insistence on making carriage horses wear canvas diapers? Or somebody snogging my woman."

"Snogging," he said.

"I didn't want to start at too basic a level, but fine: screwing, Nick. Didn't your parents explain these things to you when you were small?"

"Jo *hasn't* talked to you, then."

"I don't know that she needs to, now."

He moved his hands as if to help me pour some language out. But I was jamming my finger sandwich into my mouth. I was chewing and pulping and sliding the slimy sandwich down. I saw Jo and Brenda across the long, pale, chilly room ringed with colors sprayed in geometric patterns. They were watching us, I realized. So Brenda, probably, also knew. I saw how much like the Susan Hayward of Portland, Maine, my daughter looked.

"Okay," I said to him as the sandwich paused beneath my breastbone. "Good pictures. Striking pictures. You probably have a mildly guilty conscience, and you probably give money to street people when they ask. All right. But I wish you'd have stuck to loving *yourself.* He humps best who humps his own. You bastard."

Bernie, on the telephone, said, "You left it at that?"

"I figured, why not take impotence as far as I could, Bern."

I was in my apartment, and it was late. I held a package of fig newtons in my left hand as if it were a loaded, cocked gun. My former lover and my former child were wherever in New York they'd got to without me. The fig newtons weren't open yet.

Bernie said, "The husband's the last to know. Or boyfriend, whatever."

"I knew."

"How long?"

"Don't ask."

"So—look: Billy. Consider that at least you don't have to wait until she moves her clothes and furniture out. You don't have to sit there and watch her do it with what's his name."

"I am blessed."

"It's a small consideration, but I *would* consider it a blessing, yes."

"I'm going to do that." I sat back and laid the cookie packet across my chest.

"And you'll stick to the diet," he said.

"I will?"

"Yeah," he said, "you should do that. I like you trim and healthy."

"And you?"

"Me, too," he said. "Now that we're both miserable, it'll be easier for me."

"I'm glad to help, kid."

"You'll be all right, Billy?"

"You need to go to sleep."

"If you're okay."

"I'm fine. I'll cry tomorrow."

"Who *said* that?"

"Susan Hayward," I said, landing on the punch line with my paws.

I was working on an article about billing practices that I owed the *New York Law Reporter,* and I was reviewing once again the Seven Hundred Signs—the indications I now knew

I'd known I knew that Joanne had showed me over four months, proving we'd been an impermanence from the start. I was also framing a note, drafting something spontaneous, to send Brenda:

> *Here's 20 bucks, baby. Please take a cab instead of the subway from Port Authority to your dorm late at night.*

It didn't ask why she was arriving on buses at dawn, or where the buses were coming from. It didn't go into details about the sullen phone call from Susan Hayward, asking why she, in Maine, knew scary facts about the safety of the child whom I, in New York, should be protecting. I mistakenly wiped out a line about legal accounting procedures for international matters and told the machine to save what was left, and I went downstairs for the Saturday mail.

The warning from American Express about my overdue payments made me, literally, blush. I hated to disappoint the man in Phoenix who had written about my history with the firm. The postcard, addressed in Bernie's hand, made me smile: on fiscal matters, we were co-conspirators. The reproduction on the front of the card was of a graceful, naked Diana by Saint-Gaudens, poised on the ball of her golden left foot, aiming a long-shafted, heavy-headed arrow at Bernie or me. The message:

> *B—*
> *Busted the diet last night with a grown-up woman.*
> *Long-awaited calories did not meet my expectations.*
> *Nor I hers.*
>
> *B*

I went upstairs and fried three eggs in butter and ate three dripping sandwiches. I spent the rest of the afternoon lugging my stomachache from the screen showing the Texas Tech game to the screen that showed me what I'd managed to save.

But Bernie and I, while we are mildly sorrowful people, also, often, are capable adults. Brenda's a whacked-out late-night drifter, but also a college kid with some sense. And her parents do love her. You always manage to pay American Express, and they always forgive you. People try to understand.

So imagine us, then, in Pennsylvania Station—not the arc of iron and glass that Bernie and I knew as boys, but a large enough place for people and trains and their echoes—as we wait for Bernie's arrival on the Washington-to-Philly-to-New York. It's early November. I'm wearing a Burberry lined raincoat that costs as much as a car, and Brenda, hair the color of neon strawberries, in her dark leather fleece-collared bombardier jacket that falls below her hips, with sleeves so long her fingertips barely protrude, looks nothing but terrific. Her mother's face every now and again shows forth, and I can only think, though I never want to say it, *Susan: not so bad.*

Bernie walks toward us, now. He's wearing the khaki fatigue jacket that our father brought home from the service. He's lost enough weight to fasten it over his sport coat, which hangs out. He's closed the jacket as our father did, snapped it and zipped it to the knot of his tie. His toes point outward as he walks, and I can see as if from the less soaring and less gorgeous ceiling how alike we seem in motion and bulk.

As if from that reduced height, I watch Brenda hug his neck and kiss his cheek, and then I watch Bernie and me embrace; our big, though smaller, bellies collide. Brenda walks between us, a little in front of us, impatient, of course. I'm back down now where I ought to be. We're going out to eat. We will watch our step. We'll look at each other, Bernie and I, and we'll see ourselves eat with a little restraint. But I'll insist on a bottle of excellent wine, and we'll take turns, I predict, encouraging Brenda with similar voices in similar tones to ask for anything she wants. Terrine of duck, the sautéed caviar, the hot scallop and avocado salad. "Anything," one of us will say.

The Brief Wondrous Life
of Oscar Wao

Oscar de León was not one of those Dominican cats every-body's always going on about. He wasn't no player. Except for one time, he'd never had much luck with women.

He'd been seven then.

It's true: Oscar was a carajito who was into girls mad young. Always trying to kiss them, always coming up behind them during a merengue, the first nigger to learn the perrito and the one who danced it every chance he got. Because he was a Dominican boy raised in a relatively "normal" Dominican family, his nascent pimp-liness was encouraged by family and friends alike. During the parties—and there were many, many parties in those long-ago seventies days, before Washington Heights was Washington Heights, before the Bergenline became a straight shot of Spanish for almost a hundred blocks—some drunk relative inevitably pushed Oscar onto some little girl, and then everyone would howl as boy and girl approximated the hipmotism of the adults.

You should have seen him, his mother sighed. He was our little Porfirio Rubirosa.

He had "girlfriends" early. (Oscar was a stout kid, heading straight to fat, but his mother kept him nice in haircuts, and be-fore the proportions of his head changed he'd had these lovely flashing eyes and these cute-ass cheeks.) The girls—his older sister's friends, his mother's friends, even his neighbor, a twenty-something postal employee who wore red on her lips and walked like she had a brass bell for an ass—all fell for him. Ese muchacho está bueno! Once, he'd even had two girlfriends at the same time, his only ménage à trois ever. With Maritza Chacón and Olga Polanca, two girls from his school.

The relationship amounted to Oscar's standing close to both girls at the bus stop, some undercover hand holding, and some very serious kissing on the lips, first Maritza, then Olga, while the three of them hid behind some bushes. (Look at that little macho, his mother's friends said. Qué hombre.)

The threesome lasted only a week. One day after school, Maritza cornered Oscar behind the swing set and laid down the law. It's either her or me! Oscar held Maritza's hand and talked seriously and at great length about his love for her and suggested that maybe they could all share, but Maritza wasn't having any of it. Maritza, with her chocolate skin and gray eyes, already expressing the Ogún energy that would chop down obstacles for her the rest of her life. Didn't take him long to decide: after all, Maritza was beautiful, and Olga was not. His logic as close to the yes/no math of insects as a nigger could get. He broke up with Olga the next day on the playground, Maritza at his side, and how Olga cried! Snots pouring out of her nose and everything! In later years, when he and Olga had both turned into overweight freaks, Oscar could not resist feeling the occasional flash of guilt when he saw Olga loping across a street or staring blankly out near the New York bus stop, wondering how much his cold-as-balls breakup had contributed to her present fuckedupness. (Breaking up with her, he would remember, hadn't felt like anything; even when she started crying, he hadn't been moved. He'd said, Don't be a baby.)

What *had* hurt, however, was when Maritza dumped *him*. The Monday after he'd shed Olga, he arrived at the bus stop only to discover beautiful Maritza holding hands with butt-ugly Nelson Pardo. At first Oscar thought it a mistake; the sun was in his eyes, he'd not slept enough the night before. But Maritza wouldn't even smile at him! Pretended he wasn't there. We should get married, she was saying to Nelson, and Nelson grinned moronically, turning up the street to look for the bus.

Oscar was too hurt to speak; he sat down on the curb and felt something overwhelming surge up from his chest, and before he knew it he was crying, and when his sister Lola walked over and asked him what was the matter he shook his head. Look at the mariconcito, somebody snickered. Somebody else kicked his beloved lunchbox. When he got on the bus, still crying, the driver, a famously reformed PCP addict, said, Christ, what a fucking *baby*.

Maybe coincidence, maybe self-serving Dominican hyperbole, but it seemed to Oscar that from the moment Maritza dumped him his life shot straight down the tubes. Over the next couple of years he grew fatter and fatter, and early adolescence scrambled his face into nothing you could call cute; he got uncomfortable with himself and no longer went anywhere near the girls, because they always shrieked and called him gordo asqueroso. He forgot the perrito, forgot the pride he felt when the women in the family had called him hombre. He did not kiss another girl for a long, long time. As though everything he had in the girl department had burned up that one fucking week. Olga caught the same bad, no-love karma. She got huge and scary—a troll gene in her somewhere—and started drinking 151 straight out of the bottle and was taken out of school because she had a habit of screaming NATAS! in the middle of homeroom. Sorry, loca, home instruction for you. Even her breasts, when they finally emerged, were huge and scary.

And the lovely Maritza Chacón? Well, as luck would have it, Maritza blew up into the flyest girl in Paterson, New Jersey, one of the queens of New Peru, and, since she and Oscar were neighbors, he saw her plenty, hair as black and lush as a thunderhead, probably the only Peruvian girl on the planet with curly hair (he hadn't heard of Afro Peruvians yet or of a town called Chincha), body fine enough to make old men forget their infirmities, and from age thirteen steady getting in or out of some roughneck's ride. (Maritza might not have been good at much—not sports, not school, not work—but she was good at boys.) Oscar would watch Maritza's getting in and out all through his cheerless, sexless adolescence. The only things that changed in those years were the models of the cars, the size of Maritza's ass, and the music volting out of the car's speakers. First freestyle, then Special Ed-era hip-hop, and right at the very end, for just a little while, Hector Lavoe and the boys.

Oscar didn't imagine that she remembered their kisses but of course he remembered.

High school was Don Bosco Tech and since Don Bosco Tech was an all-boys Catholic school run by the Salesian Fathers and Brothers and packed with a couple of hundred insecure, hyperactive adolescents it was, for a fat, girl-crazy nigger like Oscar, a source of endless anguish.

Sophomore year Oscar's weight stabilized at about two-ten (two-twenty when he was depressed, which was often), and it had become clear to everybody, especially his family, that he'd become the neighborhood pariguayo. He wore his semikink hair in a Puerto Rican Afro, had enormous Section-8 glasses (his anti-pussy devices, his boys Al and Miggs called them), sported an unappealing trace of mustache, and possessed a pair of close-set eyes that made him look somewhat retarded. The Eyes of Mingus (a comparison he made himself one day, going through his mother's record collection; she was the only old-school Dominicana he knew who loved jazz; she'd arrived in the States in the early sixties and shacked up with morenos for years until she met Oscar's father, who put an end to that particular chapter of the All-African World Party). Throughout high school he did the usual ghettonerd things: he collected comic books, he played role-playing games, he worked at a hardware store to save money for an outdated Apple IIe. He was an introvert who trembled with fear every time gym class rolled around. He watched nerd shows like "Doctor Who" and "Blake's 7," could tell you the difference between a Veritech fighter and a Zentraedi battle pod, and he used a lot of huge-sounding nerd words like "indefatigable" and "ubiquitous" when talking to niggers who would barely graduate from high school. He read Margaret Weis and Tracy Hickman novels (his favorite character was, of course, Raistlin) and became an early devotee of the End of the World. He devoured every book he could find that dealt with the End Times, from John Christopher's "Empty World" to Hal Lindsey's "The Late Great Planet Earth." He didn't date no one. Didn't even come close. Inside, he was a passionate person who fell in love easily and deeply. His affection—that gravitational mass of love, fear, longing, desire, and lust that he directed at any and every girl in the vicinity—roamed across all Paterson, affixed itself everywhere without regard to looks, age, or availability. Despite the fact that he considered his affection this tremendous, sputtering force, it was actually more like a ghost because no girl ever seemed to notice it.

Anywhere else, his triple-zero batting average with the girls might have passed unremarked, but this is a Dominican kid, in a Dominican family. Everybody noticed his lack of game and everybody offered him advice. His tío Rodolfo (only recently released from Rahway State) was especially generous in his tutelage. We wouldn't want you to turn into one of those Greenwich Village maricones, Tío Rodolfo muttered ominously. You have to grab a muchacha, broder, y méteselo. That will take care of everything. Start with a fea. Coge that fea y méteselo! Rodolfo had four kids with three different women, so the nigger was without doubt the family's resident metiéndolo expert.

Oscar's sister Lola (who I'd start dating in college) was a lot more practical. She was one of those tough Jersey Latinas, a girl soccer star who drove her own car, had her own checkbook, called men bitches, and would eat a fat cat in front of you without a speck of vergüenza. When she was in sixth grade, she was raped by an older acquaintance, and surviving that urikán of pain, judgment, and bochinche had stripped her of cowardice. She'd say anything to anybody and she cut her hair short (anathema to late-eighties Jersey Dominicans) partially, I think, because when she'd been little her family had let it grow down past her ass—a source of pride, something I'm sure her rapist noticed and admired.

Oscar, Lola warned repeatedly, you're going to die a virgin.

Don't you think I know that? Another five years of this and I'll bet you somebody tries to name a church after me.

Cut the hair, lose the glasses, exercise. And get rid of those porn magazines. They're disgusting, they bother Mami, and they'll never get you a date.

Sound counsel, which he did not adopt. He was one of those niggers who didn't have any kind of hope. It wouldn't have been half bad if Paterson and its surrounding precincts had been, like Don Bosco, all male. Paterson, however, was girls the way N.Y.C. was girls. And if that wasn't guapas enough for you, well, then, head south, and there'd be Newark, Elizabeth, Jersey City, the Oranges, Union City, West New York, Weehawken—an urban swath known to niggers every-where as Negrapolis One. He wasn't even safe in his own house; his sister's girlfriends were always hanging out, and when they were around he didn't need no *Penthouses*. Her girls were the sort of hot-as-balls Latinas who dated only weight-lifting morenos or Latino cats with guns in their cribs. (His sis-ter was the anomaly—she dated the same dude all four years of high school, a failed Golden Gloves welterweight who was ex-cruciatingly courteous and fucked her like he was playing con-nect the dots, a pretty boy she'd eventually dump after he dirty-dicked her with some Pompton Lakes Irish bitch.) His sis-ter's friends were the Bergen County All-Stars, New Jersey's very own Ciguapas: primera was Gladys, who complained con-stantly about her chest being too big; Marisol, who'd end up in M.I.T. and could out-salsa even the Goya dancers; Leticia, just off the boat, half Haitian, half Dominican, that special blend the Dominican government swears no existe, who spoke with the deepest accent, a girl so good she refused to sleep with three consecutive boyfriends! It wouldn't have been so bad if these girls hadn't treated Oscar like some deaf-mute harem guard; they blithely went on about the particulars of their sex lives while he sat in the kitchen clutching the latest issue of *Dragon*. Hey, he would yell, in case you're wondering, there's a male unit in here. Where? Marisol would say blandly. I don't see one.

Senior year found him bloated, dyspeptic, and, most cruelly, alone in his lack of a girlfriend. His two nerd boys, Al and Miggs, had, in the craziest twist of fortune, both succeeded in landing themselves girls that summer. Nothing special, skanks really, but girls nonetheless. Al had met his at Menlo Park Mall, near the arcade; she'd come on to him, he bragged, and when she informed him, after she sucked his dick, that she had a girl-friend *desperate* to meet somebody, Al had dragged Miggs away from his Atari and out to a movie, and the rest was, as they say, history. By the end of the week, Miggs had his, too, and only then did Oscar find out about any of it, while they were in his room setting up for another "hair-raising" Champions adventure against the Death-Dealing Destroyers. At first, he didn't say much. He just rolled his dice over and over. Said, You guys sure got lucky. Guess I'm next. It killed him that they hadn't thought to include him in their girl heists; he hated Al for inviting Miggs instead of him, and he hated Miggs for getting a girl, period. Al's getting a girl Oscar could comprehend; Al looked completely normal, and he had a nice gold necklace he wore everywhere. It was Miggs's girl-getting that astounded him. Miggs was an even bigger freak than Oscar. Acne galore and a retard's laugh and gray fucking teeth from having been given some medicine too young. What little faith Oscar had in the world took an SS-N-17 Snipe to the head. When, finally, he couldn't take it no more, he asked pathetically, What, these girls don't have any other friends?

Al and Miggs traded glances over their character sheets. I don't think so, dude.

And right there he realized something he'd never known: his fucked-up, comic-book-reading, role-playing, game-loving, no-sports-playing friends were embarrassed by *him*.

Knocked the architecture right out of his legs. He closed the game early—the Exterminators found the Destroyers' hideout right away; that was bogus, Al groused as Oscar showed them the door. Locked himself in his room, lay in bed for a couple of stunned hours, then got up, undressed in the bathroom he no longer had to share because his sister was at Rutgers, and examined himself in the mirror. The fat! The miles of stretch marks! The tumescent horribleness of his proportions! He looked straight out of a Daniel Clowes comic book. Like the fat, blackish kid in Beto Hernández's Palomar.

Jesus Christ, he whispered. I'm a Morlock.

Spent a week looking at himself in the mirror, turned himself every which way, took stock, didn't flinch, and then he went to Chucho's and had the barber shave his Puerto Rican 'fro off, lost the mustache, then the glasses, bought contacts, was already trying to stop eating, starving himself dizzy, and the next time Al and Miggs saw him Miggs said, Dude, what's the matter with you?

Changes, Oscar said pseudo-cryptically.

He, Miggs, and Al were never quite the same friends again. He hung out, saw movies, talked Los Brothers Hernández, Frank Miller, and Alan Moore with them but, over all, he kept his distance. Listened to their messages on the machine and resisted the urge to run over to their places. Didn't see them but once, twice a week. I've been finishing up my first novel, he told them when they asked about his absences.

In December, after all his college applications were in (Fairleigh Dickinson, Montclair, Rutgers, Drew, Glassboro State, William

Paterson; he also sent an application to N.Y.U., a one-in-a-million shot, and they rejected him so fast he was amazed the shit hadn't come back Pony Express) and winter was settling its pale, miserable ass across northern New Jersey, Oscar fell in love with a girl in his S.A.T.-prep class. Ana Acuña was a pretty, loudmouthed gordita who read Henry Miller books while she should have been learning to defeat problem sets. Their fifth class, he noticed her reading "Sexus," and she noticed him noticing and, leaning over, she showed him a passage and he got an erection like a motherfucker.

You must think I'm weird, right? she said, during the break.

You ain't weird, he said. Believe me—I'm the top expert in the state.

Ana was a talker, had beautiful Caribbean-girl eyes, pure anthracite, and was the sort of heavy that almost every Island nigger dug (and wasn't shy about her weight, either), and, like every other girl in the neighborhood, wore tight black stirrup pants and the sexiest underwear she could afford. She was a peculiar combination of badmash and little girl—even before he visited her house, he knew there'd be an avalanche of stuffed animals on the bed—and there was something in the ease with which she switched between these two Anas that convinced him that there existed a third Ana, who was otherwise obscure and impossible to know. She'd got into Miller because her ex-boyfriend Manny had given her the books before he joined the Army. She'd been thirteen when they started dating, he'd been twenty-four, a recovering coke addict—Ana talking about these things like they weren't nothing at all.

You were thirteen and your mother *let* you date some old-ass nigger?

My parents *loved* Manny, she said. My mom used to cook dinner for him.

He said, That's crazy. (And later, at home, he asked his sister, back on winter break, Would you let your thirteen-year-old daughter date some twenty-four-year-old guy? Sure, she snorted, right after they killed me. But they better cut my fucking head off because, believe me, I'd come back from the dead and get them both.)

Oscar and Ana in S.A.T. class, Oscar and Ana in the parking lot afterward, Oscar and Ana at the McDonald's, Oscar and Ana become friends. Each day, Oscar expected her to be adiós, each day she was still there. They got into the habit of talking on the phone a couple times a week, about nothing, really, spinning words out of their everyday; the first time *she* called *him*, offering him a ride to the S.A.T. class; a week later, he called her, just to try it. His heart beating so hard he thought he would die, but all she did was say, Oscar, listen to the *bullshit* my sister pulled, and off they'd go, building another one of their word-scrapers. By the fifth time he called, he no longer expected the Big Blowoff. She was the first girl outside his family who admitted to having a period, who actually said to him, I'm bleeding like a hog, an astounding confidence that he kept turning over and over in his head. Because her appearance in his life was sudden, because she'd come in under his radar, he didn't have time to raise his usual wall of nonsense or throw some wild-ass expectations her way. Maybe, after four years of not getting ass, he'd finally found his zone, because amazingly enough, instead of making an idiot of himself as one might have expected, given the hard fact that this was the first girl he'd ever had a conversation with, he actually took it a day at a time. He spoke to her plainly and without effort, and discovered that his sharp, self-deprecating world view pleased her immensely. He would say something obvious and uninspired, and she'd say, Oscar, you're really fucking smart. When she said, I *love* men's hands, he spread both of his across his face and said faux-casual-like, Oh, *really*? It cracked her up.

Man, she said, I'm glad I got to know you.

And he said, I'm glad I'm me knowing you.

One night while he was listening to New Order and trying to chug through "Clay's Ark," his sister knocked on his door. At Rutgers, she'd shaved her head down to the bone, Sinéad style, and now everybody, including their mother, was convinced she was a jota.

You got a visitor, she said.

I do?

Yup. But you might want to clean up some, she warned.

It was Ana. Standing in his foyer, in full-length leather, her trigueña skin blood-charged from the cold, her face gorgeous with eyeliner, mascara, base, lipstick, and blush.

Freezing out, she said. She had her gloves in one hand like a crumpled bouquet.

Hey, was all he managed to say. He knew his sister was up-stairs, listening.

What you doing? Ana asked.

Nothing.

Like let's go to a movie then.

Like O.K., he said.

When he went upstairs to change, his sister was jumping up and down on his bed, low screaming, It's a date, it's a date, and she jumped onto his back and nearly toppled him clean through the bedroom window.

So is this some kind of date? he said as he slipped into her car.

She smiled wanly. You could call it that.

Ana drove a Cressida, and instead of taking them to the local theatre she headed down to the Amboy Multiplex. It was so hard for Oscar to believe what was happening that he couldn't take it seriously. The whole time the movie was on, Oscar kept expecting niggers to jump out with cameras and scream, Surprise! Boy, he said, trying to remain on her map, this is some movie. Ana nodded; she smelled of a perfume, and when she pressed close the heat of her body was *vertiginous*.

On the ride home, Ana complained about having a head-ache and they didn't speak for a long time. He tried to turn on the radio but she said, No, my head's really killing me. So he sat back and watched the Hess Building and the rest of Woodbridge slide past through a snarl of overpasses. The longer they went without speaking, the more morose he became. It's just a movie, he told himself. It's not like it's a date.

Ana seemed unaccountably sad and she chewed her bottom lip, a real bembe, until most of her lipstick was on her teeth and he was going to make a comment about it, but he decided not to.

I'm reading "Dune," he said, finally.

She nodded. I *hate* that book.

They reached the Elizabeth exit, which is what New Jersey is really known for, industrial wastes on both sides of the turnpike, when Ana let loose a scream that threw him against the door.

Elizabeth! she shrieked. Close your fucking legs! Then she looked over at him, threw back her head, and laughed.

When he returned to the house, his sister said, Well?

Well, what?

Did you *fuck* her?

Jesus, Lola.

Don't lie to me. I know you Dominican men. She held up her hands and flexed the fingers in playful menace. Son pulpos.

The next day he woke up feeling like he'd been unshackled from his fat, like he'd been washed clean of his misery, and for a long time he couldn't remember why he felt this way and then finally he said her name. Little did he know that he'd entered into the bane of nerds everywhere: a let's-be-friends relationship.

In April, Oscar learned he was heading to Rutgers-New Brunswick. You'll love it, his sister promised him. I know I will, he said. I was meant for college. Ana was on her way to Penn State, honors program, full ride. It was also in April that her ex-boyfriend Manny returned from the Army—Ana told Oscar during one of their trips to Yaohan, the Japanese mall in Edgewater. Manny's sudden reappearance and Ana's joy over it shattered the hopes Oscar had cultivated. He's back, Oscar asked, like forever? Ana nodded. Apparently, Manny had got into trouble again, drugs, but this time, Ana insisted, he'd been set up by these three cocolos, a word he'd never heard her use, so he figured she'd got it from Manny. Poor Manny, she said.

Yeah, poor Manny, Oscar muttered.

Poor Manny, poor Ana, poor Oscar. Things changed quickly. First, Ana stopped being home all the time, and Oscar found himself stacking messages on her machine: This is Oscar, a bear is chewing my legs off, please call me. This is Oscar, they want a million dollars or it's over, please call me. She always got back to him after a couple of days and was pleasant about it, but still. Then she cancelled three Fridays in a row, and he had to settle for the clearly reduced berth of Sunday after church. She picked him up, and they drove out to Boulevard East and parked the car, and together they stared out at the Manhattan skyline. It wasn't an ocean, or a mountain range; it was, at least to Oscar, better.

On one of these little trips, she let slip, God, I'd forgotten how big Manny's cock is.

Like I really need to hear that, Oscar snapped.

I'm sorry, she said hesitantly. I thought we could talk about everything.

Well, it actually wouldn't be bad if you kept Manny's anatomical enormity to yourself.

With Manny and his *big cock* around, Oscar began dreaming about nuclear annihilation, how through some miracle he was first to hear about a planned attack, and without pausing to think he stole his tío's car, drove it to the store, stocked it full of supplies (shooting a couple of looters on the way), and then fetched Ana. What about Manny? she wailed. There's no time! he'd insisted, peeling out. When he was in a better mood, he let Ana discover Manny, who would be hanging from a light fixture in his apartment, his tongue bulbous in his mouth. The news of the imminent attack on the TV, a note pinned to his chest. *I koona taek it.* And then Oscar would comfort Ana and say something like, He was too weak for this hard new world.

Oscar even got—joy of joys!—the opportunity to meet the famous Manny, which was about as much fun as being called a fag during a school assembly (which had happened). Met him outside Ana's house. He was this intense emaciated guy with voracious eyes.

When they shook hands, Oscar was sure the nigger was going to smack him; he acted so surly. Manny was muy bald and completely shaved his head to hide it, had a hoop in each ear, and this leathery out-in-the-sun look of an old cat straining for youth.

So you're Ana's little friend, Manny said derisively.

That's me, Oscar said in a voice so full of cheerful innocuousness that he could have shot himself for it.

He snorted. I hope you ain't trying to chisel in on my girl.

Oscar said, Ha-ha. Ana flushed red, looked at the ground.

With Manny around, Oscar was exposed to an entirely new side of Ana. All they talked about now, the few times they saw each other, was Manny and the terrible things he did to her. Manny smacked her, Manny kicked her, Manny called her a fat twat, Manny cheated on her, she was sure, with this Cuban chickie from the middle school. They couldn't talk ten minutes without Manny beeping her and her having to call him back and assure him she wasn't with anybody else.

What am I going to do? she asked over and over, and Oscar always found himself holding her awkwardly and telling her, Well, I think if he's this bad you should break up with him, but she shook her head and said, I know I should, but I can't. I love him.

Oscar liked to kid himself that it was only cold, anthropological interest that kept him around to see how it would all end, but the truth was he couldn't extricate himself. He was totally and irrevocably in love with Ana. What he used to feel for those girls he'd never really known was nothing compared with the amor he was carrying in his heart for Ana. It had the density of a dwarf motherfucking star and at times he was a hundred per cent sure it would drive him mad. Every Dominican family has stories about niggers who take love too far, and Oscar was beginning to suspect that they'd be telling one of these stories about him real soon.

Miraculous things started happening. Once, he blacked out while crossing an intersection. Another time, Miggs was goofing on him, talking smack, and for the first time ever Oscar lost his temper and swung on the nigger, connected so hard that homeboy's mouth spouted blood. Jesus Christ, Al said. Calm down! I didn't mean to do it, Oscar said unconvincingly. It was an accident. Mudafuffer, Miggs said. Mudafuffer! Oscar got so bad that one desperate night, after listening to Ana sobbing to him on the phone about Manny's latest bullshit, he said, I have to go to church now, and put down the phone, went to his tío's room and stole his antique Dragoon pistol, that oh-so famous First Nation exterminating Colt .44, stuck its impressive snout down the front of his pants, and proceeded to stand in front of Manny's apartment. Come on, motherfucker, he said calmly. I got a nice eleven-year-old girl for you. He didn't care that he would more than likely be put away forever and that niggers like him got ass- and mouth-raped in jail, or that if the cops picked him up and found the gun they'd send his tío's ass up the river for parole violation. He didn't care about jack. His head contained nothing, it felt like it had been excavated, a perfect vacuum.

Folks started noticing that he was losing it. His mother, his tío, even Al and Miggs, not known for their solicitude, were like, Dude, what the fuck's the matter with you?

After he went on his third Manny hunt, he broke down and confessed to his sister, and she got them both on their knees in front of the altar she'd built to their dead abuela and had him swear on their mother's soul that he'd never pull anything like that again as long as he lived. She even cried, she was so worried about him.

You need to stop this, Mister.

I know I do, he said. But it's hard.

That night, he and his sister both fell asleep on the couch, she first. Her shins were covered in bruises. Before he joined her, he decided that this would be the end of it. He would tell Ana how he felt, and if she didn't come away with him then he wouldn't speak to her ever again.

They met at the Yaohan mall. Ordered two chicken-katsu curries and then sat in the large cafeteria with the view of Manhattan, the only gaijin in the whole joint.

He could tell by Ana's clothes that she had other plans that night. She was in a pair of black leather pants and had on one of those fuzzy light-pink sweaters that girls with nice chests can rock forever. Her face was so swollen from recent crying it looked like she was on cortisone.

You have beautiful breasts, he said as an opener.

Confusion, alarm. Oscar! What's the matter with you?

He looked out through the glass at Manhattan's western flank, looked out like he was some deep nigger. Then he told her.

There were no surprises. Her eyes went soft, she put a hand on his hand, her chair scraped closer, there was a strand of yellow in her teeth. Oscar, she said gently, I have a boyfriend.

So you don't love me?

Oscar. She breathed deep. I love you as a *friend*.

She drove him home; at the house, he thanked her for her time, walked inside, lay in bed. They didn't speak again.

In June, he graduated from Don Bosco. He heard in passing that, of everybody in their section of P-town, only he and Olga, poor, fucked-up Olga, had not attended even one prom. Dude, Miggs joked, maybe you should have asked her out.

He spent the summer working at the hardware store. Had so much time on his hands he started writing a novel for real. In September, he headed to Rutgers, and quickly buried himself in what amounted to the college version of what he'd majored in throughout high school: getting no ass. Despite swearing to be different, he went back to his nerdy ways, eating, not exercising, using flash words, and after a couple consecutive Fridays alone he joined the university's resident geek organization, R.U. Gamers.

The first time I met Oscar was at Rutgers. We were roommates our sophomore year, cramped up in Demarest, the university's official homo dorm, because Oscar wanted to be a writer and because I'd pulled the last number in the housing lottery. You never met more opposite niggers in your life. He was a dork, totally into Dungeons & Dragons and comic books; he had like a billion science-fiction paperbacks, all in his closet; and me, I was into girls, weight lifting, and Danocrine. (What is it with us niggers and our bodies? Not even Fanon can explain it to me.) I had this beautiful Irish–Puerto Rican girlfriend, a Plainfield girl I couldn't get enough of, a firefighter's daughter who didn't speak a word of Spanish, and I was into clubs like a motherfucker—Illusions, Foxes, Mercedes and Mink (on Springfield Ave. in Newark, the only club on the planet with a Ghettogirl Appreciation Night). Those were the Boricua Posse days, and I never got home before six in the morning, so mostly what I saw of Oscar was a big, dormant hump crashed out under a sheet. When we were in the dorm together, he was either working on his novel or talking on the phone to his sister, who I'd seen a few times at Douglass. (I'd tried to put a couple of words on her because she was no joke in the body department, but she cold-crumbed me.) Those first months, me and my boys ragged on Oscar a lot—I mean, he was a nerd, wasn't he?—and right before Halloween I told him he looked like that fat homo Oscar Wilde, which was bad news for him, because then all of us started calling him Oscar Wao. The sad part? After a couple of weeks, he started *answering* to it.

Besides me fucking with him, we never had no problems; he never got mad at me when I said shit, just sat there with a hurt stupid smile on his face. Made a brother feel kinda bad, and after the others left I would say, You know I was just kidding, right? By second semester, I even started to like the kid a little. Wasn't it Turgenev who said, Whom you laugh at you forgive and come near to loving? I didn't invite him out to no clubs, but we did start going to Brower Commons to eat, even checked out an occasional movie. We talked a little, mostly about girls, comic books, and our corny white-boy neighbors who were pussy asshole cocksuckers. Girls, though, were point zero; they were the world to Oscar. I mean, they were the world to me, too, but with him it was on some next shit. He got around a cute one and the nigger would almost start shaking. Easy to understand; our first month as roommates, he'd told me he'd never kissed one! Never! Jesus fucking Christ! The horror! It wasn't like I couldn't sympathize, but I didn't think acting like a nut around the mamacitas was going to help his case. I tried to give him advice—first off, cristiano, you have to stop gunning on the superbabes—but he wouldn't listen. He said, Nothing else works, I might as well make a fool out of myself.

It wasn't until the middle of spring semester that I ever saw Oscar really in love. Catalyn Sangre de Toro Luperón. Catalyn was this Puerto Rican Goth girl—in 1990, niggers were having trouble wrapping their heads around Goths, period, but a Puerto Rican Goth, that was as strange to us as a black Nazi. Anyway, Catalyn was her real name, but her around-the-cauldron name was La Jablesse. You think I'm kidding? Every standard a brother like me had, this girl short-circuited. Her hair she wore in this black Egypt cut, her eyes caked with eyeliner and mascara, her lips painted black, a Navajo tattoo across her whole back, and none of it mattered, because home-girl was *luminous*. She had no waist, big perfect tits, wore black spiderweb clothes, and her accent in Spanish and English was puro Guayama. Even I had been hot for Catalyn, but the one time I'd tried to mack her at the Douglass Library she picked up her books and moved to another table, and when I tried to come over to apologize she did it again.

Ice.

So: one day I caught Oscar talking to La Jablesse in Brower, and I had to watch, because I figured if I got roasted she was going to vaporize his ass. Of course, he was full on, and home-girl was holding her tray and looking at him askance, like, What the fuck does this freak want? She started walking away, and Oscar yelled out, We'll talk later, O.K.? And she shot back a Sure, all larded with sarcasm.

You have to give it to Oscar. He didn't let up. He just kept hitting on her with absolutely no regard for self or dignity, and eventually she must have decided he was harmless, because she started treating him civil. Soon enough, I saw them walking together down College Avenue. One day, I came home from classes and found La Jablesse sitting on my bed, Oscar sitting on his. I was speechless. She remembered me. You can always tell. She said, You want me to get off your bed? I said, Nah, picked up my gym bag, and ran out of there like a pussy. When I got back from the weight room, Oscar was on his computer. On page one billion of his novel.

I said, What's up with you and Miss Scarypants?

Nothing much. Then he smiled and I knew he'd heard about my lame-ass pickup attempt.

I was one sore loser; I said, Well, good luck, Wao. I just hope she doesn't sacrifice you to Beelzebub or anything.

Later, the two of them started going to movies together. Some narratives never die. She was the first person to get him to try mushrooms, and once, right at the end, when he was starting to talk about her like she was the Queen of Everything, she took him to her room, turned off the lights, lit some witchy candles, and danced for him.

What the hell was this girl thinking?

In less than a week, Oscar was in bed crying, and La Jablesse had a restraining order on his ass. Turns out Oscar walked in on Catalyn while she was "entertaining" some Goth kid, caught them both naked, probably covered with blood or something, and he berserked. Started tearing her place up, and Gothdude jumped butt-naked out the window. Same night, I found Oscar on his top bunk, bare-chested, the night he said, I fucked up real bad, Yunior.

He had to attend counselling, to keep from losing his housing, but now everybody in the dorm thought he was some kind of major psycho. This is how our year together ended. Him at his computer, typing, me being asked in the hall how I liked dorming with Mr. Crazyman.

Would probably never have chilled with him again, but then, a year later, I started speaking to his sister, Lola de León. Femme-matador. The sort of girlfriend God gives you young, so you'll know loss the rest of your life. The head of every black and brown women's progressive organization at Douglass, beloved Phi Chi hermana, blah, blah, blah. She didn't have no kind of tact and talked too much for my taste, but, man, could she move, and her smile was enough to pull you across a room. I began noticing every time she was around, it was like she was on a high wire; I couldn't keep my eyes off her. I asked my boys what they thought about her and they laughed, said, Yo, she looks like a slave. Never forgave any of them for that.

Our first night together was at her place on Commercial Ave., and before I put my face between her legs she dragged me up by my ears. Why is this the face I cannot forget? Tired from finals, swollen from kissing. She said, Don't ever cheat on me.

I won't, I promised her. Don't laugh. My intentions were good.

34

We were still together at graduation, and we took pictures with each other's families—there's even a couple of me and Oscar. We look like a couple of circus freaks: I'm muscle-bound, hands as big as hams, and Oscar's heavy, squinting into the camera like we just pulled him out of a trunk and he doesn't know where the fuck he is.

After college, Oscar moved back home. Left a virgin, returned one. Took down his childhood posters (Star Blazers, Captain Harlock) and tacked up his college ones (Akira and Terminator II). These were the early Bush years, the economy still sucked, and he kicked around doing nada for almost seven months until he started substituting at Don Bosco. A year later, the substituting turned into a full-time job. He could have refused, could have made a "saving throw" versus Death Magic, but instead he went with the flow. Watched his horizons collapse, told himself it didn't matter.

Had Don Bosco, since last we visited, been miraculously transformed by the spirit of Christian brotherhood? Had the eternal benevolence of the Lord cleansed the students of their bile? Negro, please. The only change that Oscar saw was in the older brothers, who all seemed to have acquired the inbred Innsmouth "look"; everything else (like white arrogance and the self-hate of people of color) was the same, and a familiar gleeful sadism still electrified the halls. Oscar wasn't great at teaching, his heart wasn't in it, and boys of all grades and dispositions shitted on him effusively. Students laughed when they spotted him in the halls. Pretended to hide their sandwiches. Asked in the middle of lectures if he ever got laid, and no matter how he responded they guffawed mercilessly. How demoralizing was that? And every day he found himself watching the "cool" kids torture the crap out of the fat, the ugly, the smart, the poor, the dark, the black, the unpopular, the African, the Indian, the Arab, the immigrant, the strange, the femenino, the gay—and in every one of these clashes he must have been seeing himself. Sometimes he tried to reach out to the school's whipping boys—You ain't alone, you know?—but the last thing a freak wants is a helping hand from another freak. In a burst of enthusiasm, he attempted to start a science-fiction club, and for two Thursdays in a row he sat in his classroom after school, his favorite books laid out in an attractive pattern, listened to the roar of receding footsteps in the halls, the occasional shout outside his door of Beam me up! and Nanoo-Nanoo! Then, after thirty minutes, he collected his books, locked the room, and walked down those same halls, alone, his footsteps sounding strangely dainty.

Social life? He didn't have one. Once a week he drove out to Woodbridge Mall and stared at the toothpick-thin black girl who worked at the Friendly's, who he was in love with but to whom he would never speak.

At least at Rutgers there'd been multitudes and an institutional pretense that allowed a mutant like him to approach without causing a panic. In the real world, girls turned away in disgust when he walked past. Changed seats at the cinema, and one woman on the crosstown bus even told him to stop thinking about her. I know what you're up to, she hissed. So stop it.

I'm a permanent bachelor, he told his sister.

There's nothing permanent in the world, his sister said tersely.

He pushed his fist into his eye. There is in me.

The home life? Didn't kill him, but didn't sustain him, either. His moms, smaller, rounder, less afflicted by the suffering of her youth, still the work golem, still sold second-rate clothes out of the back of her house, still allowed her Peruvian boarders to pack as many relatives as they wanted into the first floors. And Tío Rodolfo, Fofo to his friends, had reverted back to some of his hard pre-prison habits. He was on the caballo again, broke into lightning sweats at dinner, had moved into Lola's room, and now Oscar got to listen to him chicken-boning his stripper girlfriends almost every single night. Hey, Tío, he yelled out, try to use the headboard a little less.

Oscar knew what he was turning into, the worst kind of human on the planet: an old, bitter dork. He was depressed for long periods of time. The Darkness. Some mornings, he would wake up and not be able to get out of bed. Had dreams that he was wandering around the evil planet Gordo, searching for parts for his crashed rocket ship, but all he encountered were burned-out ruins. I don't know what's wrong with me, he said to his sister over the phone. He threw students out of class for breathing, told his mother to fuck off, went into his tío's closet and put the Colt up between his eyes, then lay in bed and thought about his mother fixing him his plate for the rest of his life. (He heard her say into the phone when she thought he wasn't around, I don't care, I'm happy he's here.)

Afterward—when he no longer felt like a whipped dog inside, when he could go to work without wanting to cry—he suffered from overwhelming feelings of guilt. He would apologize to his mother. He would take the car and visit Lola. She lived in the city now, was letting her hair grow, had been pregnant once, a real moment of excitement, but she aborted it because I was cheating on her with a neighbor. (Our only baby.) He went on long rides. He drove as far as Amish country, would eat alone at a roadside diner, eye the Amish girls, imagine himself in a preacher suit, sleep in the back of the car, and then drive home.

When Oscar had been at Don Bosco nearly three years, his moms asked him what plans he had for the summer. Every year, the family spent the better part of June, July, and August in Santo Domingo; Oscar hadn't accompanied them since Abuela had screamed out *Haitians!* once and died.

It's strange. If he'd said no, nigger would probably still be alive. But this ain't no Marvel Comics "What if?"—this ain't about stupid speculation, and time, as they say, is growing short. That May, Oscar was, for once, in better spirits. A couple of months earlier, after a particularly nasty bout with the Darkness, he'd started another one of his diets and combined it with long, lumbering walks around the neighborhood, and guess what? The nigger stuck with it and lost close on twenty pounds! A milagro! He'd finally repaired his ion drive; the evil planet Gordo was pulling him back but his fifties-style rocket, the Hijo de Sacrificio, wouldn't quit. Behold our cosmic explorer: eyes wide, lashed to his acceleration couch, his hand over his mutant heart.

He wasn't svelte by any stretch of the imagination, but he wasn't Joseph Conrad's wife no more, either. Earlier in the month, he'd even spoken to a bespectacled black girl on a bus, said, So, you're into photosynthesis, and she'd actually lowered her issue of *Cell* and said, Yes, I am. So what if he hadn't ever got past Earth Sciences and hadn't been able to convert that slight communication into a phone number or a date? Homeboy was, for the first time in ten years, feeling resurgent; nothing seemed to bother him, not his students, not the fact that "Doctor Who" had gone off the air, not his loneliness; he felt *insuperable,* and summers in Santo Domingo... Well, Santo Domingo summers have their own particular allure. For two months, Santo Domingo slaps the diaspora engine into reverse, yanks back as many of its expelled children as it can; airports choke with the overdressed; necks and luggage carrousels groan under the accumulated weight of that year's cadenas and paquetes; restaurants, bars, clubs, theatres, malecones, beaches, resorts, hotels, moteles, extra rooms, barrios, colonias, campos, ingenios swarm with quisqueyanos from the world over: from Washington Heights to Roma, from Perth Amboy to Tokyo, from Brijeporr to Amsterdam, from Anchorage to San Juan; it's one big party; one big party for everybody but the poor, the dark, the jobless, the sick, the Haitian, their children, the bateyes, the kids whom certain Canadian, American, German, and Italian tourists love to rape—yes, sir, nothing like a Santo Domingo summer, and so for the first time in years Oscar said, My elder spirits have been talking to me, Ma. I think I might go. He was imagining himself in the middle of all that ass-getting, imagining himself in love with an Island girl. (A brother can't be wrong forever, can he?)

So curious a change in policy was this that even Lola quizzed him about it. You never go to Santo Domingo.

He shrugged. I guess I want to try something new.

Family de León flew down to the capital on the fourteenth of June. (Oscar told his bosses, My aunt got eaten by a shark, it's horrible, so he could bail out of work early. His mother couldn't believe it. You lied to a *priest*?)

In the pictures Lola brought home—she had to leave early; her job gave her only two weeks and she'd already killed off all her aunts—there are shots of Oscar in the back of the house reading Octavia Butler, shots of Oscar on the Malecón with a bottle of Presidente in his hand, shots of Oscar at the Columbus lighthouse, where half of Villa Duarte used to stand, shots of Oscar in Villa Juana buying spark plugs, shots of Oscar trying on a hat on the Conde, shots of Oscar standing next to a burro. You can tell he's trying. He's smiling a lot, despite the bafflement in his eyes.

He's also, you might notice, not wearing his fat-guy coat.

After his initial two weeks on the Island, after he'd got somewhat used to the scorching weather and the surprise of waking up in another country, after he refused to succumb to that whisper that all long-term immigrants carry inside themselves, the whisper that says You Do Not Belong, after he'd gone to about ten clubs and, because he couldn't dance salsa or merengue or bachata, had sat and drunk his Presidentes while Lola and his cousins burned holes in the floor, after he'd explained to people a hundred times that he'd been separated from his sister at birth, after he spent a couple of quiet mornings on his own on the Malecón, after he'd given out all his taxi money to beggars and had to call his cousin to get home, after he'd watched shirtless, shoeless seven-year-olds fighting each other for the scraps he'd left on his plate at an outdoor café, after the family visited the shack in Baitoa where his moms had been born, after he had taken a dump in a latrine and wiped his ass with a corncob, after he'd got somewhat used to the surreal whirligig that was life in the capital—the guaguas, the cops, the mind-boggling poverty, the Dunkin' Donuts, the beggars, the Pizza Huts, the tígueres selling newspapers at the intersections, the snarl of streets and shacks that were the barrios, the masses of niggers he waded through every day and who ran him over if he stood still, the mind-boggling poverty, the skinny watchmen standing in front of stores with their shotguns, the music, the raunchy jokes heard on the streets, the Friday-night strolls down the Avenida, the mind-boggling poverty—after he'd gone to Boca Chica and Villa Mella, after the relatives berated him for having stayed away so long, after he heard the stories about his father and his mother, after he stopped marvelling at the amount of political propaganda plastered up on every spare wall, after the touched-in-the-head tío who'd been tortured during Balaguer's reign came over and cried, after he'd swum in the Caribbean, after Tío Rodolfo had got the clap from a puta (Man, his tío cracked, what a pisser! Har-har!), after he'd seen his first Haitians kicked off a guagua because niggers claimed they "smelled," after he'd nearly gone nuts over all the bellezas he saw, after all the gifts they'd brought had been properly distributed, after he'd brought flowers to his abuela's grave, after he had diarrhea so bad his mouth watered before each detonation, after he'd visited all the rinky-dink museums in the capital, after he stopped being dismayed that everybody called him gordo, after he'd been over-charged for almost everything he wanted to buy, after the terror and joy of his return subsided, after he settled down in his abuela's house, the house that the diaspora had built, and resigned himself to a long, dull, quiet summer, after his fantasy of an Island girlfriend caught a quick dicko (who the fuck had he been kidding? he couldn't dance, he didn't have loot, he didn't dress, he wasn't confident, he wasn't handsome, he wasn't from Europe, he wasn't fucking no Island girl), after Lola flew back to the States, Oscar fell in love with a semiretired puta.

Her name was Yvón Pimentel. Oscar considered her the start of his *real* life. (She was the end of it, too.)

She lived two houses over and was a newcomer to Mirador Norte. She was one of those golden mulatas that French-speaking Caribbeans call "chabines," that my boys call chicas de oro; she had snarled apocalyptic hair, amber eyes, and was one white-skinned relative away from jabao.

At first Oscar thought she was only a visitor, this tiny, slightly paunchy babe who was always high-heeling it out to her Pathfinder. (She didn't have the Mirador Norte wanna-be American look.) The two times Oscar bumped into her at the local café she smiled at him and he smiled at her. The second time—here, folks, is where the miracles begin—she sat at his table and chatted him up. At first he didn't know what was happening and then he realized, *Holy shit!* A girl was rapping to *him.* Turned out Yvón had known his abuela, even attended her funeral. You I don't remember. I was little, he said defensively. And, besides, that was before the war changed me.

She didn't laugh. That's probably what it is. You were a boy. On went the shades, up went the ass, out went the girl, Oscar's erection following her like a dowser's wand.

Yvón had attended the U.A.S.D. a long time ago, but she was no college girl. She had lines around her eyes and seemed, to Oscar at least, mad open, mad worldly, and had the sort of intense zipper gravity that hot middle-aged women exude effortlessly. The next time he ran into her, in front of her house (he had watched for her), she screamed, Oscar, querido! Invited him into her near-empty casa—Haven't had the time to move in yet, she said offhandedly—and because there wasn't any furniture besides a kitchen table, a chair, a bureau, a bed, and a TV, they had to sit on the bed. (Oscar peeped at the astrology books under the bed and the complete collection of Paulo Coelho's novels. She followed his gaze and said with a smile, Paulo Coelho saved my life.) She gave him a beer, had a double Scotch, then for the next six hours regaled him with tales from her life. It wasn't until midway through their chat that it hit Oscar that the job she talked so profusely about was prostitution. It was *Holy shit!* the Sequel. Even though putas were one of Santo Domingo's premier exports, Oscar had never been near one in his entire life.

Yvón was an odd, odd bird. She was talkative, the sort of easygoing woman a brother can relax around, but there was also something slightly detached about her, as though (Oscar's words now) she were some marooned alien princess who existed partially in another dimension. She was the sort of woman who, cool as she was, slipped out of your head a little too quickly, a quality she recognized and was thankful for, as though she relished the short bursts of attention she provoked from niggers, but didn't want anything sustained. She didn't seem to mind being the girl you called every couple of months at eleven at night, just to see what she was up to. As much relationship as she could handle.

Her Jedi mind tricks did not, however, work on Oscar. When it came to girls, the brother had a mind like a four-hundred-year-old yogi. He latched on and stayed latched. By the time he left her house that night and walked home through the Island's million attack mosquitoes, he was lost. He was head over heels. (Did it matter that Yvón started mixing Italian in with her Spanish after her fourth drink or that she almost fell flat on her face when she showed him out? Of course not!) He was in love.

His mother met him at the door and couldn't believe his sinvergüencería. Do you know that woman's a PUTA? Do you know she bought that house CULEANDO?

He shot back, Do you know her mother was a DOCTOR? Do you know her father was a JUDGE?

The next day at one, Oscar pulled on a clean chacabana and strolled over to her house. (Well, he sort of trotted.) A red Jeep was parked outside, nose to nose with her Pathfinder. A Policía Nacional plate. And felt like a stooge. Of course she had boyfriends. His optimism, that swollen red giant, collapsed down to a bone-crushing point of gloom. Didn't stop him coming back the next day, but no one was home, and by the time he saw her again three days later he was convinced that she had warped back to whatever Forerunner world had spawned her. Where were you? he said, trying not to sound as miserable as he felt. I thought maybe you fell in the tub or something. I thought maybe you'd got amnesia.

She smiled and gave her ass a little shiver. I was making the patria strong, mi amor.

He had caught her in front of the TV, doing aerobics in a pair of sweatpants and what might have been described as a halter top. It was hard for him not to stare at her body. When she first let him in she'd screamed, Oscar, querido! Come in! Come in!

I know what niggers are going to say. Look, he's writing Suburban Tropical now. A puta and she's not an underage, snort-addicted mess? Not believable. Should I go down to the Feria and pick me up a more representative model? Would it be better if I turned Yvón into Jahyra, a friend and a neighbor in Villa Juana, who still lives in one of those old-style pink wooden houses with a tin roof? Jahyra—your quintessential Caribbean puta, half cute, half not—who'd left home at the age of fifteen and lived in Curaçao, Madrid, Amsterdam, and Rome, has two kids and a breast job bigger than Luba's in "Love and Rockets," and who claimed, proudly, that her aparato had paved half the streets in her mother's home town. Or would it be better if I had Oscar meet Yvón at the World Famous Lavacaro, the carwash where a brother can get his head and his fenders polished (talk about convenience!). Would this be better?

But then I'd be lying. This is a true account of the Brief Wondrous Life of Oscar Wao. Can't we believe that an Yvón can exist and that a brother like Oscar might be due a little luck after twenty-three years?

This is your chance. If yes, continue. If no, return to the Matrix.

In their photos, Yvón looks young. It's her smile and the way she perks up her body for every shot as if she's presenting herself to the world, as if she's saying, ta-da, here I am, take it or leave it. It doesn't hurt that she's barely five feet tall or that she doesn't weigh nothing. She dressed young, too, but she was a solid thirty-six, a perfect age for anybody but a puta. In the closeups, you can see the crow's-feet, and the little belly she complains all the time about, and the way her breasts and her ass are starting to lose their swell, which was why, she said, she had to be in the gym five days a week. When you're sixteen, a body like this is free; when you're forty—pffft!—it's a full-time occupation. The third time Oscar came over, Yvón doubled up on the Scotches again and then took down her photo albums from the closet and showed him all the pictures of herself when she was sixteen, seventeen, eighteen, always on a beach, always in an eighties bikini, always smiling, always with her arms around some middle-aged eighties yakub. Looking at those old hairy blancos, Oscar couldn't help but feel hopeful. Each photo had a date and a place at the bottom, and this was how he was able to follow Yvón's puta's progress through Italy, Portugal, and Spain. I was so beautiful in those days, she said wistfully. It was true—her smile could have put out a sun, but Oscar didn't think she was any less fine now; the slight declensions in her appearance only seemed to add to her lustre and he told her so.

You're so sweet, mi amor. She knocked back another double and rasped, What's your sign?

How lovesick he became! He began to go over to her house nearly every day, even when he knew she was working, just in case she was sick or decided to quit the profession so she could marry him. The gates of his heart had swung open and he felt light on his feet, he felt weightless, he felt lithe. His moms steady gave him shit, told him that not even God loves a puta. Yeah, his tío laughed, but everybody knows that God loves a puto. His tío seemed thrilled that he no longer had a pájaro for a nephew. I can't believe it, he said proudly. The palomo is finally a man. He put Oscar's neck in the New Jersey State Police patented niggerkiller lock. When did it happen? What was the date? I want to play that número as soon I get home.

Here we go again: Oscar and Yvón at her house, Oscar and Yvón at the movies, Oscar and Yvón at the beach, Oscar and Yvón talking, voluminously. She told him about her two sons, Sterling and Perfecto, who lived with their grandparents in Puerto Rico, who she saw only on holidays. She told him about the two abortions she had, which she called Marisol and Pepita, and about the time she'd been jailed in Madrid and how hard it was to sell your ass, and asked, Can something be impossible and not impossible at once? She told him about her Dominican boyfriend, the Capitán, and her foreign boyfriends, the Italian, the German, and the Canadian, the three benditos, how they each visited her on different months. You're lucky they all have families, she said, or I'd have been working this whole summer. (He wanted to ask her not to talk about any of these dudes, but she would only have laughed.)

Maybe we should get married, he said once, not joking, and she said, I make a terrible wife. He was around so often that he even got to see her in a couple of her notorious "moods," when her alien princess took over and she became very cold and uncommunicative and called him an idiot americano for spilling his beer. On these days, she threw herself into bed and didn't want to do anything. Hard to be around her, but he would convince her to see a movie and afterward she'd be a little easier. She'd take him to an Italian restaurant, and no matter how much her mood had improved she'd insist on drinking herself ridiculous—so bad he'd have to put her in the truck and drive her home through a city he did not know. (Early on, he hit on a great scheme: he called Clives, the evangelical taxista his family always used, who would swing by—no sweat—and lead him home.) When he drove, she always put her head in his lap and talked to him, sometimes in Italian, sometimes in Spanish, sometimes sweet, sometimes not, and having her mouth so close to his nuts was finer than your best yesterday.

Oh, they got close, all right, but we have to ask the hard questions: Did they ever kiss in her Pathfinder? Did he ever put his hands up her super-short skirt? Did she ever push up against him and say his name in a throaty whisper? Did they ever fuck?

Of course not. Miracles go only so far. He watched her for the signs that would tell him she loved him. He began to suspect that it might not happen this summer, but already he had plans to come back for Thanksgiving and then for Christmas. When he told her, she looked at him strangely and said only his name, Oscar, a little sadly.

She liked him, it was obvious. It seemed to Oscar that he was one of her few real friends. Outside the boyfriends, foreign and domestic, outside her psychiatrist sister in San Cristóbal and her ailing mother in Sabana Iglesia, her life seemed as spare as, say, her house.

Travel light, was all she ever said about the house when he suggested buying her a lamp or something, and he suspected that she would have said the same thing about having more friends. He knew, of course, that he wasn't her only visitor. One day, he found three discarded condom foils on the floor and asked, Are you having trouble with incubuses? She smiled. This is one man who doesn't know the word quit.

Poor Oscar. At night he dreamed that his rocket ship, the Hijo de Sacrificio, was up and off but that it was heading for the Ana Acuña Barrier at the speed of light.

At the beginning of August Yvón started mentioning her ex-boyfriend the Capitán a lot more. Seems he'd heard about Oscar and wanted to meet him. He's really jealous, Yvón said, rather weakly. Just have him meet me, Oscar said. I make all boyfriends feel better about themselves. I don't know, Yvón said. Maybe we shouldn't spend so much time together. Shouldn't you be looking for a girlfriend?

I got one, he said.

A jealous Third World cop ex-boyfriend? Maybe we shouldn't spend so much time together? Any other nigger would have pulled a Scooby-Doo double take—Eeuoooorr?—would have thought twice about staying in Santo Domingo another day, but not Oscar.

Two days later, Oscar found his tío examining the front door. What's the matter? His tío showed him the door and pointed at the concrete-block wall on the other side of the foyer. I think somebody shot our house last night. He shook his head. Fucking Dominicans. Probably hosed the whole neighborhood down.

For a second, Oscar felt this strange tugging in the back of his head, what someone else might have called Instinct, but instead of hunkering down and sifting through it he said, We probably didn't hear it because of all our air-conditioners. Then he walked over to Yvón's. They were going to the Duarte that day.

In the middle of August, Oscar finally met the Capitán. Yvón had passed out again. It was super-late and he'd been following Clives in the Pathfinder, the usual routine, when a crowd of cops up ahead let Clives pass and then asked Oscar to please step out of the vehicle. These were the D.R.'s new highway police, brand-new uniforms and esprit de corps up to here. It's not my truck, he explained, it's hers. He pointed to sleeping Yvón. We understand. If you could please step out of the truck. It wasn't until these two plainclothes—who we'll call Solomon Grundy and Gorilla Grodd, for simplicity's sake—tossed him into the back of a black Volkswagen bug that he realized something was up. Wait a minute, he said as they pulled out, where the hell are you taking me? Wait! Gorilla Grodd gave him one cold glance and that was all it took to quiet his ass down. This is fucked up, he said under his breath. I didn't *do* nothing.

The Capitán was waiting for him on a noticeably unelectrified stretch of road. A skinny forty-something-year-old jabao standing near his spotless red Jeep, dressed nice in slacks and a crisply pressed white button-down, his shoes bright as scarabs. The Capitán was one of those tall, arrogant, handsome niggers that most of the planet feels inferior to. (The Capitán was also one of those very bad men who not even postmodernism can explain away.)

So you're the New Yorker, he said with great cheer. When Oscar saw the Capitán's close-set eyes he knew he was fucked. (He had the Eyes of Lee Van Cleef!) If it hadn't been for the courage of his sphincter, Oscar's lunch and his dinner and his breakfast would have whooshed straight out of him.

I didn't do anything, Oscar quailed. Then he blurted out, I'm an American citizen.

The Capitán waved away a mosquito. I'm an American citizen, too. I was sworn in in the city of Buffalo, in the State of New York.

I bought mine in Miami, Gorilla Grodd said.

Not me, Solomon Grundy lamented. I only got my damn residency.

Please, you have to believe me, I didn't do anything.

The Capitán smiled. Motherfucker even had First World teeth. Oscar was lucky; if he had looked like my pana Pedro, the

Dominican Superman, he probably would have got shot right there. But because he was a young homely slob the Capitán punched him only a couple of times, warned him away from Yvón in no uncertain terms, and then remanded him to Messrs. Grundy and Grodd, who squeezed him back into the bug and drove out to the cane fields between Santo Domingo and Villa Mella.

Oscar was too scared to speak. He was a shook daddy. He couldn't believe it. He was going to die. He tried to imagine Yvón at the funeral in her nearly see-through black sheath and couldn't. Watched Santo Domingo race past and felt impossibly alone. Thought about his mother and his sister and started crying.

You need to keep it down, Grundy said, but Oscar couldn't stop, even when he put his hands in his mouth.

At the cane fields, Messrs. Grodd and Grundy pulled Oscar out of the car, walked him into the cane, and then with their pistol butts proceeded to give him the beating to end all beatings. It was the Götterdämmerung of beatdowns, a beatdown so cruel and relentless that even Camden, the City of the Ultimate Beatdown, would have been impressed. (Yessir, nothing like getting smashed in the face with those patented Pachmayr Presentation Grips.) He shrieked, but that didn't stop the beating; he begged, but that didn't stop it, either; he blacked out, but that was no relief; the niggers kicked him in the nuts and perked him right up! It was like one of those nightmare 8 A.M. M.L.A. panels that you think will never, ever end. Man, Gorilla Grodd said, this kid is making me *sweat*. Toward the end, Oscar found himself thinking about his old dead abuela, who used to scratch his back and fry him yaniqueques; she was sitting in her rocking chair and when she saw him she snarled, What did I tell you about those putas?

The only reason he didn't lie out in that rustling endless cane for the rest of his life was because Clives the evangelical taxista had had the guts to follow the cops on the sly, and when they broke out he turned on his headlights and pulled up to where they'd last been and found poor Oscar. Are you alive? Clives whispered. Oscar said, Blub, blub. Clives couldn't hoist Oscar into the car alone so he drove to a nearby batey and recruited a couple of Haitian braceros to help him. This is a big one, one of the braceros joked. The only thing Oscar said the whole ride back was her name. *Yvón.* Broken nose, broken zygomatic arch, crushed seventh cranial nerve, three of his front teeth snapped off at the gum, concussion, alive.

That was the end of it. When Moms de León heard it was the police, she called first a doctor and then the airlines. She wasn't no fool; she'd lived through Trujillo and the Devil Balaguer; knew that the cops hadn't forgotten shit from those days. She put it in the simplest of terms. You stupid, worthless, no-good son of a whore are going home. No, he said, through demolished lips. He wasn't fooling, either. When he first woke up and realized that he was still alive, he insisted on seeing Yvón. I love her, he whispered, and his mother said, Shut up, you! Just shut up!

The doctor ruled out epidural hematoma but couldn't guarantee that Oscar didn't have brain damage. (She was a cop's girlfriend? Tío Rodolfo whistled. I'll vouch for the brain damage.) Send him home right now, homegirl said, but for four whole days Oscar resisted any attempt to be packed up in a plane, which says a lot about this fat kid's fortitude; he was eating morphine by the handful and his grill was in agony, he had an around-the-clock quadruple migraine and couldn't see squat out of his right eye; motherfucker's head was so swollen he looked like John Merrick, Jr., and anytime he attempted to stand, the ground whisked right out from under him. My God! he thought. So this is what it feels like to get your ass *kicked.* It wasn't all bad, though; the beating granted him strange insights: he heard his tío, three rooms over, stealing money from his mother's purse; and he realized that had he and Yvón not been serious the Capitán would probably never have fucked with him. Proof positive that he and Yvón had a relationship.

Yvón didn't answer her cell, and the few times Oscar managed to limp to the window he saw that her Pathfinder wasn't there. I love you, he shouted into the street. I love you! Once, he made it to her door and buzzed before his tío realized that he was gone and dragged him back inside.

And, then, on Day Three, she came. While she sat on the edge of his bed, his mother banged pots in the kitchen and said "puta" loudly enough for them to hear.

Forgive me if I don't get up, Oscar whispered. I'm having a little trouble with my face.

She was dressed in white, like an angel, and her hair was still wet from the shower, a tumult of brownish curls. Of course the Capitán had beaten the shit out of her, too; of course she had two black eyes. (He'd also put his .44 Magnum in her vagina and asked her who she really loved.) There was nothing about her that Oscar wouldn't have gladly kissed. She put her fingers on his hand and told him that she could never be with him again. For some reason, Oscar couldn't see her face; it was a blur, she had retreated completely into that other plane of hers. Heard only the sorrow of her breathing. He tried to focus but all he saw was his love for her. Yvón? he croaked, but she was already gone.

Se acabó. Oscar refused to look at the ocean as they drove to the airport. It's beautiful today, Clives remarked. On the flight over, Oscar sat between his tío and his moms. Jesus, Oscar, Rodolfo said nervously. You look like they put a shirt on a turd.

Oscar returned to Paterson. He lay in bed, he stared at his games, he read Andre Norton books, he healed. He talked to the school, and they told him not to worry about the job; it was his when he was ready. You're lucky you're alive, his mother told him. Maybe you could save up your money and get an operation for your face, his tío suggested. Oscar, his sister sighed, Oscar. On the darkest days, he sat in his tío's closet, the Dragoon on his lap, looked back over the past two decades of his life, saw nothing but cowardice and fear. So why was there still a fortress in his heart? Why did he feel like he could be Minas Tirith if he wanted to? He really tried to forget, but he couldn't. He dreamed that he was adrift, alone in his spacesuit, and that she was calling to him.

Me and Lola were living up in the Heights—this was before the white kids started their invasion, when you could walk the entire length of Harlem and see not a single "homesteader." September, October? I was home for the week, curling ninety, when Oscar buzzed me from the street. Hadn't seen him in weeks. Jesus, Oscar, I said. Come up, come up. I waited for him in the hall and when he stepped out of the elevator I put the mitts on him. How are you, bro?

I'm fine, he said, smiling sheepishly.

We sat down and I broke up a dutch, asked him how it was going.

I'm going back to Don Bosco soon.

Word? I said.

Word, he said. His face was still fucked up, the left side was paralyzed and wouldn't get better anytime soon, but he wasn't hiding it anymore. I still got the Two-Face going on bad, he said, laughing.

You gonna smoke?

Just a little. I don't want to cloud my faculties.

That last day on our couch, he looked like a man at peace with himself. You should have seen him. He was so thin, had lost all the weight, and was still, still.

I want to know, Yunior, if you can do me a favor.

Anything, bro. Just ask it.

He needed money for a security deposit, was finally moving into his own apartment, and of course I gave it to him. All I had, but if anybody was going to pay me back it was Oscar.

We smoked the dutch and talked about the problems me and Lola were having.

You should never have had carnal relations with that Paraguayan girl, he pointed out.

I know, I said, I know. He seemed confident that it would work itself out, though, and there was something in his tone that made me hopeful. You ain't going to wait for Lola?

Have to get back to Paterson. I got a date.

You're shitting me?

He shook his head, the tricky fuck.

On Saturday, he was gone.

As soon as he hit the airport exit, Oscar called Clives and homeboy picked him up an hour later. Cristiano, Clives said, eyes tearing, what are you doing here?

It's the Ancient Powers, Oscar said. They won't leave me alone.

They parked in front of her house and waited almost seven hours before she returned. Pulled up in the Pathfinder. She looked thinner. For a moment, he thought about letting the whole thing go, returning to Bosco and getting on with his life, but then she stooped over to pick up her gym bag, as if the whole world were watching, and that settled it. He winched down the window and called her name. She stopped, shaded her eyes, and then recognized him. She said his name, terrified. *Oscar.* He popped the door and walked over to where she was standing and embraced her and she said, Mi amor, you have to leave right now.

In the middle of the street, he told her how it was. He was in love with her. He'd been hurt, but now he was all right, and if he could just have a week alone with her, one short week, then everything would be fine, and he would be able to go on with his life, and he said it again, that he loved her more than the universe, and it wasn't something that he could shake, so, please, come away with him for a little while, and then it would be over if she wanted.

Maybe she did love him a little bit. Maybe in her heart of hearts she left the gym bag on the concrete and got in the taxi with him. But she'd known men like the Capitán all her life. Knew, also, that in the D.R. they called a bullet a cop's divorce. The gym bag was not left on the street.

I'm going to call him, Oscar, she said, misting up a little. So, please, go, before he gets here.

I'm not going anywhere, he said.

For twenty-seven days he chased her. He sat in front of her house, he called her on her cell, he went to the World Famous Riverside, a casa de putas where she worked. The neighbors, when they saw him on the curb, shook their heads and said, Look at that loco.

She was miserable when she saw him and miserable, she would tell him later, when she didn't, convinced that he'd been killed. He slipped long passionate letters under her gate, written in English, and the only response he got was when the Capitán and his friends called and threatened to chop him in pieces. After each threat, he recorded the time and then phoned the Embassy and told them that the Capitán had threatened to kill him, and asked, Could you please help?

She started scribbling back notes and passed them to him at the club or had them mailed to his house. Please, Oscar, I haven't slept in a week. I don't want you to end up hurt or dead. Go home.

But, beautiful girl above all beautiful girls, he wrote back. This *is* my home.

Your real home, mi amor.

A person can't have two?

Night Nineteen, she honked her horn, and he opened his eyes and knew it was her. She leaned over and unlocked the truck door, and when he got in he tried to kiss her, but she said, Please stop it. They drove out toward La Romana, where the Capitán didn't have no friends. Nothing new was discussed, but he said, I like your new haircut, and she started laughing and crying and said, Really? You don't think it makes me look cheap?

You and cheap do not compute, Yvón.

What could we do? Lola flew down to see him, begged him to come home, told him that he was only going to get Yvón and himself killed; he listened and then said angrily that she didn't understand how he felt, never had. How incredibly short are twenty-seven days.

One night, the Capitán and his friends came into the Riverside, and Oscar stared at the man for a good ten seconds and then, whole body shaking, he left. Didn't bother to call Clives, jumped in the first taxi he could find. The next night Oscar was back and, in the parking lot of the Riverside, he tried again to kiss Yvón; she turned her head away (but not her body). Please don't, she said. He'll kill us.

Twenty-seven days, and then the expected happened. One night, he and Clives were driving back from the World Famous Riverside and at a light two men got into the cab with them. It was, of course, Gorilla Grodd and Solomon Grundy. Good to see you again, Grodd said, and then they beat him as best they could, given the limited space inside the cab.

This time, Oscar didn't cry when they drove him back to the cane fields. Zafra would be here soon, and the cane had grown well and thick and in places you could hear the stalks clack-clack-clacking against each other like triffids, and you could hear the kriyol voices lost in the night. There was a moon, and Clives begged the men to spare Oscar, but they laughed. You should be worrying, Grodd said, about yourself. Oscar sent telepathic messages to his moms (I love you, Señora), to Rodolfo (Quit, Tío, and live), to Lola (I'm so sorry it happened; I always loved you), and the longest to Yvón.

They walked him into the cane and then turned him around. (Clives they left tied up in the cab.) They looked at him and he looked at them, and then he started to speak. He told them that what they were doing was wrong, that they were going to take a great love out of the world. Love was a rare thing, he told them, easily confused with a million other things, and if anybody knew this to be true it was him. He told them about Yvón and the way he loved her and how much they had risked and that they'd started to dream the same dreams and say the same words, and he told them that if they killed him they would probably feel nothing and their children would probably feel nothing, either, not until they were old and weak or about to be struck by a car, and then they would sense his waiting for them on the other side, and over there he wouldn't be no fat boy or dork or kid no girl had ever loved, over there he'd be a hero, an avenger. Because anything you can dream (he put his hand up) you can be.

They waited for him to finish, and then they shot him to pieces.

Oscar—

Lola and I flew down to claim the body. We went to the funeral. A year later, we broke up.

Four times, the family hired lawyers, but no charges were ever filed. The Embassy didn't help and neither did the government. Yvón, I hear, is still living in Mirador Norte, still dancing at the Riverside. The de Leóns sold their house a year later.

Lola swore she would never return to that terrible country, and I don't think she ever has. On one of our last nights, she said, Eight million Trujillos is all we are.

(Of course things like this don't happen in Santo Domingo no more. We have enlightened, uncorrupt politicians and a kind benevolent President and a people who are clearheaded and loving. The country is kind, no Haitian or dark-skinned person is hated, the élites fuck nobody, and the police measure their probity by the mile.)

Almost eight weeks after Oscar died, a package arrived at the house in Paterson. Two manuscripts enclosed. One was chapters of his never-to-be-completed opus, an E. E. (Doc) Smithesque space opera called "Starscourge." The other was a long letter to Lola. Turns out that toward the end the palomo *did* get Yvón away from the capital. For two whole days, they hid out on some beach in Barahona while the Capitán was away on "business," and guess what? Yvón actually kissed him! Guess what else? Yvón actually fucked him. Yahoo! He reported that he'd liked it and that Yvón's you-know-what hadn't tasted the way he had expected. She tastes like Heineken, he said. He wrote that at night Yvón had nightmares that the Capitán had found them; once, she'd woken up and said in the voice of true fear, Oscar, he's here, really believing he was, and Oscar woke up and threw himself at the Capitán but it turned out to be only a turtle shell the hotel had hung on the wall for decoration. Almost busted my nose! He wrote that Yvón had little hairs coming up almost to her bellybutton and that she crossed her eyes when she fucked but what really got him were the little intimacies that he'd never in his whole life anticipated, like combing her hair or getting her underwear off a line or watching her walk naked to the bathroom or the way she would suddenly sit on his lap and put her face into his neck. The intimacies like listening to her tell him about being a little girl and him telling her that he'd been a virgin all his life. He wrote that he couldn't believe he'd had to wait for this so goddam long. (Yvón was the one who suggested calling the wait something else. Yeah, like what? Maybe, she said, you could call it life.) He wrote: So this is what everybody's always talking about! Diablo! If only I'd known. The beauty! The beauty!

Wesley McNair

The Fat Enter Heaven

It is understood, with the clarity possible only
in heaven, that none have loved food
better than these. Angels gather to admire
their small mouths and their arms, round
as the fenders of Hudson Hornets. In their past
they have been among the world's most meek,
the farm boy who lived with his mother,
the grade-school teacher who led the flag salute
with expression, day after day. Now
their commonplace lives, the guilt
about weight, the ridicule fade and disappear.
They come to the table arrayed with perfect food
shedding their belts and girdles for the last time.
Here, where fat itself is heavenly,
they fill their plates and float upon the sky.

The Fat Girl

Her name was Louise. Once when she was sixteen a boy kissed her at a barbecue; he was drunk and he jammed his tongue into her mouth and ran his hands up and down her hips. Her father kissed her often. He was thin and kind and she could see in his eyes when he looked at her the lights of love and pity.

It started when Louise was nine. You must start watching what you eat, her mother would say. I can see you have my metabolism. Louise also had her mother's pale blonde hair. Her mother was slim and pretty, carried herself erectly, and ate very little. The two of them would eat bare lunches, while her older brother ate sandwiches and potato chips, and then her mother would sit smoking while Louise eyed the bread box, the pantry, the refrigerator. Wasn't that good, her mother would say. In five years you'll be in high school and if you're fat the boys won't like you; they won't ask you out. Boys were as far away as five years, and she would go to her room and wait for nearly an hour until she knew her mother was no longer thinking of her, then she would creep into the kitchen and, listening to her mother talking on the phone, or the footsteps upstairs, she would open the bread box, the pantry, the jar of peanut butter. She would put the sandwich under her shirt and go outside or to the bathroom to eat it.

Her father was a lawyer and made a lot of money and came home looking pale and happy. Martinis put color back in his face, and at dinner he talked to his wife and two children. Oh give her a potato, he would say to Louise's mother. She's a growing girl. Her mother's voice then became tense: If she has a potato she shouldn't have dessert. She should have both, her father would say, and he would reach over and touch Louise's cheek or hand or arm.

In high school she had two girl friends and at night and on weekends they rode in a car or went to movies. In movies she was fascinated by fat actresses. She wondered why they were fat. She knew why she was fat: she was fat because she was Louise. Because God had made her that way. Because she wasn't like her friends Joan and Marjorie, who drank milk shakes after school and were all bones and tight skin. But what about those actresses, with their talents, with their broad and profound faces? Did they eat as heedlessly as Bishop Humphries and his wife who sometimes came to dinner and, as Louise's mother said, gorged between amenities? Or did they try to lose weight, did they go about hungry and angry and thinking of food? She thought of them eating lean meats and salads with friends, and then going home and building strange large sandwiches with French bread. But mostly she believed they did not go through these failures; they were fat because they chose to be. And she was certain of something else too: she could see it in their faces: they did not eat secretly. Which she did: her creeping to the kitchen when she was nine became, in high school, a ritual of deceit and pleasure. She was a furtive eater of sweets. Even her two friends did not know her secret.

Joan was thin, gangling, and flat-chested; she was attractive enough and all she needed was someone to take a second look at her face, but the school was large and there were pretty girls in every classroom and walking all the corridors, so no one ever needed to take a second look at Joan. Marjorie was thin too, an intense, heavy-smoking girl with brittle laughter. She was very intelligent, and with boys she was shy because she knew she made them uncomfortable, and because she was smarter than they were and so could not understand or could not believe the levels they lived on. She was to have a nervous breakdown before earning her Ph.D. in philosophy at the University of California, where she met and married a physicist and discovered within herself an untrammelled passion: she made love with her husband on the couch, the carpet, in the bathtub, and on the washing machine. By that time much had happened to her and she never thought of Louise. Joan would finally stop growing and begin moving with grace and confidence. In college she would have two lovers and then several more during the six years she spent in Boston before marrying a middle-aged editor who had two sons in their early teens, who drank too much, who was tenderly, boyishly grateful for her love, and whose wife had been killed while rock-climbing in New Hampshire with her lover. She would not think of Louise either, except in an earlier time, when lovers were still new to her and she was ecstatically surprised each time one of them loved her and, sometimes at night, lying in a man's arms, she would tell how in high school no one dated her, she had been thin and plain (she would still believe that: that she had been plain; it had never been true) and so had been forced into the weekend and night-time company of a neurotic smart girl and a shy fat girl. She would say this with self-pity exaggerated by Scotch and her need to be more deeply loved by the man who held her.

She never eats, Joan and Marjorie said of Louise. They ate lunch with her at school, watched her refusing potatoes, ravioli, fried fish. Sometimes she got through the cafeteria line with only a salad. That is how they would remember her: a girl whose hapless body was destined to be fat. No one saw the sandwiches she made and took to her room when she came home from school. No one saw the store of Milky Ways, Butterfingers, Almond Joys, and Hersheys far back on her closet shelf, behind the stuffed animals of her childhood. She was not a hypocrite. When she was out of the house she truly believed she was dieting; she forgot about the candy, as a man speaking into his office dictaphone may forget the lewd photographs hidden in an old shoe in his closet. At other times, away from home, she thought of the waiting candy with near lust. One night driving home from a movie, Marjorie said: 'You're lucky you don't smoke; it's in*cred*ible what I go through to hide it from my parents.' Louise turned to her a smile which was elusive and mysterious; she yearned to be home in bed, eating chocolate in the dark. She did not need to smoke; she already had a vice that was insular and destructive.

She brought it with her to college. She thought she would leave it behind. A move from one place to another, a new room without the haunted closet shelf, would do for her what she could not do for herself. She packed her large dresses and went. For two weeks she was busy with registration, with shyness, with classes; then she began to feel at home. Her room was no longer like a motel. Its walls had stopped watching her, she felt they were her friends, and she gave them her secret. Away from her mother, she did not have to be as elaborate; she kept the candy in her drawer now.

The school was in Massachusetts, a girls' school. When she chose it, when she and her father and mother talked about it in the evenings, everyone so carefully avoided the word boys that sometimes the conversations seemed to be about nothing but boys. There are no boys there, the neuter words said; you will not have to contend with that. In her father's eyes were pity and encouragement; in her mother's was disappointment, and her voice was crisp. They spoke of courses, of small classes where Louise would get more attention. She imagined herself in those small classes; she saw herself as a teacher would see her, as the other girls would; she would get no attention.

The girls at the school were from wealthy families, but most of them wore the uniform of another class: blue jeans and work shirts, and many wore overalls. Louise bought some overalls, washed them until the dark blue faded, and wore them to classes. In the cafeteria she ate as she had in high school, not to lose weight nor even to sustain her lie, but because eating lightly in public had become as habitual as good manners. Everyone had to take gym, and in the locker room with the other girls, and wearing shorts on the volleyball and badminton courts, she hated her body. She liked her body most when she was unaware of it: in bed at night, as sleep gently took her out of her day, out of herself. And she liked parts of her body. She liked her brown eyes and sometimes looked at them in the mirror: they were not shallow eyes, she thought; they were indeed windows of a tender soul, a good heart. She liked her lips and nose, and her chin, finely shaped between her wide and sagging cheeks. Most of all she liked her long pale blonde hair, she liked washing and drying it and lying naked on her bed, smelling of shampoo, and feeling the soft hair at her neck and shoulders and back.

Her friend at college was Carrie, who was thin and wore thick glasses and often at night she cried in Louise's room. She did not know why she was crying. She was crying, she said, because she was unhappy. She could say no more. Louise said she was unhappy too, and Carrie moved in with her. One night Carrie talked for hours, sadly and bitterly, about her parents and what they did to each other. When she finished she hugged Louise and they went to bed. Then in the dark Carrie spoke across the room: 'Louise? I just wanted to tell you. One night last week I woke up and smelled chocolate. You were eating chocolate, in your bed. I wish you'd eat in front of me, Louise, whenever you feel like it.'

Stiffened in her bed, Louise could think of nothing to say. In the silence she was afraid Carrie would think she was asleep and would tell her again in the morning or tomorrow night. Finally she said Okay. Then after a moment she told Carrie if she ever wanted any she could feel free to help herself; the candy was in the top drawer. Then she said thank you.

They were roommates for four years and in the summers they exchanged letters. Each fall they greeted with embraces, laughter, tears, and moved into their old room, which had been stripped and cleansed of them for the summer. Neither girl enjoyed summer. Carrie did not like being at home because her parents did not love each other. Louise lived in a small city in Louisiana. She did not like summer because she had lost touch with Joan and Marjorie; they saw each other, but it was not the same. She liked being with her father but with no one else. The flicker of disappointment in her mother's eyes at the airport was a vanguard of the army of relatives and acquaintances who awaited her: they would see her in the streets, in stores, at the country club, in her home, and in theirs; in the first moments of greeting, their eyes would tell her she was still fat Louise, who had been fat as long as they could remember, who had gone to college and returned as fat as ever. Then their eyes dismissed her, and she longed for school and Carrie, and she wrote letters to her friend. But that saddened her too. It wasn't simply that Carrie was her only friend, and when they finished college they might never see each other again. It was that her existence in the world was so divided; it had begun when she was a child creeping to the kitchen; now that division was much sharper, and her friendship with Carrie seemed disproportionate and perilous. The world she was destined to live in had nothing to do with the intimate nights in their room at school.

In the summer before their senior year, Carrie fell in love. She wrote to Louise about him, but she did not write much, and this hurt Louise more than if Carrie had shown the joy her writing tried to conceal. That fall they returned to their room; they were still close and warm, Carrie still needed Louise's ears and heart at night as she spoke of her parents and her recurring malaise whose source the two friends never discovered. But on most week-ends Carrie left, and caught a bus to Boston where her boyfriend studied music. During the week she often spoke hesitantly of sex; she was not sure if she liked it. But Louise, eating candy and listening, did not know whether Carrie was telling the truth or whether, as in her letters of the past summer, Carrie was keeping from her those delights she may never experience.

Then one Sunday night when Carrie had just returned from Boston and was unpacking her overnight bag, she looked at

Louise and said: 'I was thinking about you. On the bus coming home tonight.' Looking at Carrie's concerned, determined face, Louise prepared herself for humiliation. 'I was thinking about when we graduate. What you're going to do. What's to become of you. I want you to be loved the way I love you. Louise, if I help you, *rea*lly help you, will you go on a diet?'

Louise entered a period of her life she would remember always, the way some people remember having endured poverty. Her diet did not begin the next day. Carrie told her to eat on Monday as though it were the last day of her life. So for the first time since grammar school Louise went into a school cafeteria and ate everything she wanted. At breakfast and lunch and dinner she glanced around the table to see if the other girls noticed the food on her tray. They did not. She felt there was a lesson in this, but it lay beyond her grasp. That night in their room she ate the four remaining candy bars. During the day Carrie rented a small refrigerator, bought an electric skillet, an electric broiler, and bathroom scales.

On Tuesday morning Louise stood on the scales, and Carrie wrote in her notebook: *October 14: 184 lbs.* Then she made Louise a cup of black coffee and scrambled one egg and sat with her while she ate. When Carrie went to the dining room for breakfast, Louise walked about the campus for thirty minutes. That was part of the plan. The campus was pretty, on its lawns grew at least one of every tree native to New England, and in the warm morning sun Louise felt a new hope. At noon they met in their room, and Carrie broiled her a piece of hamburger and served it with lettuce. Then while Carrie ate in the dining room Louise walked again. She was weak with hunger and she felt queasy. During her afternoon classes she was nervous and tense, and she chewed her pencil and tapped her heels on the floor and tightened her calves. When she returned to her room late that afternoon, she was so glad to see Carrie that she embraced her; she had felt she could not bear another minute of hunger, but now with Carrie she knew she could make it at least through tonight. Then she would sleep and face tomorrow when it came. Carrie broiled her a steak and served it with lettuce. Louise studied while Carrie ate dinner, then they went for a walk.

That was her ritual and her diet for the rest of the year, Carrie alternating fish and chicken breasts with the steaks for dinner, and every day was nearly as bad as the first. In the evenings she was irritable. In all her life she had never been afflicted by ill temper and she looked upon it now as a demon which, along with hunger, was taking possession of her soul. Often she spoke sharply to Carrie. One night during their after-dinner walk Carrie talked sadly of night, of how darkness made her more aware of herself, and at night she did not know why she was in college, why she studied, why she was walking the earth with other people. They were standing on a wooden foot bridge, looking down at a dark pond. Carrie kept talking; perhaps soon she would cry. Suddenly Louise said: 'I'm sick of lettuce. I never want to see a piece of lettuce for the rest of my life. I hate it. We shouldn't even buy it, it's immoral.'

Carrie was quiet. Louise glanced at her, and the pain and irritation in Carrie's face soothed her. Then she was ashamed. Before she could say she was sorry, Carrie turned to her and said gently: 'I know. I know how terrible it is.'

Carrie did all the shopping, telling Louise she knew how hard it was to go into a supermarket when you were hungry. And Louise was always hungry. She drank diet soft drinks and started smoking Carrie's cigarettes, learned to enjoy inhaling, thought of cancer and emphysema but they were as far away as those boys her mother had talked about when she was nine. By Thanksgiving she was smoking over a pack a day and her weight in Carrie's notebook was one hundred and sixty-two pounds. Carrie was afraid if Louise went home at Thanksgiving she would lapse from the diet, so Louise spent the vacation with Carrie, in Philadelphia. Carrie wrote her family about the diet, and told Louise that she had. On the plane to Philadelphia, Louise said: 'I feel like a bedwetter. When I was a little girl I had a friend who used to come spend the night and Mother would put a rubber sheet on the bed and we all pretended there wasn't a rubber sheet and that she hadn't wet the bed. Even me, and I slept with her.' At Thanksgiving dinner she lowered her eyes as Carrie's father put two slices of white meat on her plate and passed it to her over the bowls of steaming food.

When she went home at Christmas she weighed a hundred and fifty-five pounds; at the airport her mother marvelled. Her father laughed and hugged her and said: 'But now there's less of you to love.' He was troubled by her smoking but only mentioned it once; he told her she was beautiful and, as always, his eyes bathed her with love. During the long vacation her mother cooked for her as Carrie had, and Louise returned to school weighing a hundred and forty-six pounds.

Flying north on the plane she warmly recalled the surprised and congratulatory eyes of her relatives and acquaintances. She had not seen Joan or Marjorie. She thought of returning home in May, weighing the hundred and fifteen pounds which Carrie had in October set as their goal. Looking toward the stoic days ahead, she felt strong. She thought of those hungry days of fall and early winter (and now: she was hungry now: with almost a frown, almost a brusque shake of the head, she refused peanuts from the stewardess): those first weeks of the diet when she was the pawn of an irascibility, which still, conditioned to her ritual as she was, could at any moment take command of her. She thought of the nights of trying to sleep while her stomach growled. She thought of her addiction to cigarettes. She thought of the people at school: not one teacher, not one girl, had spoken to her about her loss of weight, not even about her absence from meals. And without warning her spirit collapsed. She did not feel strong, she did not feel she was committed to and within reach of achieving a valuable goal. She felt that somehow she had lost more than pounds of fat; that some time during her dieting she had lost herself too. She tried to remember what it had felt like to be Louise before she had started living on meat and fish, as an unhappy adult may look sadly in the memory of childhood for lost virtues and hopes. She looked down at the earth far below, and it seemed to her that her soul, like her body aboard the plane, was in some rootless flight. She neither knew its destination nor where it had departed from; it was on some passage she could not even define.

During the next few weeks she lost weight more slowly and once for eight days Carrie's daily recording stayed at a hundred and thirty-six. Louise woke in the morning thinking of one hundred and thirty-six and then she stood on the scales and they echoed her. She became obsessed with that number, and there wasn't a day when she didn't say it aloud, and through the days and nights the number stayed in her mind, and if a teacher had spoken those digits in a classroom she would have opened her mouth to speak. What if that's me, she said to Carrie. I mean what if a hundred and thirty-six is my real weight and I just can't lose any more. Walking hand-in-hand with her despair was a longing for this to be true, and that longing angered her and wearied her, and every day she was gloomy. On the ninth day she weighed a hundred and thirty-five and a half pounds. She was not relieved; she thought bitterly of the months ahead, the shedding of the last twenty and a half pounds.

On Easter Sunday, which she spent at Carrie's, she weighed one hundred and twenty pounds, and she ate one slice of glazed pineapple with her ham and lettuce. She did not enjoy it: she felt she was being friendly with a recalcitrant enemy who had once tried to destroy her. Carrie's parents were laudative. She liked them and she wished they would touch sometimes, and look at each other when they spoke. She guessed they would divorce when Carrie left home, and she vowed that her own marriage would be one of affection and tenderness. She could think about that now: marriage. At school she had read in a Boston paper that this summer the cicadas would come out of their seventeen year hibernation on Cape Cod, for a month they would mate and then die, leaving their young to burrow into the ground where they would stay for seventeen years. That's me, she had said to Carrie. Only my hibernation lasted twenty-one years.

Often her mother asked in letters and on the phone about the diet, but Louise answered vaguely. When she flew home in late May she weighed a hundred and thirteen pounds, and at the airport her mother cried and hugged her and said again and again: You're so *beaut*iful. Her father blushed and bought her a martini. For days her relatives and acquaintances congratulated her, and the applause in their eyes lasted the entire summer, and she loved their eyes, and swam in the country club pool, the first time she had done this since she was a child.

She lived at home and ate the way her mother did and every morning she weighed herself on the scales in her bathroom. Her mother liked to take her shopping and buy her dresses and they put her old ones in the Goodwill box at the shopping center; Louise thought of them existing on the body of a poor woman whose cheap meals kept her fat. Louise's mother had a photographer come to the house, and Louise posed on the couch and standing beneath a live oak and sitting in a wicker lawn chair next to an azalea bush. The new clothes and the photographer made her feel she was going to another country or becoming a citizen of a new one. In the fall she took a job of no consequence, to give herself something to do.

Also in the fall a young lawyer joined her father's firm, he came one night to dinner, and they started seeing each other. He was the first man outside her family to kiss her since the barbecue when she was sixteen. Louise celebrated Thanksgiving not with rice dressing and candied sweet potatoes and mince meat and pumpkin pies, but by giving Richard her virginity which she realized, at the very last moment of its existence, she had embarked on giving him over thirteen months ago, on that Tuesday in October when Carrie had made her a cup of black coffee and scrambled one egg. She wrote this to Carrie, who replied happily by return mail. She also, through glance and smile and innuendo, tried to tell her mother too. But finally she controlled that impulse, because Richard felt guilty about making love with the daughter of his partner and friend. In the spring they married. The wedding was a large one, in the Episcopal church, and Carrie flew from Boston to be maid of honor. Her parents had recently separated and she was living with the musician and was still victim of her unpredictable malaise. It overcame her on the night before the wedding, so Louise was up with her until past three and woke next morning from a sleep so heavy that she did not want to leave it.

Richard was a lean, tall, energetic man with the metabolism of a pencil sharpener. Louise fed him everything he wanted. He liked Italian food and she got recipes from her mother and watched him eating spaghetti with the sauce she had only tasted, and ravioli and lasagna, while she ate antipasto with her chianti. He made a lot of money and borrowed more and they bought a house whose lawn sloped down to the shore of a lake; they had a wharf and a boathouse, and Richard bought a boat and they took friends waterskiing. Richard bought her a car and they spent his vacations in Mexico, Canada, the Bahamas, and in the fifth year of their marriage they went to Europe and, according to their plan, she conceived a child in Paris. On the plane back, as she looked out the window and beyond the sparkling sea and saw her country, she felt that it was waiting for her, as her home by the lake was, and her parents, and her good friends who rode in the boat and waterskied; she thought of the accumulated warmth and pelf of her marriage, and how by slimming her body she had bought into the pleasures of the nation. She felt cunning, and she smiled to herself, and took Richard's hand.

But these moments of triumph were sparse. On most days she went about her routine of leisure with a sense of certainty about herself that came merely from not thinking. But there were times, with her friends, or with Richard, or alone in the house, when she was suddenly assaulted by the feeling that she had taken the wrong train and arrived at a place where no one knew her, and where she ought not to be. Often, in bed with Richard, she talked of being fat: 'I was the one who started the friendship with Carrie, I chose her, I started the conversations. When I understood that she was my friend I understood something else: I had chosen her for the same reason I'd chosen Joan and Marjorie. They were all thin. I was always thinking about what people saw when they looked at me and I didn't want them to see two fat girls. When I was alone I didn't mind being fat but then I'd have to leave the house again and then I didn't want to look like me. But at home I didn't mind except when I was getting dressed to go out of the house and when Mother looked at me. But I stopped looking at her when she looked at me. And in college I felt good with Carrie; there weren't any boys and I didn't have any other friends and so when I wasn't with Carrie I thought about her and I tried to ignore the other people around me, I tried to make them not exist. A lot of the time I could do that. It was strange, and I felt like a spy.'

If Richard was bored by her repetition he pretended not to be. But she knew the story meant very little to him. She could have been telling him of a childhood illness, or wearing braces, or a broken heart at sixteen. He could not see her as she was when she was fat. She felt as though she were trying to tell a foreign lover about her life in the United States, and if only she could command the language he would know and love all of her and she would feel complete. Some of the acquaintances of her childhood were her friends now, and even they did not seem to remember her when she was fat.

Now her body was growing again, and when she put on a maternity dress for the first time she shivered with fear. Richard did not smoke and he asked her, in a voice just short of demand, to stop during her pregnancy. She did. She ate carrots and celery instead of smoking, and at cocktail parties she tried to eat nothing, but after her first drink she ate nuts and cheese and crackers and dips. Always at these parties Richard had talked with his friends and she had rarely spoken to him until they drove home. But now when he noticed her at the hors d'oeuvres table he crossed the room and, smiling, led her back to his group. His smile and his hand on her arm told her he was doing his clumsy, husbandly best to help her through a time of female mystery.

She was gaining weight but she told herself it was only the baby, and would leave with its birth. But at other times she knew quite clearly that she was losing the discipline she had fought so hard to gain during her last year with Carrie. She was hungry now as she had been in college, and she ate between meals and after dinner and tried to eat only carrots and celery, but she grew to hate them, and her desire for sweets was as vicious as it had been long ago. At home she ate bread and jam and when she shopped for groceries she bought a candy bar and ate it driving home and put the wrapper in her purse and then in the garbage can under the sink. Her cheeks had filled out, there was loose flesh under her chin, her arms and legs were plump, and her mother was concerned. So was Richard. One night when she brought pie and milk to the living room where they were watching television, he said: 'You already had a piece. At dinner.'

She did not look at him.

'You're gaining weight. It's not all water, either. It's fat. It'll be summertime. You'll want to get into your bathing suit.'

The pie was cherry. She looked at it as her fork cut through it; she speared the piece and rubbed it in the red juice on the plate before lifting it to her mouth.

'You never used to eat pie,' he said. 'I just think you ought to watch it a bit. It's going to be tough on you this summer.'

In her seventh month, with a delight reminiscent of climbing the stairs to Richard's apartment before they were married, she returned to her world of secret gratification. She began hiding candy in her underwear drawer. She ate it during the day and at night while Richard slept, and at breakfast she was distracted, waiting for him to leave.

She gave birth to a son, brought him home, and nursed both him and her appetites. During this time of celibacy she enjoyed her body through her son's mouth; while he suckled she stroked his small head and back. She was hiding candy but she did not conceal her other indulgences: she was smoking again but still she ate between meals, and at dinner she ate what Richard did, and coldly he watched her, he grew petulant, and when the date marking the end of their celibacy came they let it pass. Often in the afternoons her mother visited and scolded her and Louise sat looking at the baby and said nothing until finally, to end it, she promised to diet. When her mother and father came for dinners, her father kissed her and held the baby and her mother said nothing about Louise's body, and her voice was tense. Returning from work in the evenings Richard looked at a soiled plate and glass on the table beside her chair as if detecting traces of infidelity, and at every dinner they fought.

'Look at you,' he said. 'Lasagna, for God's sake. When are you going to start? It's not simply that you haven't lost any weight. You're gaining. I can see it. I can feel it when you get in bed. Pretty soon you'll weigh more than I do and I'll be sleeping on a trampoline.'

'You never touch me anymore.'

'I don't want to touch you. Why should I? Have you *looked* at yourself?'

'You're cruel,' she said. 'I never knew how cruel you were.'

She ate, watching him. He did not look at her. Glaring at his plate, he worked with fork and knife like a hurried man at a lunch counter.

'I bet you didn't either,' she said.

That night when he was asleep she took a Milky Way to the bathroom. For a while she stood eating in the dark, then she turned on the light. Chewing, she looked at herself in the mirror; she looked at her eyes and hair. Then she stood on the scales and looking at the numbers between her feet, one hundred and sixty-two, she remembered when she had weighed a hundred and thirty-six pounds for eight days. Her memory of those eight days was fond and amusing, as though she were recalling an Easter egg hunt when she was six. She stepped off the scales and pushed them under the lavatory and did not stand on them again.

It was summer and she bought loose dresses and when Richard took friends out on the boat she did not wear a bathing suit or shorts, her friends gave her mischievous glances, and Richard did not look at her. She stopped riding on the boat. She told them she wanted to stay with the baby, and she sat inside holding him until she heard the boat leave the wharf. Then she took him to the front lawn and walked with him in the shade of the trees and talked to him about the blue jays and mockingbirds and cardinals she saw on their branches. Sometimes she stopped and watched the boat out on the lake and the friend skiing behind it.

Every day Richard quarrelled, and because his rage went no further than her weight and shape, she felt excluded from it, and she remained calm within layers of flesh and spirit, and watched his frustration, his impotence. He truly believed they were arguing about her weight. She knew better: she knew that beneath the argument lay the question of who Richard was. She thought of him smiling at the wheel of his boat, and long ago courting his slender girl, the daughter of his partner and friend. She thought of Carrie telling her of smelling chocolate in the dark and, after that, watching her eat it night after night. She smiled at Richard, teasing his anger.

He is angry now. He stands in the center of the living room, raging at her, and he wakes the baby. Beneath Richard's voice she hears the soft crying, feels it in her heart, and quietly she rises from her chair and goes upstairs to the child's room and takes him from the crib. She brings him to the living room and sits holding him in her lap, pressing him gently against the folds of fat at her waist. Now Richard is pleading with her. Louise thinks tenderly of Carrie broiling meat and fish in their room, and walking with her in the evenings. She wonders if Carrie still has the malaise. Perhaps she will come for a visit. In Louise's arms now the boy sleeps.

'I'll help you,' Richard says. 'I'll eat the same things you eat.'

But his face does not approach the compassion and determination and love she had seen in Carrie's during what she now recognizes as the worst year of her life. She can remember nothing about that year except hunger, and the meals in her room. She is hungry now. When she puts the boy to bed she will get a candy bar from her room. She will eat it here, in front of Richard. This room will be hers soon. She considers the possibilities: all these rooms and the lawn where she can do whatever she wishes. She knows he will leave soon. It has been in his eyes all summer. She stands, using one hand to pull herself out of the chair. She carries the boy to his crib, feels him against her large breasts, feels that his sleeping body touches her soul. With a surge of vindication and relief she holds him. Then she kisses his forehead and places him in the crib. She goes to the bedroom and in the dark takes a bar of candy from her drawer. Slowly she descends the stairs. She knows Richard is waiting but she feels his departure so happily that, when she enters the living room, unwrapping the candy, she is surprised to see him standing there.

Crash Diet

Kenneth left me on a Monday morning before I'd even had the chance to mousse my hair, and I just stood there at the picture window with the drapes swung back and watched him get into that flashy red Mazda, which I didn't want him to get anyway, and drive away down Marnier Street, and make a right onto Seagrams. That's another thing I didn't want, to live in a subdivision where all the streets are named after some kind of liquor. But Kenneth thought that was cute because he runs a bartending school, which is where he met Lydia to begin with.

"I'll come back for the rest of my things," he said, and I wondered just what he meant by that. What was his and what was mine?

"Where are you going to live, in a pup tent?" I asked and took the towel off of my head. I have the kind of hair that will dry right into big clumps of frosted-looking thread if I don't comb it out fast. Once, well before I met Kenneth at the Holiday Inn lounge where he was giving drink-mixing lessons to the staff, I wrote a personal ad and described myself as having angel hair, knowing full well that whoever read it would picture flowing blond curls, when what I really meant was the stuff that you put on a Christmas tree or use to insulate your house. I also said I was average size, which at the time I was.

"I'm moving in with Lydia," he said in his snappy, matter-of-fact way, like I had just trespassed on his farmland. Lydia. It had been going on for a year and a half though I had only known of it for six weeks. *LYDIA*, a name so old-sounding even my grandmother wouldn't have touched it.

"Well, give her my best," I said like you might say to a child who is threatening to run away from home. "Send me a postcard," I said and laughed, though I already felt myself nearing a crack, like I might fall right into it, a big dark crack, me and five years of Kenneth and liquor streets and the microwave oven that I'd just bought to celebrate our five years of marriage and the fact that I had finally started losing some of the weight that I had put on during the first two years.

"Why did you do this?" he asked when he came home that day smelling of coconut because he had been teaching piña coladas, and approached that microwave oven that I had tied up in red ribbon.

"It's our anniversary," I said and told him that he was making me so hungry for macaroons or those Hostess Snoballs with all that pink coconut. I'd lost thirty pounds by that time and needed to lose only ten more and they were going to take my "after" picture and put me on the wall of the Diet Center along with all the other warriors (that's what they called us) who had conquered fat.

"But this is a big investment," Kenneth said and picked up the warranty. Five years, and he stared at that like it had struck some chord in his brain that was high-pitched and off-key. Five years, that's how long it had been since we honeymooned down at Sea Island, Georgia, and drank daiquiris that Kenneth said didn't have enough rum and ate all kinds of wonderful food that Kenneth didn't monitor going down my throat like he came to do later.

"Well, sure it's an investment," I told him. "Like a marriage."

"Guaranteed for five years," he said and then got all choked up, tried to talk but cried instead, and I knew something wasn't right. I sat up half the night waiting for him to say something. *Happy anniversary, You sure do look good these days,* anything. It must have been about two A.M. when I got out of him the name Lydia, and I didn't do a thing but get up and out of that bed and start working on the mold that wedges in between those tiles in the shower stall. That's what I do when I get upset because it's hard to eat while scrubbing and because there's always mold to be found if you look for it.

"You'll have to cross that bridge when you come to it," my mama always said, and when I saw Kenneth make that right turn onto Seagrams, I knew I was crossing it right then. I had two choices: I could go back to bed or I could do something. I have never been one to climb back into the bed after it's been made, so I got busy. I moussed my hair and got dressed, and I went to my pocketbook and got out the title to that Mazda that had both our names on it. I poured a glass of wine, since it was summer vacation from teaching sixth grade, painted my toenails, and then, in the most careful way, I wrote in Kenneth's handwriting that I (Kenneth I. Barkley) gave full ownership of the Mazda to Sandra White Barkley, and then I signed his name. Even Kenneth couldn't have told that it wasn't his signature; that's just how well I forged. I finished my wine, got dressed, and went over to my friend Paula's house to get it notarized.

"Why are you doing this?" Paula asked me. She was standing there in her bathrobe, and I could hear some movement in the back where her bedroom was. I didn't know if she meant why was I stopping by her house unannounced or why I was changing the title on the car. I know it's rude to stop by a person's house unannounced and hated to admit I had done it, so I just focused on the title. Sometimes I can focus so well on things and other times I can't at all.

"Kenneth and I are separating and I get the Mazda," I told her.

"When did this happen?" Paula asked, and glanced over her shoulder to that cracked bedroom door.

"About two hours ago," I told her and sat down on the sofa. Paula just kept standing there like she didn't know what to do, like she could have killed me for just coming in and having a seat in the middle of her activities, but I didn't focus on that. "Just put your stamp on it and I'll be going." I held that title and piece of paper out to her, and she stared down at it and shook her head back and forth. "Did Kenneth write this?" she asked me, like my reputation might not be the best.

"Haven't I been through enough this morning?" I asked her and worked some tears into my eyes. "What kind of friend questions such a thing?"

"I'm sorry, Sandra," she said, her face as pink as her bathrobe. "I have to ask this sort of thing. I'll be right back." She went down the hall to her bedroom, and I got some candy corn out of her little dish shaped like a duck or something in that family. I wedged the large ends up and over my front teeth so I had fangs like little kids always do at Halloween.

"Who was that?" I heard a man say, frustrated. I could hear frustration in every syllable that carried out there to the living room, and then Paula said, "Shhh." When she came back with her little embosser, I had both front teeth covered in candy corn and grinned at her. She didn't laugh so I took them off my teeth and laid them on her coffee table. I don't eat sweets.

"I'm sorry I can't talk right now," Paula said. "You see..."

"What big eyes you have," I said and took my notarized paper right out of her hand. "Honey, go for it," I told her and pointed down the hall. "I'm doing just fine."

"I feel so guilty, though," Paula said, her hair all flat on one side from sleeping that way. "I feel like maybe you need to talk to somebody." That's what people always say when they feel like they should do something but have no intention of doing it, *I feel so bad*, or *If only*. I just laughed and told Paula I had to go to Motor Vehicles and take care of a piece of business and then I had to go to the police station and report a stolen car.

"What?" Paula asked, and her mouth fell open and she didn't even look over her shoulder when there were several frustrated and impatient knocks on her bedroom wall. "That's illegal."

"And you're my accomplice," I told her and walked on down the sidewalk and got into that old Ford Galaxy, which still smelled like the apples that Kenneth's granddaddy used to keep in it to combat his cigar smoke. If there'd been a twenty-year-old apple to be found rolling around there under the front seat, I would've eaten it.

I didn't report the car, though. By the time I had driven by Lydia's house fourteen times—the first four of which the Mazda was out front and the other ten parked two blocks away behind the fish market (hidden, they thought)—I was too tired to talk to anybody so I just went home to bed. By ten o'clock, I'd had a full night's sleep so I got up, thawed some hamburger in the microwave, and made three pans of lasagna, which I then froze because mozzarella is not on my diet.

The next day, I was thinking about going to the grocery store because I didn't have a carrot in the house, but it was as if my blood was so slow I couldn't even put on a pair of socks. I felt like I had taken a handful of Valium but I hadn't. I checked the bottle there at the back of the medicine cabinet that was prescribed for Kenneth when he pulled his back lifting a case of Kahlúa about a year ago. The bottle was there with not a pill touched, so I didn't have an excuse to be found for this heaviness. "When you feel heavy, exercise!" we warriors say, so before my head could be turned toward something like cinnamon toast, I got dressed and did my Jane Fonda routine twice, scrubbed the gasoline spots from the driveway, and then drove to the Piggly Wiggly for some carrots. It felt good being in the car with the radio going, so I didn't get out at the Piggly Wiggly but kept driving. I had never seen that rotating bar that is in a motel over in Clemmonsville, so I went there. It was not nearly as nice as Kenneth had made it sound; I couldn't even tell that I was moving at all, so I rode the glass elevator twice, and then checked into the motel across the street. It was a motel like I'd never seen, electric finger massages for a quarter and piped-in reggae. I liked it so much I stayed a week and ate coleslaw from Kentucky Fried Chicken. When I got home, I bought some carrots at the Piggly Wiggly.

"I was so worried about you!" my buddy Martha from the Diet Center said, and ran into my house. Martha is having a long hard time getting rid of her excess. "I was afraid you were binging."

"No, just took a little trip for my nerves," I told her, and she stood with her mouth wide open like she had seen Frankenstein. "Kenneth and I have split." Martha's mouth was still hanging open, which is part of her problem: oral, she's an oral person.

"Look at you," Martha said, and put her hands on my hips, squeezed on my bones there, love handles they're sometimes called if you've got somebody who loves them. "You've lost, Sandra."

"Well, Kenneth and I weren't right for each other, I guess."

"The hell with Kenneth," Martha said, her eyes filling with tears. "You've lost more weight." Martha shook my hips until my teeth rattled. She is one of those people who her whole life has been told she has a pretty face. And she does, but it makes her mad for people to say it because she knows what they mean is that she's fat, and to ignore that fact they say what a pretty face she has. Anybody who's ever been overweight has had this happen. "I'm going to miss you at the meetings," Martha said, and looked like she was going to cry again. Martha is only thirty, just five years younger than me, but she looks older; the word is *matronly,* and it has a lot to do with the kind of clothes you have to wear if you're overweight. The mall here doesn't have an oversize shop.

I went to the beauty parlor and told them I wanted the works— treatments, facials, haircut, new shampoo, mousse, spray, curling wand. I spent a hundred and fifty dollars there, and then I went to Revco and bought every color of nail polish that they had, four different new colognes because they each represented a different mood, five boxes of Calgon in case I didn't get back to Revco for a while, all the Hawaiian Tropic products, including a sun visor and beach towel. I bought a hibachi and three bags of charcoal, a hammock, some barbecue tongs, an apron that says KISS THE COOK, and one of those inflatable pools so I could stretch out in the backyard in some water. I bought one of those rafts that will hold a canned drink in a little pocket, in case I should decide to walk down to the pool in our subdivision over on Tequila Circle. Summer was well under way, and I had to catch up on things. I bought a garden hose and a hoe and a rake, thinking I might relandscape my yard even though the subdivision doesn't really like you to take nature into your own hands. I had my mind on weeping willows and crepe myrtle. I went ahead and bought fifteen azaleas while I was there, some gardening gloves, and some rubber shoes for working in the yard. Comet was on sale so I went ahead and got twenty cans. I bought a set of dishes (four place settings) because Kenneth had come and taken mine while I was in Clemmonsville; I guess Lydia didn't have any dishes. Then I thought that wouldn't be enough if I should have company, so I got two more sets so that I'd have twelve place settings. I figured if I was to have more than twelve people for dinner then I'd need not only a new dining-room set but also a new dining room. I didn't have any place mats that matched those dishes so I picked up some and some glasses that matched the blue border on my new plates and some stainless because I had always loved that pattern with the pistol handle on the knife.

They had everything in this Revco. I thought if I couldn't sleep at night I'd make an afghan, so I picked out some pretty yarn, and then I thought, well, if I was going to start making afghans at night, I could get ahead on my Christmas shopping, and so I'd make an afghan for my mama and one for Paula, who had been calling me on the phone nonstop to make sure I hadn't reported the stolen car, and one for Martha that I'd make a little bigger than normal, which made me think that I hadn't been to the Diet Center in so long I didn't even know my weight, so I went and found the digital scales and put one right on top of my seventy-nine skeins of yarn. I bought ten each of Candy Pink, Watermelon, Cocoa, Almond, Wine, Cinnamon, Lime, and only nine of the Cherry because the dye lot ran out. It made me hungry, so I got some dietetic bonbons. By the time I got to the checkout I had five carts full and when that young girl looked at me and handed me the tape that was over a yard long, I handed her Kenneth I. Barkley's MasterCard and said, "Charge it."

It was too hot to work in the yard, and I was too tired to crochet or unpack the car and felt kind of sick to my stomach. Thinking it was from the bonbon I ate on the way home, I went to the bathroom to get an Alka-Seltzer, but Kenneth had taken those too, so I just took two Valiums and went to bed.

"I feel like a yo-yo," I told the shrink when Paula suggested that I go. All of my clothes were way too big, so I had given them to Martha as an incentive for her to lose some weight and had ordered myself a whole new wardrobe from Neiman-Marcus on Kenneth I. Barkley's MasterCard number. That's why I had to wear my KISS THE COOK apron and my leotard and tights to the shrink's. "My clothes should be here any day now," I told him, and he smiled.

"No, I feel like a yo-yo, not a regular yo-yo either," I said. "I feel like one of those advanced yo-yos, the butterfly model, you know where the halves are turned facing outward and you can do all those tricks like 'walk the dog,' 'around the world,' and 'eat spaghetti.'" He laughed, just threw back his head and laughed, so tickled over "eat spaghetti"; laughing at the expense of another human being, laughing when he was going to charge me close to a hundred dollars for that visit that I was going to pay for with a check from my dual checkbook, which was what was left of Kenneth I. Barkley's account over at Carolina Trust. I had already taken most of the money out of that account and moved it over to State Employee's Credit Union. That man tried to be serious, but every time I opened my mouth, it seemed he laughed.

But I didn't care because I hadn't had so much fun since Kenneth and I ate a half-gallon of rocky-road ice cream in our room there in Sea Island, Georgia.

"Have you done anything unusual lately?" he asked. "You know, like going for long rides, spending lots of money?"

"No," I said and noticed that I had a run in my tights. After that, I couldn't think of a thing but runs and running. I wanted to train for the Boston Marathon. I knew I'd win if I entered.

Lydia was ten years younger than Kenneth, I had found that out during the six weeks when he fluctuated between snappy and choked up. That's what I knew of her, ten years younger than Kenneth and studying to be a barmaid, and that's why I rolled the trees in the yard of that pitiful-looking house she rented with eleven rolls of decorator toilet paper. My new clothes had come by then so I wore my black silk dress with the ruffled off-the-shoulder look. Lydia is thirteen years younger than me and, from what I could tell of her shadow in the window, about twenty pounds heavier. I was a twig by then. "I'd rather be an old man's darlin' than a young man's slave," my mama told me just before I got married, and I said, "You mind your own damn business." Lydia's mama had probably told her the same thing, and you can't trust a person who listens to her mama.

I stood there under a tree and hoisted roll after roll of the decorator toilet paper into the air and let it drape over branches. I wrapped it in and out of that wrought-iron rail along her steps and tied a great big bow. I was behind the shrubs, there where it was dark, when the front door opened and I heard her say, "I could have sworn I heard something," and then she said, "Just look at this mess!" She was turning to get Kenneth so I got on my stomach and slid along the edge of the house and hid by the corner. I got my dress covered with mud and pine straw, but I didn't really care because I liked the dress so much when I saw it there in the book that I ordered two. The porch light came on, and then she was out in that front yard with her hands on her hips and the ugliest head of hair I'd ever seen, red algae hair that looked like it hadn't been brushed in four years. "When is *she* going to leave us alone?" Lydia asked, and looked at Kenneth, who was standing there with what looked like a tequila sunrise in his hand. He looked terrible. "You've got to do something!" Lydia said, and started crying. "You better call your lawyer right now. She's already spent all your money."

"I'll call Sandra tomorrow," Kenneth said, and put his arm around Lydia, but she wasn't having any part of that. She twisted away and slapped his drink to the dirt.

"Call *her*?" Lydia screamed, and I wished I had my camera to catch her expression right when she was beginning to say "her"; that new camera of mine could catch anything. "What good is that going to do?"

"Maybe I can settle it all," he said. "I'm the one who left her. If it goes to court, she'll get everything."

"She already has," Lydia said, sat down in the yard, and blew her nose on some of that decorator toilet paper. "The house, the money. She has taken everything except the Mazda."

"I got the dishes," he said. "I got the TV and the stereo."

"I don't know why you didn't take your share when you had the chance," Lydia said. "I mean, you could've taken the microwave and the silver or something."

"It's going to be fine, honey," Kenneth said, and pulled her up from the dirt. "We've got each other."

"Yes," Lydia nodded, but I couldn't help but feel sorry for her, being about ten pounds too heavy for her own good. I waited until they were back inside before I finished the yard, and then walked over behind the fish market where I had parked the car. There wasn't much room in the car because I had six loads of laundry that I'd been meaning to take to the subdivision Laundromat to dry. Kenneth had bought me a washer but not a dryer, and I should have bought one myself but I hadn't; the clothes had mildewed something awful.

Not long after that all my friends at the Diet Center took my picture to use as an example of what not to let happen to yourself. They said I had gone overboard and needed to gain a little weight for my own health. I was too tired to argue with Martha, aside from the fact that she was five times bigger than me, and I just let her drive me to the hospital. I checked in as Lydia Barkley, and since I didn't know how Lydia's handwriting looked, I used my best Kenneth imitation. "Her name is Sandra," Martha told the woman, but nobody yelled at me. They just put me in a bed and gave me some dinner in my vein and knocked me out. As overweight as I had been, I had never eaten in my sleep. It was a first, and when I woke up, the shrink was there asking me what I was, on a scale of one to ten. "Oh, four," I told him. It seemed like I was there a long time. Paula came and did my nails and hair, and Martha came and confessed that she had eaten three boxes of chocolate-covered cherries over the last week. She brought me a fourth. She said that if she had a husband, she'd get a divorce, that's how desperate she was to lose some weight, but that she'd stop before she got as thin as me. I told her I'd rather eat a case of chocolate-covered cherries than go through it again.

My mama came, and she said, "I always knew this would happen." She shook her head like she couldn't stand to look at me. "A man whose business in life depends on others taking to the bottle is no kind of man to choose for a mate." I told her to mind her own damn business, and when she left, she took my box of chocolate-covered cherries and told me that sweets were not good for a person.

By the time I got out of the hospital, I was feeling much better. Kenneth stopped by for me to sign the divorce papers right before it was time for my dinner party. His timing had never been good. There I was in my black silk dress with the table set for twelve, the lasagna getting ready to be thawed and cooked in the microwave.

"Looks like you're having a party," he said, and stared at me with that same look he always had before he got choked up. I just nodded and filled my candy dish with almonds. "I'm sorry for all the trouble I caused you," he said. "I didn't know how sick you were." And I noticed he was taking me in from head to toe. "You sure look great now."

"Well, I'm feeling good, Kenneth," I told him and took the papers from his hand.

"I'm not with Lydia anymore," he said, but I focused instead on signing my name, my real name, in my own handwriting, which if it was analyzed would be the script of a fat person. Some things you just can't shake; part of me will always be a fat person and part of Kenneth will always be gutter slime. He had forgotten that when he *had* me he hadn't wanted me, and I had just about forgotten how much fun we'd had eating that half-gallon of ice cream in bed on our honeymoon.

"Well, send me a postcard," I told him when I opened the front door to see Martha coming down the walk in one of my old dresses that she was finally able to wear. And then came Paula and the man she kept in her bedroom, and my mama, who I had sternly instructed not to open her mouth if she couldn't be pleasant, my beautician, the manager of Revco, my shrink, who, after I had stopped seeing him on a professional basis, had called and asked me out to lunch. They were all in the living room, mingling and mixing drinks; I stood there with the curtains pulled back and watched Kenneth get in that Mazda that was in my name and drive down Marnier and take a left onto Seagrams. Summer was almost over, and I couldn't wait for the weather to turn cool so that I could stop working in the yard.

"I want to see you do 'eat spaghetti,'" my shrink, who by then had told me to call him Alan, said and pulled a butterfly yo-yo like I hadn't seen in years from his pocket. I did it; I did it just as well as if I were still in the seventh grade, and my mama hid her face in embarrassment while everybody else got a good laugh. Of course, I'm not one to overreact or to carry a situation on and on, and so when they begged for more tricks, I declined. I had plenty of salad on hand for my friends who were dieting so they wouldn't have seconds on lasagna, and while I was fixing the coffee, Alan came up behind me, grabbed my love handles, and said, "On a scale of one to ten, you're a two thousand and one." I laughed and patted his hand because I guess I was still focused on Kenneth and where was he going to stay, in a pup tent? Some things never change, and while everybody was getting ready to go and still chatting, I went to my bedroom and turned my alarm clock upside down, which would remind me when it went off the next day to return the title to Kenneth's name and to maybe write him a little check to help with that MasterCard bill.

I could tell that Alan wanted to linger, but so did my mama and so I had to make a choice. I told Alan it was getting a little late and that I hoped to see him real soon, *socially*, I stressed. He kissed me on the cheek and squeezed my hip in a way that made me get gooseflesh and also made me feel sorry for both Kenneth and Lydia all at the same time. "A divorce can do strange things to a person," Alan had told me on my last visit; the man knew his business. He was cute, too.

"It was a nice party, Sandra," my mama said after everybody left. "Maybe a little too much oregano in the lasagna.

You're a tad too thin still, and I just wonder what that man who calls himself a psychiatrist has on his mind."

"Look before you leap," I told her, and gave her seventy-nine skeins of yarn in the most hideous colors that I no longer had room for in my closet. "A bird in the hand is worth two in the bush."

"That's no way to talk to your mother," she said. "It's not my fault that you were overweight your whole life. It's not my fault your husband left you for a redheaded bar tramp."

"Well, send me a postcard," I said and closed the door, letting out every bit of breath that I'd held inside my whole life. I washed those dishes in a flash, and when I got in my bed, I was feeling so sorry for Kenneth, who had no birds in his hand, and sorry for Mama, who would never use up all that yarn. I hurried through those thoughts because my eyelids were getting so heavy and I wanted my last thought of the night to be of Alan, first with the yo-yo and then grabbing my hipbone. When you think about it, if your hipbones have been hidden for years and years, it's a real pleasure to have someone find them, grab hold, and hang on. You can do okay in this world if you can just find something worth holding on to.

Rhoda B. Stamell

Love for a Fat Man

She was not beautiful; she was out of place. For one, the soles of her shoes were too thin. Any piece of broken glass could cut through such thin soles. She knew that. She picked her way delicately among the broken bottles in the parking lot, the pot holes puddled with muddy water, the cans and the newspapers. She held her skirt as if it might sweep across the filthy pavement. This was in the beginning, anyway, because she changed so much that sometimes I think I am remembering someone else. In the beginning she seemed fragile but not broken. Broken was what she thought she was, but I wouldn't have started up with her if that had been true. Broken women are too dangerous. They don't care enough to be cautious. The women who worked in the clinic—City Health and Social Services—talked about her in Spanish. The nurses speculated about the cost of the buttery leather satchel that she carried. The clerks envied the paisley folds of her skirts, the ruffled silk of her blouses. Even the pediatrician, who was from Pakistan, remarked on the gold ring that she wore: "True gold, twenty-two carat, and the diamonds are not of glass, I tell you." I preside over this world of women. Aside from them there is only Xavier, who drives the van, and the medical residents who are assigned here for rotations in pediatrics and obstetrics. The residents cause me the most trouble because there aren't any barriers here between their medicine and the malnourished children; no way to separate themselves from the junkies in Prenatal, from the women who come up pregnant every ten months; from the tea-colored babies brought in by pasty-faced girls. These residents have a lot of flat tires and incidences of the flu, and I report them to their chiefs. "Medicine is about people," I tell the chiefs. It is an effective argument. I drive here from my home at the farthest edge of Detroit. The people in my neighborhood consider themselves cosmopolitan: Blacks with solid incomes, Mexicans like me who are professionals, Jews with liberal tendencies. It took me a long time to get there, to the boxed-in area bound by Seven and Eight Mile Roads, Livernois and Woodward, to the two-storied houses with three bedrooms, shuttered, with lawns that spread out like aprons. My wife drives a Volvo so that no harm will come to our sons, Rafael, Miguel, and Luis, in the event of a collision.

When I was growing up down here on 23rd Street, one of those poor streets numbered in haste, too unimportant to be named, there wasn't any clinic. My grandmother wrapped my chest in flannel, gave me tea brewed from ancient memory, and prayed in the Spanish of Indians. And I survived, unlike my mother, who was murdered by her boyfriend—probably my father—in the Jalisco Bar just a half a block from here on the corner of Fort and Junction; unlike my brother, who slammed a stolen car into an abutment on the Lodge Freeway; unlike my uncles, who died of pneumonia, undiagnosed cancer, mistaken identity, and jealous women. "Roberto," my grandmother would say to me, "Eat, Roberto. Eat what I make for you. Eat to live. Live, my baby."

And so I ate. The beans, slow-baked in the fat of pork; the soups, red with tomatoes, thick with meaty bones, dense with onions, corn, and rice. Tamales, greasy in corn husks. And I ate. Coney Islands from Duly's, hamburgers from Top Hat, chop suey from Ho Ho Gardens, baloney and white bread bought at A&P, wolfed down in Clark Park after school.

It is all the same here as it was when I grew up on a numbered street, but I don't approach it with any particular bitterness because it's not my home anymore. I can stand at the window of my office and sever the connection between me and the litter of the street. So what did she see when she came to my office that first time, up those steps that winded me to walk? What did she see that she thought she could love? A fat man whose eyes were lost in cheeks like bags of candy. A man who grew up in the streets he looked down on from a streaked window of a squat building, cold in winter, hot in summer.

I am trained to be suspicious. There was law school, but I didn't stay long enough to benefit from mistrusting what I heard and saw. There was the M.S.W. program. And always there were the numbered streets whose lessons added up, like the cross above our bed taught me suspicion, believing as I do that my wife lay beneath me during nights of love to please her Lord and his insatiable appetite for children. Once, in an argument, I called her a whore for Jesus, and the way she looked at me, not angry, but as if she understood something about herself, hurt me. For this tidy box of a house, real brick; the sturdy blue Volvo; three pale boys spared the dark Mexican sun, she would suffocate under the rolls and weight of flesh and close her eyes against the sight of my body, sloping down in cascades of fat.

So I had my reasons to be suspicious of a woman whose hands were quick, little birds that flew about her words. The delicate color of her eyelids was taken from a subtle palette. Her earrings were little pearls, irregular and starch-white. Such a woman would wear little pearls. She talked of the program she had been assigned to administer. Yes, she was new at this kind of thing, not used to the subject matter, but didn't doubt that she could work it out. Her goals were realistic, always open to re-evaluation. When her hands came to rest on the fine, woolen weave of her skirt she said, "I am in terrible pain."

Because she had eyes that didn't see me, I could do what I did. I came around my desk and took her small hands. I tasted the grief in her kiss, felt loneliness in the coolness of her skin. I thought—I remember thinking—this is like the movies. But not really—there was too much pain in that embrace. And I was afraid.

I didn't think that she would ever come back up those stairs. She wasn't like the social workers or the board members of the clinic or the R.N.s. They were people like me, from the tall houses and the narrow driveways. Thin, ravening dogs had chased them home from the bus stop after a day of work, a night at school. Women like that I could kiss in my office and not be afraid that I had dared to hold them, to touch them, a short, fat man with small features, lost in pouches and caches of fat.

I can talk about the fat now, but then, I wouldn't think about it. What I did think was that she would wipe her mouth with a quick movement of her hand as she went down the worn and waxy steps. She would shake away with little shudders the memory of my small hand, my ludicrously small hand that lifted the hem of her skirt.

Then I thought she was crazy in the way that some people are off balance all of their lives, responding to something in themselves and not to what is happening outside of them. I thought she was one of those people who came at things from an angle intensely her own.

She would hang on the door frame, wearing, for instance, a black corduroy dress with a high neck closed with jet buttons, a dress fitted to the hips and falling in rounded pleats. I loved that dress and paid compliments when she wore it, but I always thought that polyester and rayon were the materials of this place, that she offered us too rich a diet for our starved appetites. At that time she was thin, very thin, and I could imagine her pushing away a plate after a few forkfuls because she was not present enough to eat. But we never ate together.

So I took her to bed, and then I turned her away. The room was dirty, I am sure. It had the sense of too many people lying on the thin, bluish sheets; too many naked feet padding across the rough carpet, damp like moss; too many feet on the cold, sticky tiles of the bathroom. It cost twenty-eight dollars for the rag of a wash cloth and the cardboard towel, the bed where no one would go for sleeping, a lamp that crooked its neck like a malignant goose. It cost twenty-eight dollars, and she gave me twenty of it. I took it as if I expected her to pay, to make the choice hers and not mine. She sat in a chair, wearing her slip. The only light came from the bathroom, but that was too much light for me. If it had been dark, I could have pretended that we were there because we wanted each other. But as long as she could see me, I couldn't believe that she was there for me. "We don't have to do this," I said, because she looked at me for the first time in that twenty-eight dollar room. An enormous undershirt, sleeveless with a rounded neck, stretched and shapeless. Shorts—they can only be bought at Big and Tall—and my thin legs and the thin bones of my feet. Then she wasn't crazy or jittery in her high-strung way. She was solemn. Her hands lay quiet where she sat in the brown chair, the white slip shining like moonlight. She said: We came here for a reason, and we don't have much time. How you feel when you are a fat man, struggling for air on a flight of stairs, whose sacks of thighs push out your feet in a splayed, duck-like walk, and how you feel when you have disappointed a woman are very much the same. You can't think about it. You say things like, "No one messes with a big man." Like "I am going to fuck you to death." But you can't do either: protect yourself from the quick and the strong, or get close enough to a woman to fill her as she desires.

I was tender with her. I kissed the soles of her feet, and she paid me back in pleasures. But I knew.

Still, on Monday, she appeared in my office, as always pausing in the doorway so that I could see the picture she was presenting to me, a picture she had prepared for me. She wore a gray silk blouse that was almost blue with a tunic collar, one that she favored at the time, and gray slacks with a lizard belt. There were little heels on her boots, and the leather satchel hung from her shoulder. Her earrings were silver discs intersected with black lightning. I thought she looked elegant. I loved her for how she looked. I would have gone back to that mossy, humid room with her at that very moment and would have found the right way to love her. But for what she did. She kissed me like a mother kisses her child in a moment when love compels her to press her lips on that child's head. Standing above me where I sat at my desk, she kissed me in this way. It was a kiss too intimate, too tender and too kind. It was a kiss I could not accept because it had to be a lie. "You know I am married."

"Yes, but still. . . ."

"There will be too much talk, and my wife comes here."

"Then it was just to get me for that once."

"I didn't mean to do it at all. It was a mistake."

She did not come upstairs after that. She ran her classes on the first floor at the back of the clinic, and we only spoke about the security guard's duties or when the men in her groups bothered the patients. I saw her all the time even when she didn't know it. I saw how she changed. There were the thick-soled boots, orange-tan, and jeans; soft, open shirts, and the parka whose collar lay against her cheek, rosy with winter. I heard her laugh, touch kindly someone's hand, open a door for an old lady. And I wanted to be with her.

But I couldn't go to her. Could not lumber down the narrow stairs, catch my breath before I reached her door. I couldn't believe that she would want such a man as I was.

Then I fell into myself, into the maelstrom at whose center was my failing heart. I rose and fell and sank. When I knew where I was, when I knew what had happened, then I thought of nothing but the beat of my heart and its echoing pulse, the circuitous journey of my blood. I thought of nothing but rising to the moment of waking and sinking to the instant of sleep. In the night I imagined the intravenous bead poised like a bird about to drop in a downward plunge. I could hear it fall in the dark. Then, in the time of full awakening—when the bed was cranked up, and day filled the single hospital window like a painting: false sky, cardboard buildings, trees bent like wire hangers; and my wife was seated in the beige armchair as if she had been there forever—they brought me food. A small piece of chicken, a scoop of rice, some beans, deep green and soggy from the steam cart. Food for the heart patient, but I refused it. I refused the oatmeal and the unbuttered toast. The tuna and the bowl of greens. The nurse told the doctor. My wife folded her hands this way and that, imploring me in a low voice so that no one would hear.

"Roberto, how can you live if you do this? Roberto, if you die, you bring us down. Roberto, I have children. Roberto, don't do this."

I didn't want to die. I saw that food was my death, my way of dying. A different kind of death from my pretty-girl mother's and her violent brothers, but really no different from other deaths we will upon ourselves, the deaths that the nameless streets intended for us. The social worker came, and she had a name that was Greek. Her hair was black and smooth, and her eyes were innocent and kind. I could hear the accents of another language in her words. The folders she gave me described the diet of heart patients, the benign food that nourished, that would not bring you crashing down in the middle of an ordinary day when your desk was filled with messages, and the intercom called your name. But you could not answer. For her kind eyes and the foreign language at the core of her words, I ate: small forkfuls, tentative spoons lifted to my lips. But I was always afraid, not the simple fear of dying but the fear of a person so purely instrumental in his own death, so deliberate in the arrangement of his own end. I had never understood this before falling into the wide pool of pain. I had never understood the devouring monster that lived in me, intent on my destruction. Now that I knew that he—it—was there, I could not please it with my easy dying.

From the woman I received a card, humorous, impartial, no words that would alarm my wife as she arranged the plants and cards on the window ledge. "We heard you were ill," cartoon figures, and her signature. When I left the hospital and the trays of food, the small portions that never satisfied the hunger, only the need to survive, I was afraid again. Afraid of the breads, the margarine, the eggs in their top-heavy ovals. The chicken bleeding on the counter-top; the stew filling the kitchen with the rich smell of bay leaf, beef, carrots and onions. The wedge of cheese covered with plastic wrap. The cookies for the boys; the boxes of mix in the pantry; the unopened cans stacked one upon the other, red for soups, green for vegetables, yellow for fruit thick in syrup. They were menacing, tempting, everywhere in my home.

I would walk because I was supposed to and because I had to escape the murderous food. At first, it was just two blocks and home again, past the square lawns beginning to green, the doors brown and creme, shutters flown open to light and the voices of the neighbors. The sidewalks were dark with rain that had fallen in the night. I had never looked at these streets before, but now I saw them foot by foot, yard by yard, roof by roof, gray and luminous, dark and light.

One afternoon, I toasted a tortilla on the burner, flipped it over and back again, filled it with beans that had been cooked in the oven with pork fat and cheese. I wrapped the tortilla around the beans, thinking, "I am cured of this madness." But with the thought came the fear, coupled and fused: yearning and aversion. I threw the tortilla in the sink and ran from the house. The Greek social worker arranged that I join the program sponsored by the hospital for people suffering from extreme obesity. There was apology in the way she said the words, "extreme obesity," but I did not need her apologies or her delicacy. I was terrified.

The way it works is that you don't eat anymore. The food for your life comes in sealed packages, choice of five flavors: chocolate, vanilla, pineapple-banana, orange-lemon, and strawberry. Five times a day the packets are mixed in a plastic container with the measure of water. There are vitamins and herbal teas. That's all. After a lifetime of eating everything, whether it tasted good or not, whether it was raw or cooked, whether you wanted it or not, the only choices were five flavors. Beyond that, there was hunger. The walks became miles of streets and extended into another season. Other journeys were made on the stationary bicycle, the degrees of difficulty determined by a single lever. While my family ate their meals, I would pedal at number two and try not to hear the fork sing against the plate, the spoon vibrate across the bowl.

When I went back to the clinic, she was preparing to leave. Xavier was carrying boxes of materials to her car. The posters were rolled into cylinders to be spread out, flattened, and pinned up with bright, new stick pins in another place. She had been offered another site and a permanent position. She was wearing slacks of soft cotton and a white shirt with the collar open.

"Why, you look wonderful," she said. "We were so concerned." She would not say "I." That was her revenge on me, a way to take away the room, the white slip, and the hurried, clumsy moment she could not have wanted to happen to her. "I had hoped we might talk," I said.

"There isn't time anymore."

A man can wait as women wait. A man can walk the pleasant streets of the life he has made. He can go each week to his support group and tell other men and women how he felt when he ate twelve doughnuts in the alley before going in the house for dinner under a dim light in the kitchen, his grandmother filling his plate. He can decide what flavors he will mix with water at 8:00, 11:00, 1:00. He can buy two pairs of trousers until the next forty pounds are lost. He can see a thinner man emerge but never lose the outlines of the man and boy he was. He can grow thinner and thinner and still be afraid. He can be afraid even when he is as thin as he is ever going to be; when he dresses in the morning in trousers with a thirty-six inch waist and a shirt with a size fifteen collar; when he eats the oatmeal measured and sealed in a package, a safe, preordained portion. He can still be afraid. And he is afraid when he calls her after so many months, more than a year: that she will not come, that she will never know what he willed for himself against the devouring other self that lived in him. She came, herself another person. She was not the woman who stood in doorways, afraid to enter. She was a woman who hung up her coat—"Thinsulate," the label on the lining read—and who took a seat at the side of the desk. She wore her glasses and smiled when she was amused.

"I can't believe this. I would never recognize you if we met on the street."

"Most of the time I don't believe it either. I have to think about it all the time. It's like being an alcoholic. That's how it's treated."

"Meeting and confessions?"

"Doctors and diets."

"Has it changed you?"

"In a lot of ways. But not about you."

She stood up, and even in her sensible clothes, a dark dress, washable, and flat shoes, a watch with a broad band, a beige purse of sturdy leather, she was still the out-of-place woman who had picked her way across the glass-littered parking lot. Ten pounds heavier, two years older, she was still delicate. She looked out at the filthy streets, the dirt-covered windows of the low buildings, housing pawn shops, junk shops, resale shops, diners.

"Before we were like people in a play, wearing masks, saying our lines to go with the parts we were playing. No sense and no consequences. We were just outside of our lives like on a stage. And I was outrageous. I don't know who I thought I was."

"So it didn't count?"

"No, it didn't. Now, you are just a man who wants to sleep with a woman who isn't his wife, maybe once or twice a month. That's all. Just a regular man with a modest salary and a family to support. And I don't want that."

"You wanted that fat man, the man I was. Is that right?"

"I liked the play acting, the inappropriateness, the thrill of it."

"You can have it again. We can."

"It would just be sordid. Before it was dramatic. I could make you up, bigger than ordinary life. I could find reasons to love you that no one else could think of. It was romantic, even creative. Now it would just be adultery. I don't have time for adultery."

I should have known that, too. About what there is time for and when that time is over. I should have known from the brief lives of the people on this street that stretches east and west in misery. For every wretched girl who comes here with a child in her arms and one opening up like a flower within, there had been a moment when she was lovely; when she and her man were poised on the exquisite brink, a place where only falling was possible. We should have gone to the room as long as it was the place for us, but there were too many things to be afraid of. And they stood in my way. I can imagine what we would be like now: two ordinary people in a bed, making love, saying too many things, and then the anger that springs from such meetings. I should be content with the memory of her quiet posture and her folded hands. I shouldn't know any more about her.

ALLISON JOSEPH

Full Figure

Other women's bodies are too thin to me,
    the size threes and fives who dart through
        every department store alien in narrow

clothes, strange as they try on sleek
    bodysuits, short hemlines. I see them eye
        my floral tent dress, clucking tongues,

nodding disapproval, avoiding me as I try on
    a pair of drawstring pants, elastic ones too tight.
        Unforgiving of heavy flesh, they step away

aghast, afraid of catching whatever virus
    fuels my fat, whatever disease makes me
        this bulky, this large. They wonder who

could love a woman so obviously lacking
    in restraint, too hefty for a seat on the bus,
        in the theater. They'd prefer I just stay home,

out of sight, far from mirrored fitting rooms
    and salons, spas and steam baths, beaches,
        pools, malls—any place I might infect

with hugeness, my body more than ample,
    proud to claim more space than they
        could ever know, ever fathom.

Ax of the Apostles

After four hours spent locked in his office, gorging on cookies and grading sophomore philosophy papers, Father Thomas Murray seethed. His students, future priests who would lead the church into the next century, were morons.

"Kant's idea of the Universal Law might have made sense back in his time, but today we live in a complex, multicultural world where one man's universal law is another man's poison, if you know what I mean." *So there are no absolutes?* Father Murray wrote in the margin, pressing so hard the letters were carved into the paper. *Peculiar notion, for a man who wants to be a priest.*

They didn't know how to *think*. Presented with the inexhaustibly rich world, all its glory, pity, and terror, they managed to perceive only the most insipid pieties. If he asked them to discuss the meaning of the crucifixion, they would come back with *Suffering is a mystery, and murder is bad.* Father Murray looked at the paper before him and with difficulty kept from picking up his pen and adding *Idiot*.

He had planned on spending no more than two hours grading; he would do well to go over to the track and put in a couple of overdue miles. But flat-footed student prose and half-baked student logic had worked him into a silent fury, and the fury itself became a kind of joy, each bad paper stoking higher the flames of his outrage. He reached compulsively for the next paper in the stack, and then the next, his left hand snagging another of the cookies he'd taken last night from the kitchen. Not good—lackluster oatmeal, made with shortening instead of butter—but enough to keep him going. *What makes you think,* he wrote, *that Kant's age was any less complex than yours?*

Still reading, he stretched his back against the hard office chair, which shrieked every time he moved, and started to count off the traits lacked by the current generation of seminarians: Historical understanding. Study skills. Vocabulary. Spelling. From down the hall he heard a crash and then yelps of laughter. "Oh, Alice!" someone cried. Father Murray closed his eyes.

A month ago one of the students had sneaked into the seminary a mannequin with eyelashes like fork tines and a brown wig that clung to its head like a bathing cap. Since then the mannequin had been popping up every day, in the showers, the library, at meals. Students mounted it on a ladder so that its bland face, a cigarette taped to its mouth, could peer in classroom windows; twice in one week Father Murray had had to look around to see why his students were giggling. Now a campaign to turn the mannequin into the seminary's mascot was afoot. Savagely, Father Murray bit into another bad cookie, then stood, took a deep breath, and left his office.

At the bend in the hallway, where faculty offices gave way to dormitory rooms, five students clustered beside an open door. The mannequin, dressed in towels, half reclined in the doorway to Quinn's room. Blonde, morose Quinn, a better student than most, tugged the towel higher up the mannequin's bosom. The customary cigarette had fallen from the doll's pink plastic mouth and now dangled by a long piece of tape. "You should have seen your *face,*" Adreson was saying to Quinn. Father Murray knew and loathed the sort of priest Adreson would become: loved by the old ladies, peppy, and brain-dead. "I thought you were going to faint. I thought we were going to lose you."

"Jumped a foot," added Michaels. "At least a foot."

"Went up like a firecracker," Father Murray suggested, and the seminarians turned, apparently delighted he had joined them.

"A Roman candle," Adreson said.

"Like a shooting star," Father Murray said. "Like a rocket. Like the Challenger. Boom."

The laughter slammed to a halt; Adreson stepped back, and Father Murray said, "You men sound, in case you're interested, like a fraternity out here. I would not like to be the one explaining to the bishop what tomorrow's priests are doing with a big plastic doll. Although I could always tell him that you were letting off some steam after your titanic academic struggles. Then the bishop and I could laugh."

"She fell right onto Brian," Adreson murmured. "Into his arms. It was funny."

Father Murray remembered a paper Adreson had written for him the year before in which Adreson had called Aquinas "The Stephen Hawking of the 1300s," not even getting the century right. In that same paper Adreson had made grave reference to the "Ax of the Apostles." From any of the other men Father Murray would have allowed the possibility that the citation was a joke. Now he looked at his student, twenty years old and still trying to subdue a saddle of pimples across his cheeks. "You have developed a genius for triviality."

"Sorry, Father."

"I'm giving you a piece of information. Think about it."

"Thank you, Father."

"Don't bother thanking me until you mean it."

"Oh, I mean it, Father." Adreson pursed his mouth—an odd, old-maidish expression. "Sorry we disturbed you. Guess we're too full of beans tonight. Hey—you want to go over to the track?"

Father Murray felt a plateful of oatmeal cookies churn in his stomach. "Another time. I've still got work to do."

"*Corpore sano*, Father."

Father Murray snorted and turned back toward his office. He cherished a measure of low satisfaction that the one Latin phrase Adreson seemed to know came from the YMCA slogan.

———

He should, of course, have taken up Adreson's offer. By ten o'clock his stomach was violent with oatmeal cookies; his error had been in eating even one. As soon as he'd taken that first bite, it was Katy bar the door. Tomorrow he would have to be especially strict with himself.

Strictness, as everyone at St. Boniface knew, was Father Murray's particular stock-in-trade. Fourteen months before, his doctor had called him in to discuss blood sugar and glucose intolerance. "You have a family history, is that right?"

Father Murray nodded. His mother—bloated, froglike, blind. Groping with her spongy hand to touch his face. He had held still, even when she pressed her thumb against his eye, and hadn't said a word. "Doesn't everybody have a family history?" he said.

"This is no joke. You are at risk," the doctor said. "You could start needing insulin injections. Your legs could be amputated. You could die. Do you understand that?"

Father Murray considered reminding the doctor that a priest's job entailed daily and exquisite awareness of his mortality. Nevertheless, he took the doctor's point: Father Murray's forty-five-inch waist, the chin that underlaid his chin, his fingers too pudgy for the ring his father had left him. If he let the disease take hold he would deteriorate in humiliating degrees, relying on others to walk for him when his feet failed, to read to him when the retinopathy set in. A life based wholly on charity—not just the charity of God, which Father Murray could stomach, but the charity of the men around him. The next day he began to walk, and a month later, to run.

For a solid year he held himself to eleven hundred exacting calories a day, eating two bananas for breakfast and a salad with vinegar for lunch. His weight plummeted; his profile shrank from Friar Tuck to Duns Scotus, and the waist of his trousers bunched like a paper bag. The night Father Murray hit one-fifty, ten pounds below his target weight, Father Radziewicz told him, "You're a walking wonder." They were standing, plates in hand, in line for iced tea. Father Radziewicz's eye rested on Father Murray's piece of pork loin, slightly smaller than the recommended three ounces, stranded on the white plate. "How much have you lost now?"

"One hundred twenty-four pounds."

"Enough to make a whole other priest. Think of it."

"I'm condensed," Father Murray said. "Same great product; half the packaging."

"Think of it," Father Radziewicz said. His plate held three pieces of pork, plus gravy, potatoes, two rolls. "I couldn't do it," he added.

"It's just a matter of willpower," Father Murray said. "To the greater glory of God."

"Still, isn't it time to stop? At least slow down. Maybe you've glorified God enough."

"I've never felt better in my life."

The statement was largely true. He had never in his life been quite so satisfied with himself, although his knees sometimes hurt so much after a twelve-mile run that he could hardly walk. He bought ibuprofen in 500-count bottles and at night, in bed, rested his hands on the bones of his hips, the corded muscles in his thighs. Out of pure discipline he had created a whole new body, and he rejoiced in his creation.

So he was unprepared for the muscular cravings that beset him shortly after his conversation with Father Radziewicz. They came without warning, raging through the airy space below his rib cage. The glasses of water, the repetitions of the daily office, all the tricks Father Murray had taught himself now served only to delay the hunger—five minutes, fifteen, never enough.

One night he awoke from a dream of boats and anchors to find himself pushing both fists against his twisting stomach. Brilliantly awake, heart hammering, he padded around the seminary, glancing into the chapel, the storage room that held raincoats and wheelchairs for needy visitors, the underused weight room. Finally, giving in, he let his hunger propel him to the kitchen, just so that he'd be able to get back to sleep.

Holding open the refrigerator door, he gazed at cheesecake left over from dinner. He was ten pounds underweight. He had left himself a margin; probably he was getting these cravings because he actually needed some trace of fat and sugar in his system. And the next day he could go to the track early and run off whatever he took in tonight. He ate two and a half pieces of cheesecake, went back to bed, and slept as if poleaxed.

Since then Father Murray had hardly gone a night without stealing downstairs for some snack—cookies, cake, whatever the seminarians and other priests, those wolves, had left. He stored his cache in a plastic bag and kept the bag in his desk drawer, allowing himself to nibble between classes, in the long afternoon lull before dinner, whenever the hunger roared up in him. Twice he broke the hour-long fast required before taking Communion; each time he sat, stony faced, in his pew, while the other priests filed forward to take the Host.

At meals he continued to take skimpy portions of lean foods; sometimes he was so stuffed with cookies even the plate of bitter salad seemed too much to get through. Father Bip, a Vietnamese priest he had often run with, told him that he was eating like a medieval monk. Father Murray slapped himself hard on the rump. "Brother Ass," he said. That rump was noticeably fleshier than it had been two months before, and he vowed again that he would recommence his diet the next day. That night, anticipating the stark hunger, he quietly walked the half-mile to a drugstore and bought a bag of peanut butter cups, several of which he ate on the way home.

As he lay in bed, his teeth gummy with chocolate and peanut butter paste, his days of crystalline discipline seemed very close. The choice was simple, and simply made; he remembered the pleasure of a body lean as a knife, a life praiseworthy and coherent. Yet the next night found him creeping back to the kitchen, plastic bag in hand, not exactly hungry anymore but still craving. Already his new black pants nipped him at the waist.

After his one o'clock Old Testament class the next afternoon, Father Murray returned to his office to find Adreson waiting for him. The young man, who had been absently fingering a flaming blemish beside his nose, held out his hand toward Father Murray, who shook it gingerly and ushered Adreson into his office.

"How was your class, Father?"

"We entertained the usual riotous dispute over Jerome's interpretation of 2 Kings." Then, looking at Adreson, he added, "It was fine."

"Your O.T. class has a real reputation. Men come out of there knowing their stuff."

"That's the basic idea."

"Sorry. I'm nervous, I guess. I want to apologize for making all that racket in the hallway last night."

"Thank you."

"I knew we were being—"

"—childish," Father Murray offered.

"—immature. I just thought you should know that there was a reason. Brian's mother has multiple sclerosis. He just found out last week. She's at home by herself with four kids, and she keeps falling down. I know it's killing Brian, but he won't talk about it. He just keeps going to class and services. It isn't healthy. That's why we put Alice in his room."

"He may find it comforting to keep up his usual schedule. This may be his way of coping," Father Murray said, autopilot words. Genuine shock kept him from asking Adreson how a towel-wrapped mannequin was supposed to help Quinn manage his sorrow.

"He needs to talk, Father. If he talks to people, we can help him."

"You have a lot of faith in yourself."

"We're here to help each other." His hand fluttered up toward his face, then dropped again. "If it were me, I'd want to know I could count on the guys around me. I'd want to know I wasn't alone."

"He prays, doesn't he? He may be getting all the support he needs. Not everything has to be talked out."

"We're not hermits, Father."

"That is abundantly true."

A burst of anger flashed across Adreson's face, and Father Murray leaned forward in the chair, which let out a squeal; he was more than ready to take the boy on. But after a complicated moment Adreson's mouth and eyes relaxed. "Of course you're right. I thought I should apologize for disturbing you." He straightened, clearly relieved to have put the moment behind him. "I'm going for a run this afternoon. Want to join me?"

"You're doing a lot of running lately. I'd suggest you take a few laps around the library."

"You're great, Father. You don't ever miss a lick." He pulled up another grin from his ready-made, toothy stockpile. "Track meet's coming up. I'm running the relay and the 440. That's your event, isn't it?"

"Distance," Father Murray said.

"I'm a little obsessed about that 440. Sometimes in practice I can get close to the conference record, so now it's my goal: I want to break the record, put St. Boniface in the books."

"Generations of the faithful will thank you."

"I'll have plenty of time to be pastoral later. Right now, running's the best talent I've got." He winked. "I know what you're going to say: Not a very priestly talent, is it?"

"I wasn't going to say anything like that. You are the model of today's seminarian."

Father Murray waited for Adreson to leave the office before he swiveled to gaze at the maple outside his window. Hundreds of tender spring leaves unfurled like moist hands, a wealth of pointless beauty. Where, he wondered, was Quinn's father? Had he run off after the fifth child, or had he died, snatched away in mid-breath or left to dwindle before the eyes of his many children? Cancer, heart attack, mugging. So many paths to tragedy. Now Quinn's mother, trapped inside a body that buckled and stumbled. Before long she would rely on others to cook for her, drive for her, hold a glass of water at her mouth.

"Too much," he muttered, his jaw so tight it trembled. He didn't blame Quinn for not wanting to talk to Adreson, who knew nothing about pain, which he believed could be eased by conversation. He didn't have a clue of sorrow's true nature or purpose: to grind people down to faceless surfaces, unencrusted with desire or intent. Only upon a smooth surface could the hand of God write. Every priest used to know that. Father Murray knew it. Quinn, bitterly, was learning it.

Father Murray hit his leg with his fist. Turning to the desk, he began to reach for the stale cookies in his drawer, then pushed back his chair. If an overdue visit to the track hurt, so much the better. He couldn't take on any of Quinn's suffering, but at least he could join him in it.

Weeks had passed since Father Murray had last gone for a run; his legs were wooden stumps, his breath a string of gasps; he flailed as if for a life preserver when he rounded the track the fourth time. Adreson, out practicing his 440, yelled, "Come on—pick 'em up, pick 'em up!" and Father Murray felt his dislike for the boy swell. After six laps he stopped and bent over. Adreson sailed around twice more. Father Murray waited for his lungs to stop feeling as if they were turning themselves inside out, then straightened and began again.

At dinner he stood in line for a slice of pineapple cake. "Oho," said Father Bip. "You are coming down to earth to join us?"

"I should be earthbound after this, all right."

"Should you be eating cake?" Father Radziewicz asked. "Wouldn't a piece of fruit be better?"

"Of course it would be better, Patrick," Father Murray snapped. "Look, one piece of cake isn't going to make my feet fall off."

Father Radziewicz shrugged, and Father Murray stomped across the dining room to a table where Father Tinsdell, a sharp young number imported this year from Milwaukee to teach canon law, was holding forth. "You're all thinking too small. We can sell this as an apparition. Trot Alice out after Mass and get the weeping women claiming that their migraines have gone away and their rosaries have turned to gold. We'll have the true believers streaming in. Pass the collection basket twice a day; next thing you know, we're all driving new cars. We'll buy one for the bishop, too."

Father Antonin leaned toward Father Murray. "He found the mannequin in his office. Hasn't shut up since."

"The women are always grousing about how there isn't enough of a feminine presence in the church," Father Tinsdell said. "Well, here they go. Five feet, six inches of miracle-working doll. We can put her in the fountain outside. Stack some rocks around her feet: Voila! Lourdes West. Bring us your lame, your hurt. If enough people come, somebody's bound to get cured. That should keep us rolling for the next century."

"You know," Father Murray said, setting his fork beside his cleaned plate, "Rome does recognize the existence of miracles."

"Somebody always stiffens up when you start talking marketing." The man's face was a series of points: the point of his needly nose, the point of his chin, the point of his frown set neatly above the point of his cool smile, directed at Father Murray. "Don't get in a twist. I'm up to date on church doctrine."

"People have been cured at Lourdes."

"I know it." Father Tinsdell leaned forward. "Have you ever seen a miracle?"

"Nope," said Father Murray.

"There are all kinds of miracles," Father Antonin broke in.

Without even glancing at the man, Father Murray knew what was coming: the miracle of birth, the miracle of sunrise, those reliable dodges. He looked at Father Tinsdell. Father Point. "Never. Not once. You?"

"Yup. Saw a fifteen-year-old girl pull out of renal failure. She was gone, kidneys totally shot. Her eyeballs were yellow. Even dialysis couldn't do much. For days her grandmother was in the hospital room saying rosaries. She got the whole family in on it. And then the girl turned around. Her eyes cleared. Her kidneys started to work again."

Father Murray stared at the other man. "That can't happen."

"I know. But I was there. I saw it."

Father Murray pondered Tinsdell's mocking gaze. How could a man see a miracle, a girl pulled from the lip of the grave, and still remain such a horse's ass? "I envy you," Father Murray said.

"Keep your eyes open. No telling what you might see." Father Tinsdell stood. He was thin as a ruler. "I'm getting some more coffee. Do you want more cake?"

"Yes," said Father Murray, though he did not, and would ignore the piece when it appeared.

Several times in the next week Father Murray paused outside of Quinn's door, his mouth already filled with words of compassion. But Quinn's door remained closed, separate from the easy coming and going between the other men's rooms. Father Murray respected a desire for solitude, the need for some kind of barrier from the relentless high jinks of all the Adresons. He pressed his hand against the doorframe, made ardent prayers for Quinn's mother, and left without knocking.

He should, he knew, have saved at least one of those heartfelt prayers for himself. His hunger was becoming a kind of insanity. Food never left his mind; when he taught he fingered the soft chocolates in his pocket, and at meals he planned his next meal. Nightly he ate directly from the refrigerator, shoveling fingerfuls of leftover casserole into his mouth, wolfing slice after slice of white bread. He dunked cold potatoes through the gravy's mantle of congealed fat, scooped up leathery cheese sauce. He ate as if he meant to disgust himself, but disgust eluded him. Instead, he awakened deep in the night, his stomach blazing with indigestion, and padded back to the kitchen for more food.

In the dining room he carried on the pretense of lettuce and lean meat; his plate held mingy portions of baked fish and chopped spinach unlightened by even a sliver of butter. He ate as if the act were a grim penance. For a week now he hadn't been able to button his trousers.

One night after dry chicken and half of a baked potato, he made his ritual pause outside of Quinn's door, then continued down the hall to his own room. Fourteen papers on the autonomy of will were waiting, and promised to provide ugly entertainment. But when he opened his door he jumped back: Propped against the frame stood the mannequin, wearing his running shoes, his singlet and jacket, and his shorts, stuffed with towels to hold them up. From down the hall came a spurt of nervous laughter, like a cough.

Father Murray waited for the laughter to die down, which didn't take long. Adreson and three other men edged out of the room where they'd positioned themselves; they looked as if they expected to be thrashed.

"My turn, I see," Father Murray said.

"We didn't want you to feel left out," said Adreson.

"Well, heavens to Betsy. *Thank* you."

"We thought you'd like the athletic motif. It was a natural."

"An inspiration, you might say."

"I was the one who thought of having Alice running,"

Adreson said. "Some of the other men suggested your clothes. Hope you don't mind." He leaned against the wall, hands plunged into the pockets of his jeans. The others, relaxed now, ringed loosely around him.

"Did Quinn have suggestions for this installation?" Father Murray looked at the mannequin's narrow plastic heels rising from his dirty running shoes, the wig caught back in his dark blue sweatband, the face, of course, unperturbed.

"Didn't you know? He's gone home to help out." His voice shifted, taking on a confiding, talk-show-host smoothness. "I don't think it was a good idea. His mom may be getting around now, but over the long run, he needs to make arrangements. Immersing himself in the situation will give him the sense that he's doing something, but he isn't addressing the real problems."

"Maybe he wants to be there."

"Not exactly a healthy desire, Father. Multiple sclerosis, for Pete's sake. I don't want to be brutal, but she isn't going to get better."

"No," Father Murray said.

"But you know Brian. He said he had to go where he's needed. I told him that he has to weigh needs. He needs to ask, 'Where can I do the most good?' He can't fix everything in the world."

"You weren't listening to him. Every need is a need," Father Murray said, chipping each word free from his mouth. "If you're hungry and you remember that children in Colombia are starving, do you feel any less hungry?"

"Sure. When I'm on vacation I always skip lunch and put that money in the box. And you know, I never feel hungry."

"One of these days," Father Murray began, then paused. His voice trembled, surprising him; he felt quite calm. Filled with distilled, purified hatred for the boy, but calm. "One of these days you'll find that your path isn't clear. Choices won't be obvious. Sacrifices won't be ranked. Needs will be like beads on a necklace, each one the same size and weight. It won't matter what you do in the world—there will still be more undone."

"My dark night of the soul." Adreson nodded.

"Your first experience of holiness," Father Murray corrected him.

"Zing," Adreson said. His friends looked at their shoes.

"Pay attention. I'm trying to get you to see. If you could take on Quinn's mother's disease for her, would you do that?"

"We each have our own role to play, Father. That's not mine."

"I know that. Would you reach for this other role?"

Angry, mute, Adreson stared at the carpet. Father Murray understood that the young man was exercising a good deal of willpower to keep from asking, *Would you? Would you?* and he meant to ensure that Adreson remained silent. If the young man asked, Father Murray would be forced to confess, *Yes. Yes, I would,* his desire caustic and bottomless.

"I'll go ahead and get Alice out of your room, Father," Adreson was saying.

"Leave it for now."

"I'm sorry. It was just supposed to be a joke."

"I know that. I'm not trying to punish you." Father Murray watched the ring of young men shrink away from him. "It's something new in my life. I'll bring it down to your room tomorrow. Besides, I need to get my clothes back."

The men retreated toward the student lounge, where they would drink Cokes and discuss Father Murray's bitterness, such a sad thing to see in a priest. None of them, Adreson least of all, would imagine himself capable of becoming like Father Murray, and in fact, none of them would become like Father Murray. Only Quinn, and he was gone.

Father Murray turned and studied the mannequin, which looked awkward, its angles all wrong. When he adjusted one of the arms, the mannequin started to tip; its center of balance was specific and meant for high-heeled shoes. Quickly he tried to straighten it, but it inclined to the right. In the end, the best he could do was prop the plastic doll against the bureau. He thought of Quinn. He wondered how often the young man would have to steady his mother on her way to the bathroom or the kitchen. Father Murray's singlet had slipped over the mannequin's shoulder; he pulled it up again.

Adreson and the others must have gotten a passkey and skipped dinner so they could sneak in and rifle his bureau drawers. Father Murray didn't mind—he kept no secret magazines that could be discovered, no letters or photographs. Then he remembered the nest of candy wrappers, the thick dust of cake crumbs. And he himself, talking to Adreson about hunger.

"Mother of *God*." He paced the room in three familiar steps, turned, paced back. The mannequin's head was tilted so that the face gazed up, toward the flat ceiling light, its expressionlessness not unlike serenity. A bit of paper lingered where a cigarette was usually taped, and Father Murray leaned forward to scrape it off. But the paper didn't come from a cigarette. Carefully folded and tucked above the mannequin's mouth, as precise as a beauty mark, was placed a streamer from a chocolate kiss; when Father Murray touched it, the paper unfurled and dangled over the corner of the mannequin's mouth like a strand of drool, and the doll pitched forward into his arms.

He thrust her back, resisting the impulse to curse. Her balance, he finally saw, was thrown off by extra weight in the pockets of her clothes. The pockets were distended—how had he not noticed this?—stuffed. Father Murray stabilized the mannequin with one hand and rifled the pockets with the other, his heart thundering.

He knew upon the first touch. Handfuls of dainty chocolate kisses, fresh-smelling, the silver wrappers still crisp. He dropped them on the bureau and let them shower around his feet. The air in the room thickened with chocolate; he imagined it sealing his lungs. A full minute might have passed before he fished out the last piece and sank to the floor beside the pool of candy.

Adreson: grinning, amiable, dumb. Seminary record-holder in the 440, possessor of a young, strong body. He didn't look capable of malice. He didn't look capable of spelling it. But above Adreson's constant, supplicating smile sat tiny eyes that never showed pleasure. They were busy eyes, the eyes of a bully or a thug. Eyes like Adreson's missed nothing, and Father Murray had been a fool to think otherwise. He had attributed the nervous gaze to self-consciousness, even to a boyish desire to make good, a miscalculation that might have been Christlike if it weren't so idiotic. Like mistaking acid for milk.

Pressing his fist against his forehead, he saw himself illuminated in the silent midnight kitchen, the overhead light blazing as he shoveled food into his mouth: a fat man making believe he had dignity, and the community of men around him charitably indulging his fantasy. Only Adreson withheld charity.

He fingered the candies on the floor. Unwrapping one, he placed it on his tongue, the taste waxy. He unwrapped a second and held it in his hand until it softened.

The next day, seated in his office at the far end of the hall, Father Murray wasn't able to see Adreson's face when he entered his room. But he knew what Adreson was confronting. The mannequin, clean now of Father Murray's clothes, sat in a wheelchair under the ceiling light. Father Murray had had to break the legs with a hammer to get them to bend; plastic shards jutted like shivs. The head was twisted to the right, a painful angle that made the unengaged expression look like a mask over hidden suffering.

"Vicious. Really vicious. The action of a sick man." Adreson seemed to know Father Murray was listening; perhaps he hoped that others were, too. His voice was loud enough to carry to the end of the corridor. Father Murray clasped his hands and leaned forward, intent on hearing every word his student had to say. "A man like this has no place in a seminary. The bishop won't think so, if he hears. He won't want us to be taught viciousness."

Father Murray shook his head. Once again Adreson was getting his lesson wrong, missing the point. On Father Murray's desk shone a pile of foil. His pockets, his hands, were empty.

Fat

Wait. What you see is another person
hanging here. I am the girl who jumps
the Hodgmans' fence so quick they never see me.
Skipping rope, I always do hot peppers.
But once on the way home I got in a strange
car. I screamed and beat on the windows,
but they smiled and held me. They said I could go
when I put on the costume, so I climbed
into it, pulled up the huge legs,
globby with veins, around my skinny shins,
pulled on this stomach that flops over itself,
I pushed my arm past the hanging elbow fat
down into the hands and fingers, tight
like a doctor's glove stuffed with Vaseline.
I hooked the top behind my neck, with these
two bladders bulging over my flat chest.
Then I pulled the rubber mask down over
my head and tucked in the cheek and chin
folds at the neck hiding the seam. I hate
the smell. When they pushed me out of the car,
I slipped and staggered as though the street
was wet with fish oil. You see what this costume is.
If you will undo me, if you will loan me a knife,
I will step out the way I got in.
I will run on home in time for supper.

STEPHEN DUNN

Power

It comes to this: dwarf-throwing contests,
dwarfs for centuries given away
as gifts, and the dwarf-jokes

at which we laugh in our big, proper bodies.
And people so fat they can't
scratch their toes, so fat

you have to cut away whole sides of their homes
to get them to the morgue.
Don't we snicker, even as the paramedics work?

And imagine the small political base
of a fat dwarf. Nothing to stop us
from slapping our knees, rolling on the floor.

Let's apologize to all of them, Roberta said
at the spirited dinner table. But by then
we could hardly contain ourselves.

The Fat Man in History

1.

His feet are sore. The emporium seems endless as he shuffles an odd-legged shuffle with the double-bed sheets under his arm. It is like a nightmare—the exit door in sight but not coming any closer, the oppressive heat, the constant swarm of bodies flowing towards him like insects drawn towards, then repelled by, a speeding vehicle.

He is sweating badly, attempting to look calm. The sheets are badly wrapped. He wrapped them himself, surprising himself with his own nerve. He took the sheets (double, because there were no singles in blue) and walked to the wrapping counter where he pulled out a length of brown paper and set to work. To an assistant looking at him queryingly he said, smiling meekly, "You don't object?" The assistant looked away.

His trousers are large, floppy, and old-fashioned. Fortunately they have very large pockets and the pockets now contain several tins of smoked oysters. The smoked oysters are easy, always in big tubs outside the entrance to the self-service section. He has often wondered why they do this, why put them outside? Is it to make them easier to steal, because they are difficult to sell? Is it their way of providing for him and his friends? Is there possibly a fat man who has retained his position in the emporium? He enjoys himself with these theories, he has a love of such constructions, building ideas like card-houses, extending them until he gets dizzy and trembles at their heights.

Approaching the revolving door he hesitates, trying to judge the best way to enter the thing. The door is turning fast, spewing people into the store, last-minute shoppers. He chooses his space and moves forward, bustling to get there in time. Deidre, as tiny and bird-like as she always was, is thrown out of the revolving door, collides with him, hisses "slob" at him, and scurries into the store, leaving him with a sense of dull amazement, surprise that such a pretty face could express such fear and hatred so quickly.

Of course it wasn't Deidre. But Alexander Finch reflects that it could have been. As he sadly circles inside the revolving door and walks slowly along the street he thinks how strange it is that the revolution should have produced this one idea that would affect his life so drastically: to be fat is to be an oppressor, to be greedy, to be pre-revolutionary. It is impossible to say if it arose from the people or was fed to them by the propaganda of the revolution. Certainly in the years before the revolution most fat men were either Americans, stooges for the Americans, or wealthy supporters of the Americans. But in those years the people were of a more reasonable mind and could accept the idea of fat men like Alexander Finch being against the Americans and against the old Danko regime.

Alexander Finch had always thought of himself as possessing a lovable face and figure. He had not thought this from any conceit. At school they had called him "Cuddles", and on the paper everyone called him "Teddy" or "Teddy Bear". He had signed his cartoons "Teddy" and when he included himself in a cartoon he was always a bewildered, rotund man with a large bum, looking on the antics of the world with smiling, fatherly eyes.

But somehow, slowly, the way in which the world looked at Alexander Finch and, in consequence, the way Alexander Finch looked at himself, altered. He was forced to become a different cartoon, one of his own "Fat Americans": grotesque, greedy, an enemy of the people.

But in the early days after the revolution the change had not taken place. Or, if it had, Finch was too busy to notice it. As secretary of the Thirty-second District he took notes, recorded minutes, wrote weekly bulletins, drafted the ten-day reports to the Central Committee of Seventy-five, and still, somehow, found time to do a cartoon for his paper every day and to remember that General Kooper was spelt with a "K" and not a "C" (Miles Cooper being one of the infamous traitors of the revolution). In addition he was responsible for inspecting and reporting on the state of properties in the Thirty-second District and investigating cases of hardship and poverty wherever he found them. And if, during these early days, he occasionally became involved in unpleasant misunderstandings he regarded them as simply that, nothing more. People were accustomed to regarding all fat officials as either American or Danko men, because only the Americans and their friends had had enough food to become fat on. Occasionally Finch attempted to explain the nature of glandular fat and to point out that he wasn't a real official but rather the cartoonist "Teddy" who had always been anti-Danko.

Finch was occasionally embarrassed by his fatness in the early days when the people were hungry. But, paradoxically, it wasn't until the situation improved, when production had reached and passed the pre-revolutionary figure and when the distribution problems had finally been more or less ironed out, that the fat question came to the fore. And then, of course, food was no problem at all. If anything there was a surfeit and there was talk of dumping grain on the world market. Instead it was dumped in the sea.

Even then the district committees and the Committee of Seventy-five never passed any motions directly relating to fat men. Rather the word "fat" entered slyly into the language as a new adjective, as a synonym for greedy, ugly, sleazy, lazy, obscene, evil, dirty, dishonest, untrustworthy. It was unfair. It was not a good time to be a fat man.

Alexander Finch, now secretary of the clandestine "Fat Men Against The Revolution", carries his stolen double-bed sheets and his cans of smoked oysters northwards through the hot city streets. His narrow slanting eyes are almost shut and he looks out at the world through a comforting curtain of eyelashes. He moves slowly, a fat man with a white cotton shirt, baggy grey trousers, and a slight limp that could be interpreted as a waddle. His shirt shows large areas of sweat, like daubs, markings deliberately applied. No one bumps him. At the traffic lights he stands to one side, away from the crowds. It seems to be a mutual arrangement.

The sheets under his arm feel heavy and soggy. He is not sure that he has gotten away with it. They may be following him still (he dares not look around), following him to the house, to discover what else he may have stolen. He smiles at the thought of all those empty cans of smoked oysters in the incinerator in the back yard, all those hundreds of cans they will find. And the beer keg Fantoni stole. And the little buddha he stole for Fantoni's birthday but somehow kept for himself, he felt so sorry for (or was it fond of?) the little fat statue. He accuses himself of self-love but reflects that a little self-love is tonic for a fat man in these times.

Two youths run past him, bumping him from either side. He assumes it was intentional but is uncertain. His whole situation is like that, a tyranny of subtlety. To be fired from his job with the only newspaper that had been continually sympathetic to Kooper and his ideas for "slovenliness" and "bad spelling". He had laughed out loud. "Bad spelling." It was almost a tradition that cartoonists were bad spellers. It was expected of them and his work was always checked carefully for literals. But now they said his spelling was a nuisance and wasteful of time, and anyway he was "generally slovenly in dress and attitude". Did "slovenly" really mean "fat"? He didn't ask them. He didn't wish to embarrass them.

2.

Milligan's taxi is parked in front of the house. The taxi is like Milligan: it is very bright and shiny and painted in stripes of iridescent blue and yellow. Milligan spray-painted it himself. It looks like a dodgem car from Luna Park, right down to the random collection of pink stars stencilled on the driver's door.

Milligan is probably asleep.

Behind Milligan's taxi the house is very still and very drab, painted in the colours of railway stations and schools: hard green and dirty cream. Rust shows through the cream paint on the cast-iron balcony and two pairs of large baggy underpants hang limply from a line on the upstairs verandah.

It is one of six such houses, all identical, surrounded by high blocks of concrete flats and areas of flat waste land where dry thistles grow. The road itself is a major one and still retains some of its pre-revolutionary grandeur: rows of large elms form an avenue leading into the city.

The small front garden is full of weeds and Glino's radishes. Finch opens the front door cautiously, hoping it will be cooler inside but knowing that it won't be. In the half-dark he gropes around on the floor, feeling for letters. There are none— Fantoni must have taken them. He can still make out the dark blotches on the door where May sat and banged his head for three hours. No one has bothered to remove the blood.

Finch stands in the dark passage and listens. The house has the feeling of a place where no one works, a sort of listlessness. May is upstairs playing his Sibelius record. It is very scratched and it makes May morose, but it is the only record he has and he plays it incessantly. The music filters through the heavy heat of the passage and Finch hopes that Fantoni is not in the kitchen reading his "correspondence"—he doesn't wish Fantoni to see the sheets. He shuffles slowly down the passage, past the foot of the high, steep stairs, through the strange little cupboard where Glino cooks his vegetarian meals in two battered aluminium saucepans, and enters the kitchen where Fantoni, wearing a florid Hawaiian shirt and smoking a cigar, is reading his "correspondence" and tugging at the large moustache which partially obscures his small mouth. Finch has often thought it strange that such a large man should have such a small mouth. Fantoni's hands are also small but his forearms are large and muscular. His head is almost clean shaven, having the shortest of bristles covering it, and the back of his head is divided by a number of strange creases. Fantoni is the youngest of the six fat men who live in the house. An ex-parking officer, aged about twenty-eight, he is the most accomplished thief of them all. Without Fantoni they would all come close to starving, eking out a living on their pensions. Only Milligan has any other income.

Fantoni has connections everywhere. He can arrange food. He can arrange anything. He can arrange anything but the dynamite he needs to blow up the 16 October Statue. He has spent two months looking for the dynamite. Fantoni is the leader and driving force of the "Fat Men Against The Revolution". The others are like a hired army, fighting for Fantoni's cause which is to "teach the little monkeys a lesson".

Fantoni does not look up as Finch enters. He does not look up when Finch greets him. He does nothing to acknowledge Finch's presence. Because he is occupied with "my correspondence", the nature of which he has never revealed to anyone. Finch, for once, is happy that Fantoni doesn't look up, and continues out on to the porch with the green fibreglass sunroof, past Fantoni's brand new bicycle and Glino's herbs, along the concrete path, past the kitchen window, and comes to what is known as "the new extensions".

"The new extensions" are two bedrooms that have been added on to the back of the house. Their outside walls are made from corrugated iron, painted a dark, rusty red. Inside they are a little more pleasant. One is empty. Finch has the other. Finch's room is full of little pieces of bric-a-brac—books, papers, his buddha, a Rubens print, postcards from Italy with reproductions of Renaissance paintings. He has an early map of Iceland on the wall above the plywood bedhead, a grey goatskin rug covering the biggest holes in the maroon felt carpet, a Chinese paper lantern over the naked light globe.

He opens the door, steps back a pace, and pulls a huge comic fatman's face to register his disgust to some invisible observer.

The room has no insulation. And with each day of heat it has become hotter and hotter. At 4 a.m. it becomes a little cooler and at 7 a.m. it begins to heat up again. The heat brings out the strange smells of previous inhabitants, strange sweats and hopes come oozing out in the heat, ghosts of dreams and spilt Pine-o-Cleen.

The window does not open. There is no fly-wire screen on the door. He can choose between suffocation and mosquitoes.

Only a year ago he did a series of cartoons about housing conditions. He had shown corrugated iron shacks, huge flies, fierce rats, and Danko himself pocketing the rent. Danko's men had called on him after the fourth one had appeared. They threatened to jail him for treason, to beat him up, to torture him. He was very frightened, but they did nothing.

And now he is living in a corrugated iron room with huge blow-flies and the occasional rat. In a strange way it pleases him that he is no longer an observer, but it is a very small pleasure, too small to overcome the sense of despair that the smells and the suffocating heat induce in him.

He opens the roughly wrapped parcel of sheets and arranges them on the bed. The blue is cool. That is why he wanted the blue so badly because it is cooler than white, and because it doesn't show the dirt so badly. The old sheets have turned a disgusting brown. If they were not listed in the inventory he would take them out and burn them. Instead he rolls them up and stuffs them under the bed.

If Fantoni had seen the sheets there would have been a row. He would have been accused, again, of self-indulgence, of stealing luxuries instead of food. But Fantoni can always arrange sufficient food.

He peels off the clinging, sweat-soaked clothes and throws them on to the goatskin rug. Bending over to remove his socks he catches sight of his body. He stands slowly, in amazement. He is Alexander Finch whose father was called Senti but who called himself Finch because he sold American cigarettes on the black market and thought the name Finch very American. He is Alexander Finch, thirty-five years old, very fat, very tired, and suddenly, hopelessly sad. He has four large rolls of fat descending like a flesh curtain suspended from his navel. His spare tyres. He holds the fat in his hand, clenching it, wishing to tear it away. He clenches it until it hurts, and then clenches harder. For all the Rubens prints, for all the little buddhas, he is no longer proud or even happy to be fat. He is no longer Teddy. But he is not yet Fantoni or Glino—he doesn't hate the little monkeys. And, as much as he might pretend to, he is never completely convincing. They suspect him of mildness.

He is Finch whose father was called Senti, whose father was not fat, whose mother was not fat, whose grandfather may well have been called Chong or Ching—how else to explain the narrow eyes and the springy black hair?

3.

There are six fat men in the house: Finch, Fantoni, May, Milligan, Glino, and one man who has never divulged his name. The-man-who-won't-give-his-name has been here from the beginning. He is taller, heavier, and stronger than any of the others, Fantoni included. Finch has estimated his weight at twenty-two stone. The-man-who-won't-give-his-name has a big tough face with a broken nose. Hair grows from him everywhere, it issues from his nose, his ears, flourishes in big bushy white eyebrows, on his hands, his fingers and, Finch has noticed, on his large rounded back. He is the only original tenant. It was because of him that Florence Nightingale suggested the place to Fantoni, thinking he would find a friend in another fat man. Fantoni offered accommodation to Milligan. A month or so later Finch and May were strolling along 16 October Avenue (once known as Royal Parade) when they saw three men talking on the upstairs balcony outside Fantoni's room. Fantoni waved. May waved back, Milligan called to them to come up, and they did. Glino moved in a week later, having been sent with a letter of introduction from Florence Nightingale.

It was Fantoni who devised the now legendary scheme for removing the other tenants. And although the-man-who-won't-give-his-name never participated in the scheme, he never interfered or reported the matter to the authorities.

The-man-who-won't-give-his-name says little and keeps to himself. But he always says good morning and goodnight and once discussed Iceland with Finch on the day Finch brought home the map. Finch believes he was a sailor, but Fantoni claims that he is Calsen, an academic who was kicked out of the university for seducing one of "the little scrawnies".

Finch stands in front of the mirror, his hands digging into his stomach. He wonders what Fantoni would say if he knew that Finch had been engaged to two diminutive girls, Deidre and Anne, fragile girls with the slender arms of children who had both loved him with a total and unreasonable love, and he them, before the revolution.

4.

May turns his Sibelius record to side two and begins one more letter to his wife. He begins, Dear Iris, just a short note to say everything is all right.

5.

Finch is sitting in the kitchen leafing through the Botticelli book he has just bought. It took half the pension money. Everyone is out. He turns each page gently, loving the expensive paper as much as the reproductions.

Behind him he hears the key in the front door. He puts the book in the cupboard under the sink, among the saucepans, and begins to wash up the milk bottles; there are dozens of them, all dirty, all stinking.

There is cursing and panting in the passage. He can hear Fantoni saying, the little weed, the little fucker. Glino says something. There is an unusual sense of urgency in their voices. They both come into the kitchen at once. Their clothes are covered with dirt but Fantoni is wearing overalls.

Glino says, we went out to Deer Park.

There is an explosives factory at Deer Park. Fantoni has discussed it for months. No one could tell him what sort of explosive they made out there, but he was convinced it was dynamite.

Fantoni pushes Finch away from the sink and begins to wash the dirt off his hands and face. He says, the little weeds had guns.

Finch looks at Glino who is leaning against the door with his eyes closed, his hands opening and closing. He is trembling. There is a small scratch on one of his round, smooth cheeks and blood is seeping through his transparent skin. He says, I thought I was going in again, I thought we'd gone for sure.

Fantoni says, shut-up Glino.

Glino says, Christ, if you've ever been inside one of those places you'll never want to see one again.

He is talking about prison. The fright seems to have overcome some of his shyness. He says, Christ I couldn't stand it.

Finch, handing Fantoni a tea towel to dry himself with, says, did you get the dynamite?

Fantoni says, well, what do *you* think! It's past your bed time.

Finch leaves, worrying about the Botticelli book.

6.

Florence Nightingale will soon be here to collect the rents. Officially she arrives at 8 p.m., and at 7.30 she will arrive secretly, entering through the backyard, and visit Finch in "the new extensions".

Finch has showered early and shaved carefully. And he waits in his room, the door closed for privacy, checking with nervous eyes to see that everything is tidy.

These visits are never mentioned to the others, there is an unspoken understanding that they never will be.

There is a small tap on the door and Florence Nightingale enters, smiling shyly. She says, wow, the heat. She is wearing a simple yellow dress and leather sandals that lace up her calves Roman style. She closes the door with an exaggerated sort of care and tip-toes across to Finch who is standing, his face wreathed in a large smile.

She says, hello Cuddles, and kisses him on the cheek. Finch embraces her and pats her gently on the back. He says, the heat...

As usual Finch sits on the bed and Florence Nightingale squats yoga style on the goatskin rug at his feet. Finch once said, you look as if Modigliani painted you. And was pleased that she knew of Modigliani and was flattered by the comparison. She has a long straight face with a nose that is long vertically but not horizontally. Her teeth are straight and perfect, but a little on the long side. But now they are not visible and her lips are closed in a strange calm smile that suggests melancholy. They enjoy their melancholy together, Finch and Florence Nightingale. Her eyes, which are grey, are very big and very wide and she looks around the room as she does each time, looking for new additions.

She says, it got to 103 degrees... the steering wheel was too hot to touch.

Finch says, I was shopping. I got a book on Botticelli.

Her eyes begin to circle the room more quickly. She says, where, show me?

Finch giggles. He says, it's in the kitchen cupboard. Fantoni came back while I was reading it.

She says, you shouldn't be frightened of Fantoni, he won't eat you. You've got blue sheets, *double* blue sheets. She raises her eyebrows.

He says, no significance, it was just the colour.

She says, I don't believe you. *Double* blue sheets. Florence Nightingale likes to invent a secret love life for him but he doesn't know why. But they enjoy this, this sexual/asexual flirtation. Finch is never sure what it is meant to be but he has never had any real hopes regarding Florence Nightingale, although in sleep and half-sleep he has made love to her many times. She is not quite frail enough. There is a strength that she attempts to hide with little girl's shyness. And sometimes there is a strange awkwardness in her movements as if some logical force in her mind is trying to deny the grace of her body. She sits on the floor, her head cocked characteristically on one side so her long hair falls over one eye. She says, how's the Freedom Fighter?

The Freedom Fighter was Finch's name for Fantoni. Finch says, oh nothing, we haven't done anything yet, just plans.

She says, I drove past the 16 October Statue—it's still there.

Finch says, we can't get the explosive. Maybe we'll just paint it yellow.

Florence Nightingale says, maybe you should eat it.

Finch loves that. He says, that's good, Nancy, that's really good.

Florence Nightingale says, it's your role isn't it? The eaters? You should behave in character, the way they expect you to. You should eat everything. Eat the Committee of Seventy-five. She is rocking back and forth on the floor holding her knees, balancing on her arse.

Finch tries not to look up her skirt. He says, a feast.

She cups her hands to make a megaphone and says, The Fat Men Against The Revolution have eaten General Kooper.

He says, and General Alvarez.

She says, the Central Emporium was devoured last night, huge droppings have been discovered in 16 October Avenue.

He says, you make me feel like the old days, good fat, not bad fat.

She says, I've got to go. I was late tonight. I brought you some cigars, some extra ones for you.

She has jumped up, kissed him, and departed before he has time to thank her. He remains on the bed, nursing some vague disappointment, staring at the goatskin rug.

Slowly he smiles to himself, thinking about eating the 16 October Statue.

7.

Florence Nightingale will soon be here to collect the rents. With the exception of Fantoni, who is in the shower, and Glino, who is cooking his vegetarian meal in his little cupboard, everyone is in the kitchen.

Finch sits on a kerosene drum by the back annexe, hoping to catch whatever breeze may come through.

Milligan, in very tight blue shorts, yellow T-shirt, and blue-tinted glasses, squats beside him smiling to himself and rubbing his hands together. He has just finished telling a very long and involved story about a prostitute he picked up in his cab and who paid him double to let her conduct her business in the back seat. She made him turn his mirror back to front. No one cares if the story is true or not.

Milligan says, yep.

Milligan wears his clothes like corsets, always too tight. He says it is good for his blood, the tightness. But his flesh erupts in strange bulges from his thighs and stomach and arms. He looks trussed up, a grinning turkey ready for the oven.

Milligan always has a story. His life is a continual charade, a collection of prostitutes and criminals, "characters", beautiful women, eccentric old ladies, homosexuals, and two-headed freaks. Also he knows many jokes. Finch and May sit on the velvet cushions in Milligan's room and listen to the stories, but it is bad for May who becomes depressed. The evenings invariably end with May in a fury saying, Jesus, I want a fuck, I want a fuck so badly it hurts. But Milligan just keeps laughing, somehow never realizing how badly it affects May.

May, Finch, Milligan, and the-man-who-won't-give-his-name lounge around the kitchen drinking Glino's homemade beer. Finch has suggested that they wash the dirty milk bottles before Florence Nightingale arrives and everyone has agreed that it is a good idea. However they have all remained seated, drinking Glino's homemade beer. No one likes the beer, but of all the things that are hard to steal alcohol is the hardest. Even Fantoni cannot arrange it. Once he managed to get hold of a nine-gallon keg of beer but it sat in the back yard for a year before Glino got hold of a gas cylinder and the gear for pumping it out. They were drunk for one and a half days on that lot, and were nearly arrested en masse when they went out to piss on the commemorative plaque outside the offices of the Fifty-fourth District.

No one says much. They sip Glino's beer from jam jars and look around the room as if considering ways to tidy it, removing the milk bottles, doing something about the rubbish bin— a cardboard box which was full a week ago and from which eggshells, tins, and breadcrusts cascade on to the floor. Every now and then May reads something from an old newspaper, laughing very loudly. When May laughs, Finch smiles. He is happy to see May laughing because when he is not laughing he is very sad and liable to break things and do himself an injury. May's forehead is still scarred from the occasion when he battered it against the front door for three hours. There is still blood on the paintwork.

May wears an overcoat all the time, even tonight in this heat. His form is amorphous. He has a double chin and a drooping face that hangs downwards from his nose. He is balding and worries about losing hair. He sleeps for most of the day to escape his depressions and spends the nights walking around the house, drinking endless glasses of water, playing his record, and groaning to himself as he tries to sleep.

May is the only one who was married before the revolution. He came to this town when he was fired from his job as a refrigerator salesman, and his wife was to join him later. Now he can't find her. She has sold their house and he is continually writing letters to her, care of anyone he can think of who might know her whereabouts.

May is also in love with Florence Nightingale, and in this respect he is no different from the other five, even Fantoni who claims to find her skinny and undernourished.

Florence Nightingale is their friend, their confidante, their rent collector, their mascot. She works for the revolution but is against it. She will be here soon. Everybody is waiting for her. They talk about what she will wear.

Milligan, staring intently at his large Omega watch, says, peep, peep, peep, on the third stroke...

The front door bell rings. It is Florence Nightingale.

The-man-who-won't-give-his-name springs up. He says, I'll get it, I'll get it. He looks very serious but his broken, battered face appears to be very gentle. He says, I'll get it. And sounds out of breath. He moves with fast heavy strides along the passage, his back hunched urgently like a jungle animal, a rhino, ploughing through undergrowth. It is rumoured that he is having an affair with Florence Nightingale but it doesn't seem possible.

They crowd together in the small kitchen, their large soft bodies crammed together around the door. When Florence Nightingale nears the door there is much pushing and shoving and Milligan dances around the outside of the crowd, unable to get through, crying "make way there, make way for the lady with the big blue eyes" in his high nasal voice, and everyone pushes every way at once. Finally it is Fantoni who arrives from his shower and says, "For Christ's sake, give a man some *room*."

Everybody is very silent. They don't like to hear him swear in front of Florence Nightingale. Only Fantoni would do it, no one else. Now he nods to her and indicates that she should sit down on one of the two chairs. Fantoni takes the other. For the rest there are packing cases, kerosene tins, and an empty beer keg which is said to cause piles.

Fantoni is wearing a new safari suit, but no one mentions it. He has sewn insignia on the sleeves and the epaulettes. No one has ever seen this insignia before. No one mentions it. They pretend Fantoni is wearing his white wool suit as usual.

Florence Nightingale sits simply with her hands folded in her lap. She greets them all by name and in turn; to the-man-who-won't-give-his-name she merely says "Hello". But it is not difficult to see that there is something between them. The-man-who-won't-give-his-name shuffles his large feet and suddenly smiles very broadly. He says, "Hello".

Fantoni then collects the rent which they pay from their pensions. The rent is not large, but the pensions are not large either. Only Milligan has an income, which gives him a certain independence.

Finch doesn't have enough for the rent. He had meant to borrow the difference from Milligan but forgot. Now he is too embarrassed to ask in front of Fantoni.

He says, I'm a bit short.

Florence Nightingale says, forget it, try and get it for next week. She counts the money and gives everyone a receipt. Finch tries to catch Milligan's eye.

Later, when everyone is smoking the cigars she has brought and drinking Glino's home brew, she says, I hate this job, it's horrible to take this money from you.

Glino is sitting on the beer keg. He says, what job would you like? But he doesn't look at Florence Nightingale. Glino never looks at anyone.

Florence Nightingale says, I would come and look after you. We could all live together and I'd cook you crêpes suzettes.

And Fantoni says, but who would bring us cigars then? And everybody laughs.

8.

Everyone is a little bit drunk.

Florence Nightingale says, Glino play us a tune.

Glino says nothing, but seems to double up even more so that his broad shoulders become one with his large bay window. His fine white hair falls over his face.

Everybody says, come on Glino, give us a tune. Until, finally, Glino takes his mouth organ from his back pocket and, without once looking up, begins to play. He plays something very slow. It reminds Finch of an albatross, an albatross flying over a vast, empty ocean. The albatross is going nowhere. Glino's head is so bowed that no one can see the mouth organ, it is sandwiched between his nose and his chest. Only his pink, translucent hands move slowly from side to side.

Then, as if changing its mind, the albatross becomes a gipsy, a pedlar, or a drunken troubador. Glino's head shakes, his foot taps, his hands dance.

Milligan jumps to his feet. He dances a sailor's dance, Finch thinks it might be the hornpipe, or perhaps it is his own invention, like the pink stars stencilled on his taxi door. Milligan has a happy, impish face with eyebrows that rise and fall from behind his blue-tinted glasses. If he weighed less his face might even be pretty. Milligan's face is half-serious, half-mocking, intent on the dance, and Florence Nightingale stands slowly. They both dance, Florence Nightingale whirling and turning, her hair flying, her eyes nearly closed. The music becomes faster and faster and the five fat men move back to stand against the wall, as if flung there by centrifugal force. Finch, pulling the table out of the way, feels he will lose his balance. Milligan's face is bright red and streaming with sweat. The flesh on his bare white thighs shifts and shakes and beneath his T-shirt his breasts move up and down. Suddenly he spins to one side, drawn to the edge of the room, and collapses in a heap on the floor.

Everyone claps. Florence Nightingale keeps dancing. The clapping is forced into the rhythm of the music and everyone claps in time. May is dancing with Florence Nightingale. His movements are staccato, he stands with his feet apart, his huge overcoat flapping, slaps his thighs, claps his hands together above his head, stamps his feet, spins, jumps, shouts, nearly falls, takes Florence Nightingale around the waist and spins her around and around, they both stumble, but neither stops. May's face is transformed, it is living. The teeth in his partly open mouth shine white. His overcoat is like some magical cloak, a swirling beautiful thing.

Florence Nightingale constantly sweeps long hair out of her eyes.

May falls. Finch takes his place but becomes puffed very quickly and gives over to the-man-who-won't-give-his-name.

The-man-who-won't-give-his-name takes Florence Nightingale in his arms and disregards the music. He begins a very slow, gliding waltz. Milligan whispers in Glino's ear. Glino looks up shyly for a moment, pauses, then begins to play a Strauss waltz.

Finch says, the "Blue Danube". To no one in particular.

The-man-who-won't-give-his-name dances beautifully and very proudly. He holds Florence Nightingale slightly away from him, his head is high and cocked to one side. Florence Nightingale whispers something in his ear. He looks down at her and raises his eyebrows. They waltz around and around the kitchen until Finch becomes almost giddy with embarrassment. He thinks, it is like a wedding.

Glino once said (of prisons), "If you've ever been inside one of those places you wouldn't ever want to be inside one again."

Tonight Finch can see him lying on his bunk in a cell, playing the "Blue Danube" and the albatross and staring at the ceiling. He wonders if it is so very different from that now: they spend their days lying on their beds, afraid to go out because they don't like the way people look at them.

The dancing finishes and the-man-who-won't-give-his-name escorts Florence Nightingale to her chair. He is so large, he treats her as if she were wrapped in crinkly cellophane, a gentleman holding flowers.

Milligan earns his own money. He asks Fantoni, why don't you dance?

Fantoni is leaning against the wall smoking another cigar. He looks at Milligan for a long time until Finch is convinced that Fantoni will punch Milligan.

Finally Fantoni says, I can't dance.

9.

They all walk up the passage with Florence Nightingale. Approaching the front door she drops an envelope. The envelope spins gently to the floor and everyone walks around it. They stand on the porch and wave goodnight to her as she drives off in her black government car.

Returning to the house Milligan stoops and picks up the envelope. He hands it to Finch and says, for you. Inside the official envelope is a form letter with the letterhead of the Department of Housing. It says, Dear Mr. Finch, the department regrets that you are now in arrears with your rent. If this matter is not settled within the statutory seven days you will be required to find other accommodation. It is signed, Nancy Bowlby.

Milligan says, what is it?

Finch says, it's from Florence Nightingale, about the rent.

Milligan says, seven days?

Finch says, oh, she has a job to do, it's not her fault.

10.

May has the back room upstairs. Finch is lying in bed in "the new extensions". He can hear Milligan calling to May.

Milligan says, May?

May says, what is it?

Milligan says, come here.

Their voices, Milligan's distant, May's close, seem to exist only inside Finch's head.

May says, what do you want?

Milligan shouts, I want to tell you something.

May says, no you don't, you just want me to tuck you in.

Milligan says, no. No, I don't.

Fantoni's loud raucous laugh comes from even further away.

The-man-who-won't-give-his-name is knocking on the ceiling of his room with a broom. Finch can hear it going, bump, bump, bump. The Sibelius record jumps. May shouts, quit it.

Milligan says, I want to tell you something.

May shouts, no you don't.

Finch lies naked on top of the blue sheets and tries to hum the albatross song but he has forgotten it.

Milligan says, come *here*. May? May, I want to tell you something.

May says, tuck yourself in, you lazy bugger.

Milligan giggles. The giggle floats out into the night.

Fantoni is in helpless laughter.

Milligan says, May?

May's footsteps echo across the floorboards of his room and cross the corridor to Milligan's room. Finch hears Milligan's laughter and hears May's footsteps returning to May's room.

Fantoni shouts, what did he want?

May says, he wanted to be tucked in.

Fantoni laughs. May turns up the Sibelius record. The-man-who-won't-give-his-name knocks on the ceiling with a broom. The record jumps.

11.

It is 4 a.m. and not yet light. No one can see them. As May and Finch leave the house a black government car draws away from the kerb but, although both of them see it, neither mentions it.

At 4 a.m. it is cool and pleasant to walk through the waste lands surrounding the house. There are one or two lights on in the big blocks of flats, but everyone seems to be asleep.

They walk slowly, picking their way through the thistles.

Finally May says, you were crazy.

Finch says, I know.

They walk for a long time. Finch wonders why the thistles grow in these parts, why they are sad, why they only grow where the ground has been disturbed, and wonders where they grew originally.

He says, do they make you sad?

May says, what?

He says, the thistles.

May doesn't answer. Finally he says, you were crazy to mention it. He'll really do it. He'll *really* do it.

Finch stubs his toe on a large block of concrete. The pain seems deserved. He says, it didn't enter my mind—that he'd think of Nancy.

May says, he'll really do it. He'll bloody-well eat her. Christ, you know what he's like.

Finch says, I know, but I didn't mention Nancy, just the statue.

May wraps his overcoat around himself and draws his head down into it. He says, he *looks* evil, he *likes* being fat.

Finch says, that's reasonable.

May says, I can still remember what it was like being thin. Did I tell you, I was only six, but I can remember it like it was yesterday. Jesus it was nice. Although I don't suppose I appreciated it at the time.

Finch says, shut-up.

May says, he's still trying to blow up that bloody statue and he'll get caught. Probably blow himself up. Then we'll be the ones that have to pinch everything. And we'll get caught, or we'll starve more like it.

Finch says, help him get some dynamite and then dob

him in to the cops. While he's in jail he couldn't eat Florence Nightingale.

May says, and we wouldn't eat anything. I wouldn't mind so much if he just wanted to screw her. I wouldn't mind screwing her myself.

Finch says, maybe he is. Already.

May pulls his overcoat tightly around himself and says, no, it's whatshisname, the big guy, that's who's screwing her. Did you see them dancing? It's him.

Finch says, I like him.

May says nothing. They have come near a main road and they wordlessly turn back, keeping away from the street lights, returning to the thistles.

Finch says, it was Nancy's idea. She said why don't we eat the statue.

May says, you told me already. You were nuts. She was nuts too but she was only joking. You should have known that he's serious about everything. He really wants to blow up everything, not just the fucking statue.

Finch says, he's a fascist.

May says, what's a fascist?

Finch says, like Danko...like General Kooper...like Fantoni. He's going to dig a hole in the backyard. He calls it the barbecue.

12.

In another two hours Finch will have earned enough money for the rent. Fantoni is paying him by the hour. In another two hours he will be clear and then he'll stop. He hopes there is still two hours' work. They are digging a hole among the dock weeds in the backyard. It is a trench like a grave but only three feet deep. He asked Milligan for the money but Milligan had already lent money to Glino and May.

Fantoni is wearing a pair of May's trousers so he won't get his own dirty. He is stripped to the waist and working with a mattock. Finch clears the earth Fantoni loosens; he has a long-handled shovel. Both the shovel and the mattock are new, they have appeared miraculously, like anything that Fantoni wants.

They have chosen a spot outside Finch's window, where it is completely private, shielded from the neighbouring houses. It is a small private spot which Fantoni normally uses for sunbathing.

The top of Fantoni's bristly head is bathed in sweat and small dams of sweat have caught in the creases on the back of his head; he gives strange grunts between swings and carries out a conversation with Finch who is too exhausted to answer.

He says, I want the whole thing...in writing, OK?...write it down...all the reasons...just like you explained it to me.

Finch is getting less and less earth on the shovel. He keeps aiming at the earth and overshooting it, collecting a few loose clods on the blade. He says, yes.

Fantoni takes the shovel from him. He says, you write that now, write all the reasons like you told me and I'll count that as time working. How's that?

And he pats Finch on the back.

Finch is not sure how it is. He cannot believe any of it. He cannot believe that he, Alexander Finch, is digging a barbecue to cook a beautiful girl called Florence Nightingale in the backyard of a house in what used to be called Royal Parade. He would not have believed it, and still cannot.

He says, thanks Fantoni.

Fantoni says, what I want, Finch, is a thing called a rationale...that's the word isn't it...they're called rationales.

13.

Rationale by A. Finch

The following is a suggested plan of action for the "Fat Men Against The Revolution".

It is suggested that the Fat Men of this establishment pursue a course of militant love, by bodily consuming a senior member of the revolution, an official of the revolution, or a monument of the revolution (e.g. the 16 October Statue).

Such an act would, in the eyes of the revolution, be in character. The Fat Men of this society have been implicitly accused of (among other things) loving food too much, of loving themselves too much to the exclusion of the revolution. To eat a member or monument of the revolution could be seen as a way of turning this love towards the revolution. Eating is a total and literal act of consummation. The Fat Men would incorporate in their own bodies all that could be good and noble in the revolution and excrete that which is bad. In other words, the bodies of Fat Men will purify the revolution.

Alexander Finch shivers violently although it is very hot. He makes a fair copy of the draft. When he has finished he goes upstairs to the toilet and tries, unsuccessfully, to vomit.

Fantoni is supervising the delivery of a load of wood, coke, and kindling in the backyard. He is dressed beautifully in a white suit made from lightweight wool. He is smoking one of Florence Nightingale's cigars.

As Finch descends the stairs he hears a loud shout and then, two steps later, a loud crash. It came from May's room. And Finch knows without looking that May has thrown his bowl of goldfish against the wall. May loved his goldfish.

14.

At dinner Finch watches Fantoni eat the omelette that Glino has cooked for him. Fantoni cuts off dainty pieces. He buries the dainty pieces in the small fleshy orifice beneath his large moustache.

15.

May wakes him at 2 a.m. He says, I've just realized where she is. She'll be with her brother. That's where she'll be. I wrote her a letter.

Finch says, Florence Nightingale.

May says, my wife.

16.

Glino knows. Milligan knows. May and Finch know. Only the-man-who-won't-give-his-name is unaware of the scheme. He asked Fantoni about the hole in the backyard. Fantoni said, it is a wigwam for a goose's bridle.

17.

The deputation moves slowly on tip-toes from Finch's room. In the kitchen annexe someone trips over Fantoni's bicycle. It crashes. Milligan giggles. Finch punches him sharply in the ribs. In the dark, Milligan's face is caught between laughter and surprise. He pushes his glasses back on the bridge of his nose and peers closely at Finch.

The others have continued and are now moving quietly through the darkened kitchen. Finch pats Milligan on the shoulder. He whispers, I'm sorry. But Milligan passes on to join the others where they huddle nervously outside the-man-who-won't-give-his-name's room.

Glino looks to Finch, who moves through them and slowly opens the door. Finch sums up the situation. He feels a dull soft shock. He stops, but the others push him into the room. Only when they are all assembled inside the room, very close to the door, does everybody realize that the-man-who-won't-give-his-name is in bed with Florence Nightingale.

Florence Nightingale is lying on her side, facing the door, attempting to smile. The-man-who-won't-give-his-name is climbing from the bed. Finch is shocked to see that he is still wearing his socks. For some reason this makes everything worse.

The-man-who-won't-give-his-name seems very slow and very old. He rummages through the pile of clothes beside the bed, his breathing the only sound in the room. It is hoarse, heavy breathing that only subsides after he has found his underpants. He trips getting into them and Finch notices they are on inside out. Eventually the-man-who-won't-give-his-name says, it is generally considered good manners to knock.

He begins to dress now. No one knows what to do. They watch him hand Florence Nightingale her items of clothing so she can dress beneath the sheet. He sits in front of her then, partially obscuring her struggles. Florence Nightingale is no longer trying to smile. She looks very sad, almost frightened.

Eventually Finch says, this is more important, I'm afraid, more important than knocking on doors.

He has accepted some new knowledge and the acceptance makes him feel strong although he has no real idea of what the knowledge is. He says, Fantoni is planning to eat Florence Nightingale.

Florence Nightingale, struggling with her bra beneath the sheet, says, we know, we were discussing it.

Milligan giggles.

The-man-who-won't-give-his-name has found his dressing-gown in the cupboard in the corner. He remains there, like a boxer waiting between rounds.

Florence Nightingale is staring at her yellow dress on the floor. Glino and May bump into each other as they reach for it at the same moment. They both retreat and both step forward again. Finally it is Milligan who darts forward, picks up the garment, and hands it to Florence Nightingale, who disappears under the sheets once more. Finch finds it almost impossible not to stare at her. He wishes she would come out and dress quickly and get the whole thing over and done with.

Technically, Florence Nightingale has deceived no one.

Glino says, we got to stop him.

Florence Nightingale's head appears from beneath the sheets. She smiles at them all. She says, you are all wonderful... I love you all.

It is the first time Finch has ever heard Florence Nightingale say anything so insincere or so false. He wishes she would unsay that.

Finch says, he must be stopped.

Behind him he can hear a slight shuffling. He looks around to see May, his face flushed red, struggling to keep the door closed. He makes wild signs with his eyes to indicate that someone is trying to get in. Finch leans against the door, which pushes back with the heavy weight of a dream. Florence Nightingale slides sideways out of bed and Glino pushes against Finch, who is sandwiched between two opposing forces. Finally it is the-man-who-won't-give-his-name who says, let him in.

Everybody steps back, but the door remains closed. They stand, grouped in a semi-circle around it, waiting. For a moment it seems as if it was all a mistake. But, finally, the door knob turns and the door is pushed gently open. Fantoni stands in the doorway wearing white silk pyjamas.

He says, what's this, an orgy?

No one knows what to do or say.

18.

Glino is still vomiting in the drain in the backyard. He has been vomiting since dawn and it is now dark. Finch said he should be let off, because he was a vegetarian, but the-man-who-won't-give-his-name insisted. So they made Glino eat just a little bit.

The stench hangs heavily over the house.

May is playing his record.

Finch has thought many times that he might also vomit.

The blue sheet which was used to strangle Fantoni lies in a long tangled line from the kitchen through the kitchen annexe and out into the backyard, where Glino lies retching and where the barbecue pit, although filled in, still smokes slowly, the smoke rising from the dry earth.

The-man-who-won't-give-his-name had his dressing-gown

ruined. It was soaked with blood. He sits in the kitchen now, wearing Fantoni's white safari suit. He sits reading Fantoni's mail. He has suggested that it would be best if he were referred to as Fantoni, should the police come, and that anyway it would be best if he were referred to as Fantoni. A bottle of scotch sits on the table beside him. It is open to anyone, but so far only May has taken any.

Finch is unable to sleep. He has tried to sleep but can see only Fantoni's face. He steps over Glino and enters the kitchen.

He says, may I have a drink please, Fantoni?

It is a relief to be able to call him a name.

19.

The-man-who-won't-give-his-name has taken up residence in Fantoni's room. Everybody has become used to him now. He is known as Fantoni.

A new man has also arrived, being sent by Florence Nightingale with a letter of introduction. So far his name is unknown.

20.

"Revolution in a Closed Society—A Study of Leadership among the Fat"
By Nancy Bowlby

Leaders were selected for their ability to provide materially for the welfare of the group as a whole. Obviously the same qualities should reside in the heir-apparent, although these qualities were not always obvious during the waiting period; for this reason I judged it necessary to show favouritism to the heir-apparent and thus to raise his prestige in the eyes of the group. This favouritism would sometimes take the form of small gifts and, in those rare cases where it was needed, shows of physical affection as well.

A situation of "crisis" was occasionally triggered, *deus ex machina,* by suggestion, but usually arose spontaneously and had only to be encouraged. From this point on, as I shall discuss later in this paper, the "revolution" took a similar course and "Fantoni" was always disposed of effectively and the new "Fantoni" took control of the group.

The following results were gathered from a study of twenty-three successive "Fantonis". Apart from the "Fantoni" and the "Fantoni-apparent", the composition of the group remained unaltered. Whilst it can be admitted that studies so far are at an early stage, the results surely justify the continuation of the experiments with larger groups.

Nouveau Big

Katya dreams she is a sumo wrestler,
but not Japanese. She is an Islander, Samoan, and she is
huge. In training she cultivates
the blank mind of a baby. She considers the distances
inside herself—from the green fields
of her ankle bone
to the fountains playing sweetly before the kiosk
inside her wide, wide forehead. Can anyone
call this fat? she thinks, tracing the curves
of her own rotund torso (nothing
like a pregnant woman's body,
which looks unbalanced, tilted, which is dedicated
solely to getting the thing inside
out). In this body Katya grapples
with her opponent, the friction of all that flesh
struggling like two mountains
to remain immovable and still
push the other from the dohyo
giving off a fierce heat.

But before the first year
is over—perhaps back in her bed Katya moves
her knee, slightly—she begins to feel
what she has given up for sumo. She misses
lu'au, with its fresh taro and coconut cream. They feed her
mostly bowls of chanko and rice, in great quantities,
to keep her weight solid. She feels cramped
among the lean buildings of frenzied Japan, she misses

just breathing beside the warm, indefinite ocean. And then
there's the chafing—those damn mawashis
do leave the inner thighs to rub together, and even
an active fat man still has fat there. And she has just
sworn in Samoan to give it all up, has bowed
quite gracefully and turned towards the arena door
when she rolls onto her back and feels
large, under her leaf-patterned quilt,
and substantive, and capable
of anything.

The Six Hundred Pound Man

Of the six hundred pound man on two beds,
nothing remains,
not the bleariness with which he moved his eyes
nor the warm oil curling in his beard.

Though the sheets and plastic bags are gone,
his grunts, his kind acceptance gone,
I see him now, rising in the distance,
an island, mountainous
and hooded with impenetrable vine.

When I awaken to the death
of the six hundred pound man
and cannot sleep again,
I paddle to his shore

in search of those flamboyant trees
that flame his flanks,
in search of bougainvillea
blossoming his thighs,
of women who rise to touch him
tenderly with ointment,

in search of healers, singers
who wrestle souls of old bodies
back to bones, back to dirt, and back back
to their beginnings.

As I enter for the first time
this medicine circle,

bearing chickens in honor of the god,
words dancing from my lips,

spirit like the plume of a child's volcano
rises

and then the medicine, the medicine is good
and the tongues, the tongues are dancing
and the fathers, oh! the fathers are dancing

and this worthless and alien body,
this six hundred pound man,
I discover him beautiful.

Hungry Self

The stars were beginning above the lake, and the boats with their tiny pilot lights were entering the bay through the channel to dock for the night. Johnny, Ngoc's son, was lighting the red evening candles with half an eye on me, because he liked to keep an eye on the help, or maybe because his mother had taught him to. I had a layer of oil on my face. My apron was shiny with duck sauce, and my pockets were puffy with crumpled dollar bills. We'd had Buffet Day earlier. On Buffet Day we got a lot of families and fat people who came because the other people who came were fat and no one was too embarrassed to load up a really tall plate, and people stayed a few hours to double-eat and left bunches of ones for tips.

I was watching Johnny glide across the dark-red carpet, menus in hand, to seat someone at the last booth in the lakeside row. Like me, he was watching the boats. I was terribly in love with him, but we were separated by race and by the fact that he hated me. Johnny was nineteen, which was my age, and we had both spent every night of the summer here—I did it because I was broke and Johnny did it because Ngoc was a widow and needed him to help her run this restaurant she'd maintained after her husband's death so that Johnny could maintain it after her own. He lit the little red candle in the booth, where he'd seated a lonely and enormous woman, and nodded at me on his way to the kitchen. I went over to the table and put down some dry noodles and a stained silver teapot and turned over a white china cup and poured some tea in it, and the woman swivelled her body toward me and gave me the smile you give a waitress if you're the kind of person who is nice to a waitress, and I saw that the woman was my ex-psychiatrist. I knocked over the cup and the tea spilled onto the table and then into her lap.

I'm sorry, I said, I'm sorry.

I watched her face go through a set of "If A, then B; if B, then C; A, therefore C," after which she said, Hi, how *are* you, as if to say, Is everything O.K. now? with an element of I am neither your mother nor your relative but I do care for you to the degree that my highly stretched human resources allow, and I said, Good, good, to mean Everything is good, your efforts were successful, and please feel happy about the energy you invested in me.

The next day was the start of Bike Week, a five-day festival during which a hundred thousand bikers would arrive and celebrate being bikers in our very small and beautiful town. On the last night of that week, I would have fourteen tables and I would tell them their food was almost ready but that would be a lie, since I'd mismatched three tables' worth of orders and none of them would eat sooner than an hour after being sat, and they would each tip me nothing, to say, You are worth nothing, or one dollar, to say, You are worth crap; except for those people who were nicest and least likely to complain and whom I would therefore serve last. They would not eat for an hour and a half. These people would tip me a twenty and I would wonder at their foolishness and give the twenty to Ken the cook, who sold coke in the basement, and who'd been shipped in by Ngoc from China and housed in a rat-shack next door. He knew how to say "shitfucker" and "asslick" and had a habit of wiping his dick with his hands then not washing them and telling me about it, charades style.

Ngoc knew about this but couldn't do much. She was old and strange-looking and dyed her hair black and wore rhinestone-studded mauve gowns that she thought added elegance to the general atmosphere of the restaurant. The restaurant was very red and very gold. Ngoc bussed tables, and supervised the kitchen, and the bar, and us, and at night I watched her bending over the counter in front, adding columns of figures without a calculator. She couldn't control the cooks, but she kept them on because they were illegal and worked cheap. All of the cooks were wrinkled and small and had perms; once a month, they pitched in and took a cab downtown, where they bought hookers and sat for their perms.

Ken the cook cut five wide lines for a twenty in a boxed-goods room behind the meat rack in the basement, which is where Ngoc would find us, and Ngoc would be in an intolerant mood that night because the same bikers who came every year, a group of them, fat and bearded and staggering drunk, had stopped her in the lobby and chanted, Ngoc, Ngoc, Ngoc, give us a chink hug, Ngoc, give us a chink hug, and Ngoc had had to totter on over in her heels and her Elvira dress and scream, So good to see you! So good to see you! and press herself against each one of their enormous bodies. When Ngoc found the cook and me doing lines in the basement she'd have some things to say to us in Cantonese and then some things to say to us in English, which would be that there is one kind of trash and there is another kind of trash and neither kind was trash that she wanted in her Eating Establishment.

But this shift was slow. I'd spent most of it putting purple tissue umbrellas in drinks and asking customers what they'd seen in town so far and telling them where they might want to go. And, even though they did not want and had not ordered dessert, I'd been bringing out ten fortune cookies on an egg-roll plate with a pile of pineapple chunks topped by whipped cream and my specialty, umbrella-lodged-in-cherry; because I remembered, when I was a kid, how excited I'd been whenever we went out to eat Chinese, and how despite the fact that we took ten minutes to study the menu we always knew exactly what we would order, which was pork fried rice, sweet-and-sour chicken, egg foo yung, and beef teriyaki, none of which were really Chinese, and I remembered how the waitress would bring out, for the finale, a plate heaped with cherries and pineapple chunks and fortune cookies, and once my sister's cookie had said, "You will discover great wealth," and then in the parking lot she found a dime and for years after that I waited for my cookies to come true.

The cherries and umbrellas came from Jud the bartender and Jud did not like my taking them, but he let me because he was short and missing two teeth and wanted to fuck me. He had a boat and a house on the promenade and was one of those people who sat on their widow's walk on bright days and watched the tourists, evaluating their stupidity or their level of ugliness. I'm going boating this week, he'd say. Want to go boating? Next week, I'd say, and he'd say, Remind me. He looked a little like Don Johnson, some people had told him, and this is what kept him happy, I think.

In the kitchen I found towels to clean up the tea. My ex-psychiatrist was my ex-counsellor, really, ex-family counsellor, one in a long line of psychiatrists that at first my family, and then just I, had consulted. She was a fat ugly lesbian. Her partner, or maybe just her lover, had arrived while I was fetching the towels. I say "lover" because they seemed to be on a date. They were nervous with happiness and had elected to sit next to each other, on the same side of the booth, facing one of the restaurant's decorative highlights, a red-and-gold dragon gleefully humping a column. I figured this side-by-side seating to be an announcement of love, a fuck-you to the world, and I was embarrassed for them, and for myself, to be serving my ex-psychiatrist here in this shitty place, and for her, to be eating here in this shitty place, because she weighed two hundred and sixty pounds and there was nothing on our menu that it was a good idea for her to eat. She'd never told me what she weighed but I knew anyway because I was an excellent evaluator of body weight; this ability was, in part, why three years ago I had driven weekly to her horrible office.

I was standing with my waitress notepad at my chest. The

boats were sliding into their places at the docks. Johnny was looking on from the lobby, to make sure I did not spill any more tea, and I thought about pleading stomach ache so I could leave early and not have to serve dinner to my ex-shrink, but that would have sounded as if I had my period, which would have been gross, and Johnny liked me little enough already.

My ex-psychiatrist said, This is my friend Angela. Then we had a round of inquiry and solicitation which was not strictly necessary since we would probably not see each other again. This woman had sat across from me for six months and told me repeatedly that I was not a bad person, was in fact a good person, and because I do not like to talk and managed to get her to talk instead, she told me that people had been unkind to her all her life and that she had suffered great sadness and once tried to end it all with some cooking oil and a match, but ended up with a fist-size patch of blackness on her skull and soft white skin grafts on her calves, and that she was now dealing with an eating disorder herself, which was obesity, and that she found that Harry's Diet Pretzels were a wonderful help and made you feel full and at peace, as if you did not need anything else, and she gave me an extra bag that she happened to have in her purse because the sadness could come upon you at any time, and it was best to have Harry's Diet Pretzels with you when it did.

I took their orders. I recommended lo mein. I said, Everyone likes it. I did not say, Everyone likes it because it is noodles in oil, and you will like it, too. They ordered lo mein and Szechuan grand worbar, a fancy chicken thing that sizzles over a blue flame on an iron plate in front of the customer, which I normally liked to serve because it guaranteed a good tip. I did not want a good tip. I wanted a shitty tip. I wanted a shitty tip so I could have a reason for hating the fat ugly lesbian, a reason other than that she had once seen me cry.

The lover was polite in a cold, challenging way. I said Ngoc's special tea was shipped straight from Shanghai and that

our cook was famous in Hong Kong, and she nodded as if
something unpleasant had just been confirmed. I guessed how
their pre-soup conversation would go.

Former patient?

Yes.

Bad one?

Yes.

Think she's better now?

Probably not. I hope so. She means well.

I delivered a pineapple plate to a family of seven who had ordered cheap and were excited to see it. Johnny was waiting for
me in the kitchen, leaning against the industrial tea bins.

You know those women?

I had a tray full of chicken bones and half-eaten egg foo
yung from the happy family. I set my tray on the wash counter
and removed the plates and started slopping them off and immediately got some of the slop on my shirt.

You know them? he repeated.

Nope.

What'd they order? Lo mein?

Yup.

He took the tray from me and stashed it with the other
trays.

Last party. You're off for the night.

Great. I kept slopping.

You going out?

I racked my dishes and wiped myself.

I don't know.

You got some gravy on your shirt.

I wiped myself again.

Let me know if there's anything going on.

Sure, I said. There was not anything going on, but I wondered what constituted Going On and how I could spin a night
of nothing going on into something Going On, and if he would

like that, and if he did like that, if he'd like me. But I knew that he did not like me. He was a color in the sea of white which was this state, and he seldom spoke and had no friends, although he worked out all the time and was beautiful. When he mowed the littered and weedy lawn that sloped from the restaurant to the lake, the other waitresses and I found reasons to walk by the open windows every ten minutes or so. Once, at the end of a day when Ngoc had been ill and Johnny had spent twelve hours ferrying unsatisfied customers in and out of the enormous red dining room, I found him sitting at the waitress station with a pile of pink drink umbrellas he'd ruined by pushing them open too forcefully. He'd said, I hate this, meaning this place, and I could tell he hated us, the staff, just as Ngoc hated us, and I guessed Ngoc would import a wife for him as she had for his regarded brother, who was twenty-nine and watched cartoons in the lobby and told knock-knock jokes and did not know how to fuck his wife and actually liked us.

I went downstairs to the basement. It was vast and unlit and I liked it, because down there I was just a person in the basement of a Chinese restaurant. I made my way around the meat racks, which were the size of twin beds and held whole bloody sides of beef. Between dark aisles of boxed goods, there were gallon cans of sweet-and-sour sauce and plastic bags of dry noodles, and one aisle was full of weird figurines—Buddhas and dull golden phoenixes. Ken the cook was sitting there, in the dark, on a cardboard box, hands limp in his lap.

Hi, honey, he said. When he smiled, his mouth was a black pit with white spots. I pulled the chain of the light bulb.

Shitfuck, he screamed.

I pulled the chain again. I didn't really need light.

Hey, he said.

What, I said.

He pointed at the box where he'd set up the lines. You every ten minute. Kill yourself. Stupid. Then he started talking again, but this time he wasn't talking to me and I didn't understand what he was saying anyway. I went ahead, but took less than my share, to prove I wasn't stupid.

I brought my ex-psychiatrist and her lover their soup. It was egg drop, the soup most likely to have a roach at the bottom. All the soups are left out uncovered overnight, but egg drop is thick and yellow and made primarily of yolk, so that the roaches remain undetected at the bottom of the cup until the soup has been eaten. I should add that this wasn't Ngoc's fault. Once a month, Ngoc made us move all the cups and plates and stuff into the dining room, and the exterminators would arrive with their hoses and spray and we'd put the stuff back, but this didn't make a difference. You could pick up a platter or a pile of napkins or a cookie and there'd be a roach underneath.

When their soup came back, the cups looked O.K.: no roaches. My ex-psychiatrist and her lover were happy. They were holding hands. Apparently, my ex-psychiatrist was right-handed and her lover was left-handed and they could hold hands and eat at the same time. When I brought their dinner plates, my ex-psychiatrist asked me, Was I at school and how did I like it, meaning, Was I better? I would take a year off school that fall and move in with an ex-attorney who was dealing some to finance his business-school fees, and my one year off would stretch into five; but I did not know that yet and I said, Yes, I was at school, and I liked it.

In the kitchen, Ken asked did I want to lick his cock, which was one of the things he knew how to say, and I said, Lao shi, which I thought meant Asshole but which I later learned meant Teacher. My other tables had finished their dinners. I was nearly done for the night. I stood in the kitchen hoping Johnny might come in, because I felt I was ready to tell him there was something going on. Ngoc and her retarded son and the cooks were playing mah-jongg on the floor. Ngoc had lit the kitchen shrine—a candle in front of a foot-high Buddha, with three or-anges at its base. She had a glass of something from the bar and was screeching and laughing periodically, which seemed to indicate that she was lessening her vigilance, but when she saw me standing and waiting for Johnny she said I could polish pupu platters or fold napkins if I wasn't busy, so I ducked back into the dining room.

In the dark, the lit globes on the tables looked elegant. Outside the pilot lights of the boats were still moving slowly through the channel. At midnight, there would be fireworks you could watch from the water or the beach. This happened every Friday night; it was part of the town's effort to make itself attractive to summer vacationers and perhaps to itself. I was living on a nearby island with two girls, twins, whose parents had money and let them live in this house that was connected to the mainland by a bridge. When these girls finished college, they would decide not to be investment bankers after all but to move to Venice Beach to try to break into movies, and then television, and then commercials. I'm still waiting to see them in commercials. I would like for something to happen for these girls, particularly because that night I decided people should come over to the house, lots of people, and I would in fact begin inviting people at the restaurant and continue doing so all the way home, walking along the boulevard in my skirt, so that there would be something going on to bring Johnny to, and this party would end in a fire that would climb from a guest bedroom to the attic and the roof, and which would make this the last summer these girls spent on this island.

I set up my prep tray by the lesbians' table so that when their food was ready they could see their Szechuan grand worbar flame up in front of them. This woman, my former psychiatrist, or former family counsellor, and her partner, or lover, were talking so intently, about something so deeply philosophical (I gathered from the few words I caught), that I felt a certain sadness. She no longer pretended to be obliged to talk to me, as if she knew it was a larger kindness simply to let me be her waitress and not someone she had once known.

The first time we met, my entire family had driven out to her home. There was a "Welcome Friends" wreath on the door and decorative wooden ducks in the hall. We sat in her living room and my father made her cry. She asked some questions, which I answered, and my father said some things that were not answers to the questions, and she told him please to refrain from interrupting others or speaking in a loud, angry tone, and he said she really knew nothing about our family, since she was not part of our family, and that she in fact had interrupted him, and that so far her ideas were crazy, and that in this family, since he was the father, he would speak when he wanted to speak and say what he wanted to say.

My mother nodded and put a hand on his leg and said his name in the tone of voice in which someone says Stop, but which really meant "I am your partner in life and I love you whatever you do," because when she spoke she told the lesbian, We need you to work with us. You are not working with us. Then the lesbian said that perhaps it was a good idea for each of my parents, my father particularly, to come individually for counselling, as there seemed to be some issues all around that might bear discussion, and then my father had some things to say about this house we were in and this lesbian counsellor and what he thought of her effectiveness, her intelligence, and her persona, and then the lesbian took a time-out break.

We sat in silence and heard her blubber in the bathroom. It was the happiest time we had known. My mother's hand was on my father's knee. I might have been smirking a little, I don't know why, except that in times of great tension or truthtelling I smirk; also I was pleased to see my father's attention directed at someone else for an extended duration of time.

After that first appointment, at the lesbian's insistence, I was told to go with either my mother or my father, not both, to her office, not her home. But that only happened once, because my father made her cry again. During our second visit, he called her a Monstrous Fat Pig. I had picked up a book about menopause and was reading it because I was pleased that my father and the lesbian had found plenty to talk about by themselves, when my father said, You must weigh . . .

He turned to me. What does she weigh?

Two-sixty, I said.

Two-sixty, he said. You weigh two-sixty and you think you can tell me what to do, how to discipline my own daughter, how to talk to my own daughter? The lesbian counsellor cried pretty soon after that. There might have been more words on my father's part—"manipulative," maybe "controlling," "disappointing," and "freakish aberration of nature." These were words that we both liked. We drove home in a happy silence, almost a camaraderie, in which he said, Beautiful day, and How is school, and How is track—a mood which would last approximately until midnight, when I would puke in the sink and he would walk downstairs from where he had not been sleeping and tell me that I was a shitty little mess who was destroying the family, which was his family, and had I not considered taking myself away to somewhere not this house, because if I did not he surely would take himself away, and how did I imagine my brothers and mother would feel about that?

My order was up. I got the chicken worbar into its vat and trucked the hot iron plate out and set it down on the tray and produced a Sterno can from my pocket. I held the match high for drama before I lit it, and when the Sterno caught the two women clapped. Then I put the can on the plate and poured the chicken from the vat onto the plate, being careful not to pour any into the can itself.

If there's anything else I can do, I said, let me know. Then I went to fold napkins. I did this at a hidden station in the corner of the dining room. I was secretly watching them. They were talking about something I'm sure they did not give a shit about, but they clearly liked each other, and not in a sex way or a passing way but with some deep and generous mutual admiration, enough that they assumed, if they saw me at all, that I was only folding napkins or watching the bow lights of the boats jostling for dock space at the pier, and not watching them, waiting for them to be done.

Johnny came over and sat with me. I kept folding.

Hey, he said.

Hey, I said. He took a pile and folded. I think there's something going on, I said. I told him the people I lived with were having a party. I said Jud would be there. I said other people that he knew would be there. I said he should come. I said that I, in particular, hoped he would come.

He said he had a few other things going on. Then he said maybe he'd come. He paused. Then he said he'd come when he got off work. I got up and left the table because I didn't know what to say next.

The lesbians were looking at me the way you look at a waitress when you're too content to crook your finger at her. I went over to their table. They said they would like, if it was not too much trouble, to take their food home in a box. I tried not to think, while I packed the box, that they would be better off without the extra food, or wonder whether they would eat it that night, individually or together, or how many hours would pass before the sadness would come back.

It was after my father called my shrink a pig that I began going to see her alone and that she suggested the special pretzels. For twenty weeks this counsellor woman saw me at half rate, because my parents would not pay more, and listened to me talk about school or books or people I liked or did not like and what I wished I had done at a certain time or what I wished I had not done, and handed me tissues when she finally got me to cry, and told me that I was a good person, a smart person, a person with whom she liked to talk, and I said, Thank you, thank you, at the end of each hour, and she said, Hug me, and I did, and once she gave me a book, which I was supposed to return by mail but never did, which was pink and called "Healing the Hungry Self" and had careful marginalia at important places in her handwriting, where I wrote, What a fat pig, go on a diet, fat pig, a book I read three times in the hope of being cured.

That night the party would happen. In just a few hours many people would arrive on the island in many cars and carry many bottles of alcohol into the house, which would be lit up, every room, and bottles and lamps would get broken and someone would have brass knuckles and someone else would have a gun and it would get so that Johnny and I had to go outside, down to the beach, and sit on the sand and watch the sky, dizzy with light, and the water, candy-fish bright. There was an anchored dock floating about thirty feet out, and I fixed on the idea of our spending the night on our backs, not talking or touching, but silently being together, and I would open my backpack, there at the beach, the air was still enough, and take out the stash I'd borrowed off Ken and say, I like to do this sometimes, and he'd say, I don't think I want to do that, and I'd say, Don't, then, and leave him a line, and he would say, Why not, and he would like it.

My ex-shrink and her lover were waiting. I brought them the super pineapple dish. I watched them spear pineapple. Ngoc was cursing in the kitchen because she was losing at mah-jongg and the cooks were taking her money again. I heard the resounding low note of a fry pan hitting a soup vat and then the thud of an industrial tea bin crashing against the tiles. The copper lights of the promenade were blinking above the water and a firework flared up prematurely and failed to ignite and the dust cloud spread out against the sky and fell across the waiting white boats.

My ex-psychiatrist came over and took my hand on her way out. I was still folding napkins.

It was so good to see you, she said.

It was good to see you, too, I said. But I didn't mean it.

Their table was neat, pre-cleaned, as if they had foreseen the work I would have to do and wanted to help. The little umbrellas, chopstick wrappers, and soiled napkins were piled on their plates and their chopsticks and silverware were neatly crossed. The tip was good, so as to say, We like you, but not too good, so as to say, We feel bad for you; obviously, you are not cured; obviously, you have failed yourself and us. She'd left a cookie at the edge of the table and I took it and ate it. Then I saw the note she'd left, in familiar blue pen, on the check, as if I were someone she knew well or someone she still wanted to help. It said, You are kindhearted, gentle, and beloved.

DOROTHY ALLISON

Dumpling Child

A southern dumpling child
    biscuit eater, tea sipper
    okra slicer, gravy dipper,
I fry my potatoes with onions
    stew my greens with pork

And ride my lover high up
on the butterfat shine of her thighs
where her belly arches and sweetly tastes
of rock salt on watermelon
sunshine sharp teeth bite light
and lick slow like mama's
favorite dumpling child.

The Fat Man

I call everyone
shriveled. Dried apples
fit for cellars,
nothing more.
They have no folds,
no flesh to touch—
gangling reminders
of the grave.

Existence melts
in my mouth.
I relish, I taste
the sweet jams of life;
I gorge and worship
the place of love:
all kitchens everywhere.

Diet is sin:
an effort
to turn limbs

to razors that slice
a lover's hands.
Right angles
pierce my eye;
I love the arc,
soft ovals, the curve—
things molded
to be touched,
the soothers of sight.

I feel at least
ten souls
swimming in my flesh.
I feed them
with both hands.
Someday
I will become
a mountain.
I eat the world.

The 400-Pound CEO

At noon another load of raccoons comes in and Claude takes them out back of the office and executes them with a tire iron. Then he checks for vitals, wearing protective gloves. Then he drags the cage across 209 and initiates burial by dumping the raccoons into the pit that's our little corporate secret. After burial comes prayer, a personal touch that never fails to irritate Tim, our ruthless CEO. Before founding Humane Raccoon Alternatives, Tim purposely backed his car over a frat boy and got ten-to-twelve for manslaughter. In jail he earned his MBA by designing and marketing a line of light-up Halloween lapel brooches. Now he gives us the brooches as performance incentives and sporadically trashes a bookshelf or two to remind us of his awesome temper and of how ill-advised we would be to cross him in any way whatsoever.

Post-burial I write up the invoices and a paragraph or two on how overjoyed the raccoons were when we set them free. Sometimes I'll throw in something about spontaneous mating beneath the box elders. No one writes a better misleading letter than me. In the area of phone inquiries I'm also unsurpassed. When a client calls to ask how their release went, everyone in the office falls all over themselves transferring the call to me. I'm reassuring and joyful. I laugh until tears run down my face at the stories I make up regarding the wacky things their raccoon did upon gaining its freedom. Then, as per Tim, I ask if they'd mind sending back our promotional materials. The brochures don't come cheap. They show glossies of raccoons in the wild, contrasted with glossies of poisoned raccoons in their death throes. You lay that on a housewife with perennially knocked-over trash cans and she breathes a sigh of relief. Then she hires you. Then you get a 10 percent commission.

These days commissions are my main joy. I'm too large to attract female company. I weigh four hundred. I don't like it but it's beyond my control. I've tried running and rowing the stationary canoe and hatha-yoga and belly staples and even a muzzle back in the dark days when I had it bad for Freeda, our document placement and retrieval specialist. When I was merely portly it was easy to see myself as a kind of exuberant sportsman who overate out of lust for life. Now no one could possibly mistake me for a sportsman.

When I've finished invoicing I enjoy a pecan cluster. Two, actually. Claude comes in all dirty from the burial and sees me snacking and feels compelled to point out that even my sub-rolls have sub-rolls. He's right but still it isn't nice to say. Tim asks did Claude make that observation after having wild sex with me all night. That's a comment I'm not fond of. But Tim's the boss. His T-shirt says: I HOLD YOUR PURSE STRINGS IN MY HOT LITTLE HAND.

"Ha, ha, Tim," says Claude. "I'm no homo. But if I was one, I'd die before doing it with Mr. Lard."

"Ha, ha," says Tim. "Good one. Isn't that a good one, Jeffrey?"

"That's a good one," I say glumly.

What a bitter little office.

My colleagues leave hippo refrigerator magnets on my seat. They imply that I'm a despondent virgin, which I'm not. They might change their tune if they ever spoke with Ellen Burtomly regarding the beautiful night we spent at her brother Bob's cottage. I was by no means slim then but could at least buy pants off the rack and walk from the den to the kitchen without panting. I remember her nude at the window and the lovely seed helicopters blowing in as she turned and showed me her ample front on purpose. That was my most romantic moment. Now for that kind of thing it's the degradation of Larney's Consenting Adult

Viewing Center. Before it started getting to me I'd bring boot-loads of quarters and a special bottom cushion and watch hours and hours of Scandinavian women romping. It was shameful. Finally last Christmas I said enough is enough, I'd rather be sexless than evil. And since then I have been. Sexless and good, but very very tense. Since then I've tried to live above the fray. I've tried to minimize my physical aspects and be a selfless force for good. When mocked, which is nearly every day, I recall Christ covered with spittle. When filled with lust, I remember Gandhi purposely sleeping next to a sexy teen to test himself. After work I go home, watch a little TV, maybe say a rosary or two.

Thirty more years of this and I'm out of it without hurting anybody or embarrassing myself.

But still. I'm a human being. A little companionship would be nice. My colleagues know nothing of my personal life. They could care less that I once had a dog named Woodsprite who was crushed by a backhoe. They could care less that my dad died a wino in the vicinity of the Fort Worth stockyards. In his last days he sent me a note filled with wonder:

"Son," he wrote, "are you fat too? It came upon me suddenly and now I am big as a house. Beware, perhaps it's in our genes. I wander cowboy sidewalks of wood, wearing a too-small hat, filled with remorse for the many lives I failed to lead. Adieu. In my mind you are a waify-looking little fellow who never answered when I asked you a direct question. But I loved you as best I could."

What do my colleagues know of Dad? What do they know of me? What kind of friend gets a kick out of posting in the break room a drawing of you eating an entire computer? What kind of friend jokes that someday you'll be buried in a specially built container after succumbing to heart strain?

I'm sorry, but I feel that life should offer more than this. As a child my favorite book was *Little Red-Faced Cop on the Beat*. Everyone loved the Little Red-Faced Cop. He knew what was what. He donned his uniform in a certain order every morning. He chased bad guys and his hat stayed on. Now I'm surrounded by kooks. I'm a kook myself. I stoop down and tell raccoons to take it like a man. I drone on and on to strangers about my weight. I ogle salesgirls. I double back to pick up filthy pennies. When no one's around I dig and dig at my earwax, then examine it. I'm huge, and terrified of becoming bitter.

Sometimes I sense deep anger welling up, and have to choke it back.

Sadly, I find my feelings for Freeda returning. I must have a death wish. Clearly I repulse her. Sometimes I catch her looking at my gut overhangs with a screwed-up face. I see her licking her lips while typing, and certain unholy thoughts go through my head. I hear her speaking tenderly on the phone to her little son, Len, and can't help picturing myself sitting on a specially reinforced porch swing while she fries up some chops and Len digs in the muck.

Today as we prepare mailers she says she's starting to want to be home with Len all the time. But there's the glaring problem of funds. She makes squat. I've seen her stub. There's the further problem that she suspects Mrs. Rasputin, Len's baby-sitter, is a lush.

"I don't know what to do," Freeda says. "I come home after work and she's sitting there tipsy in her bra, fanning herself with a *Racing Form*."

"I know how you feel," I say. "Life can be hard."

"It has nothing to do with life," she says crossly. "It has to do with my drunken baby-sitter. Maybe you haven't been listening to me."

Before I know what I'm saying I suggest that perhaps we should go out for dinner and offer each other some measure of comfort. In response she spits her Tab out across her cubicle. She says now she's heard it all. She goes to fetch Tim and Claude so they can join her in guffawing at my nerve. She faxes a comical note about my arrogance to her girlfriend at the DMV. All afternoon she keeps looking at me with her head cocked.

Needless to say, it's a long day.

Then at five, after everyone else is gone, she comes shyly by and says she'd love to go out with me. She says I've always been there for her. She says she likes a man with a little meat on his bones. She says pick her up at eight and bring something for Len. I'm shocked. I'm overjoyed.

My knees are nearly shaking my little desk apart.

I buy Len a football helmet and a baseball glove and an aquarium and a set of encyclopedias. I basically clean out my pitiful savings. Who cares. It's worth it to get a chance to observe her beautiful face from across a table without Claude et al. hooting at me.

When I ring her bell someone screams come in. Inside I find Len behind the home entertainment center and Mrs. Rasputin drunkenly poring over her grade-school yearbook with a highlighter. She looks up and says: "Where's that kid?" I feel like saying: How should I know? Instead I say: "He's behind the home entertainment center."

"He loves it back there," she says. "He likes eating the lint balls. They won't hurt him. They're like roughage."

"Come out, Len," I say. "I have gifts."

He comes out. One tiny eyebrow cocks up at my physical appearance. Then he crawls into my lap holding his MegaDeath-Dealer by the cowl. What a sweet boy. The Dealer's got a severed human head in its hand. When you pull a string the Dealer cries, "You're dead and I've killed you, Prince of Slime," and sticks its Day-Glo tongue out. I give Len my antiviolence spiel. I tell him only love can dispel hate. I tell him we were meant to live in harmony and give one another emotional support. He looks at me blankly, then flings his DeathDealer at the cat.

Freeda comes down looking sweet and casts a baleful eye on Mrs. Rasputin and away we go. I take her to Ace's Volcano Island. Ace's is an old service station now done up Hawaiian. They've got a tape loop of surf sounds and some Barbies in grass skirts climbing a papier-mâché mountain. I'm known there. Every Friday night I treat myself by taking up a whole booth and ordering the Broccoli Rib Luau. Ace is a gentle aging beatnik with mild Tourette's. When the bad words start flying out of his mouth you never saw someone so regretful. One minute he'll be quoting the Bhagavad Gita and the next roughly telling one of his patrons to lick their own bottom. We've talked about it. He says he's tried pills. He's tried biting down on a pencil eraser. He's tried picturing himself in the floodplain of the Ganges with a celestial being stroking his hair. Nothing works. So he's printed up an explanatory flyer. Shirleen the hostess hands it out pre-seating. There's a cartoon of Ace with lots of surprise marks and typographic symbols coming out of his mouth.

"My affliction is out of my hands," it says. "But please know that whatever harsh words I may direct at you, I truly treasure your patronage."

He fusses over us by bringing extra ice water and sprinting into the back room whenever he feels an attack looming. I purposely starve myself. We talk about her life philosophy. We talk about her hairstyle and her treasured childhood memories and her paranormally gifted aunt. I fail to get a word in edgewise, and that's fine. I like listening. I like learning about her. I like putting myself in her shoes and seeing things her way.

I walk her home. Kids in doorways whistle at my width. I handle it with grace by shaking my rear. Freeda laughs. A kiss seems viable. It all feels too good to be true.

Then on her porch she shakes my hand and says great, she can now pay her phone bill, courtesy of Tim. She shows me their written agreement. It says: "In consideration of your consenting to be seen in public with Jeffrey, I, Tim, will pay you, Freeda, the sum of fifty dollars."

She goes inside. I take a week of vacation and play Oil Can Man nonstop. I achieve Level Nine. I master the Hydrocarbon

Dervish and the Cave of Dangerous Lubrication. I cream Mr. Grit and consistently prohibit him from inflicting wear and tear on my Pistons. There's something sick about the amount of pleasure I take in pretending Freeda's Mr. Grit as I annihilate him with Bonus Cleansing Additives. At the end of night three I step outside for some air. Up in the sky are wild clouds that make me think of Tahiti and courageous sailors on big sinking wooden ships. Meanwhile here's me, a grown man with a joystick-burn on his thumb.

So I throw the game cartridge in the trash and go back to work. I take the ribbing. I take the abuse. Someone's snipped my head out of the office photo and mounted it on a bride's body. Tim says what the heck, the thought of the visual incongruity of our pairing was worth the fifty bucks.

"Do you hate me?" Freeda asks.

"No," I say. "I truly enjoyed our evening together."

"God, I didn't," she says. "Everyone kept staring at us. It made me feel bad about myself that they thought I was actually with you. Do you know what I mean?"

I can't think of anything to say, so I nod. Then I retreat moist-eyed to my cubicle for some invoicing fun. I'm not a bad guy. If only I could stop hoping. If only I could say to my heart: Give up. Be alone forever. There's always opera. There's angel-food cake and neighborhood children caroling, and the look of autumn leaves on a wet roof. But no. My heart's some kind of idiotic fishing bobber.

My invoices go very well. The sun sinks, the moon rises, round and pale as my stupid face.

I minimize my office time by volunteering for the Carlisle entrapment. The Carlisles are rich. A poor guy has a raccoon problem, he sprinkles poison in his trash and calls it a day. Not the Carlisles. They dominate bread routes throughout the city. Carlisle supposedly strong-armed his way to the top of the bread heap, but in person he's nice enough. I let him observe me laying out the rotting fruit. I show him how the cage door coming down couldn't hurt a flea. Then he goes inside and I wait patiently in my car.

Just after midnight I trip the wire. I fetch the Carlisles and encourage them to squat down and relate to the captured raccoon. Then I recite our canned speech congratulating them for their advanced thinking. I describe the wilderness where the release will take place, the streams and fertile valleys, the romp in the raccoon's stride when it catches its first whiff of pristine air.

Mr. Carlisle says thanks for letting them sleep at night sans guilt. I tell him that's my job. Just then the raccoon's huge mate bolts out of the woods and tears into my calf. I struggle to my car and kick the mate repeatedly against my wheelwell until it dies with my leg in its mouth. The Carlisles stand aghast in the carport. I stand aghast in the driveway, sick at heart. I've trapped my share of raccoons and helped Claude with more burials than I care to remember, but I've never actually killed anything before.

I throw both coons in the trunk and drive myself to the emergency room, where I'm given the first of a series of extremely painful shots. I doze off on a bench post-treatment and dream of a den of pathetic baby raccoons in V-neck sweaters yelping for food.

When I wake up I call in. Tim asks if I'm crazy, kicking a raccoon to death in front of clients. Couldn't I have gently lifted it off, he asks, or offered it some rotting fruit? Am I proud of my ability to fuck up one-car funerals? Do I or do I not recall Damian Flaverty?

Who could forget Damian Flaverty? He'd been dipping into the till to finance his necktie boutique. Tim blackjacked him into a crumpled heap on the floor and said: Do you think I spent nine years in the slammer only to get out and be fleeced by your ilk? Then he broke Damian's arm with an additional whack. I almost dropped my mug.

I tell Tim I'm truly sorry I didn't handle the situation more effectively. He says the raccoon must've had a sad last couple of minutes once it realized it had given up its life for the privilege of gnawing on a shank of pure fat. That hurts. Why I continue to expect decent treatment from someone who's installed a torture chamber in the corporate basement is beyond me. Down there he's got a Hide-A-Bed and a whip collection and an executioner's mask with a built-in Walkman. Sometimes when I'm invoicing late he'll bring in one of his willing victims. Usually they're both wasto. I get as much of me under my desk as I can. Talk about the fall of man. Talk about some father somewhere being crestfallen if he knew what his daughter was up to. Once I peeked out as they left and saw a blonde with a black eye going wherever Tim pointed and picking up his coat whenever he purposely dropped it.

"You could at least take me for coffee," she said.

"I'd like to spill some on your bare flesh," Tim said.

"Mmm," she said. "Sounds good."

How do people get like this, I thought. Can they change back? Can they learn again to love and be gentle? How can they look at themselves in the mirror or hang Christmas ornaments without overflowing with self-loathing?

Then I thought: I may be obese but at least I'm not cruel to the point of being satanic.

Next day Tim was inducted into Rotary and we all went to the luncheon. He spoke on turning one's life around. He spoke on the bitter lessons of incarceration. He sang the praises of America and joked with balding sweetheart ophthalmologists, and after lunch hung his Rotary plaque in the torture chamber stairwell and ordered me to Windex it daily or face extremely grim consequences.

Tuesday a car pulls up as Claude and I approach the burial pit with the Carlisle raccoons. We drag the cage into a shrub and squat panting. Claude whispers that I smell. He whispers that if he weighed four hundred he'd take into account the people around him and go on a diet. The sky's the purple of holy card

Crucifixion scenes, the rending of the firmament and all that. A pale girl in a sari gets out of the car and walks to the lip of the pit. She paces off the circumference and scribbles in a notebook. She takes photos. She slides down on her rear and comes back up with some coon bones in a Baggie.

After she leaves we rush back to the office. Tim's livid and starts baby-oiling his trademark blackjack. He says no more coons in the pit until further notice. He says we're hereby in crisis mode and will keep the coons on blue ice in our cubicles and if need be wear nose clips. He says the next time she shows up he may have to teach her a lesson about jeopardizing our meal ticket. He says animal rights are all well and good but there's a substantive difference between a cute bunny or cat and a disgusting raccoon that thrives on carrion and trash and creates significant sanitation problems with its inquisitiveness.

"Oh, get off it," Claude says, affection for Tim shining from his dull eyes. "You'd eliminate your own mother if there was a buck in it for you."

"Undeniably," Tim says. "Especially if she knocked over a client trash can or turned rabid."

Then he hands me the corporate Visa and sends me to HardwareNiche for coolers. At HardwareNiche you can get a video of *Bloodiest Crimes of the Century Reenacted*. You can get a video of Great Bloopers made during the filming of *Bloodiest Crimes of the Century Reenacted*. You can get a bird feeder that plays "How Dry I Am" while electronically emitting a soothing sensation birds love. You can get a Chill'n'Pray, an overpriced cooler with a holographic image of a famous religious personality on the lid. I opt for Buddha. I can almost hear Tim sarcastically comparing our girths and asking since when has cost control been thrown to the wind. But the Chill'n'Prays are all they've got. I'm on Tim's shit list if I do and on Tim's shit list if I don't. He has an actual shit list. Freeda generated it and enhanced it with a graphic of an angry piece of feces stamping its feet.

I buy the coolers, hoping in spite of myself that he'll applaud my decisiveness. When I get back to the office everyone's gone for the night. The Muzak's off for a change and loud whacks and harsh words are floating up from the basement via the heat ducts. Before long Tim tromps up the stairs swearing. I hide pronto. He shouts thanks for nothing, and says he could have had more rough-and-tumble fun dangling a cat over a banister, and that there's nothing duller than a clerk with the sexual imagination of a grape.

"Document placement and retrieval specialist," Freeda says in a hurt tone.

"Whatever," Tim says, and speeds off in his Porsche.

I emerge overwhelmed from my cubicle. Over her shoulder and through the plate glass is a shocked autumnal moon. Freeda's cheek is badly bruised. Otherwise she's radiant with love. My mouth hangs open.

"What can I say?" she says. "I can't get enough of the man."

"Good night," I say, and forget about my car, and walk the nine miles home in a daze.

All day Wednesday I prepare to tell Tim off. But I'm too scared. Plus he could rightly say she's a consenting adult. What business is it of mine? Why defend someone who has no desire to be defended? Instead I drop a few snots in his coffee cup and use my network access privileges to cancel his print jobs. He asks can I work late and in spite of myself I fawningly say sure. I hate him. I hate myself. Everybody else goes home. Big clouds roll in. I invoice like mad. Birds light on the Dumpster and feed on substances caked on the lid. What a degraded cosmos. What a case of something starting out nice and going bad.

Just after seven I hear him shout: "You, darling, will rot in hell, with the help of a swift push to the grave from me!" At first I think he's pillow-talking with Freeda by phone. Then I look out the window and see the animal rights girl at the lip of our pit with a camcorder.

Admirable dedication, I think, wonderful clarity of vision.

Tim runs out the door with his blackjack unsheathed.

What to do? Clearly he means her harm. I follow him, leaving behind my loafers to minimize noise. I keep to the shadows and scurry in my socks from tiny berm to tiny berm. I heave in an unattractive manner. My heart rate's in the ionosphere. To my credit I'm able to keep up with him. Meanwhile she's struggling up the slope with her hair in sweet disarray, backlit by a moon the color of honey, camcorder on her head like some kind of Kenyan water jug.

"Harlot," Tim hisses, "attempted defiler of my dream," and whips his blackjack down. Am I quick? I am so quick. I lunge up and take it on the wrist. My arm bone goes to mush, and my head starts to spin, and I wrap Tim up in a hug the size of Tulsa.

"Run," I gasp to the girl, and see in the moonlight the affluent white soles of her fleeing boat-type shoes.

I hug hard. I tell him drop the jack and to my surprise he does. Do I then release him? To my shame, no. So much sick rage is stored up in me. I never knew. And out it comes in one mondo squeeze, and something breaks, and he goes limp, and I lay him gently down in the dirt.

I CPR like anything. I beg him to rise up and thrash me. I do a crazy little dance of grief. But it's no good.

I've killed Tim.

I sprint across 209 and ineffectually drag my bulk around Industrial Grotto, weeping and banging on locked corporate doors. United KneeWrap's having a gala. Their top brass are drunkenly lip-synching hits of the fifties en masse and their foot soldiers are laughing like subservient fools, so no one hears my frantic knocking. I prepare to heave a fake boulder through the plate glass. But then I stop. By now Tim's beyond help. What do I gain by turning myself in? Did I or did I not save an innocent girl's life? Was he or was he not a cruel monster? What's done is done. My peace of mind is gone forever. Why spend the remainder of my life in jail for the crime of eliminating a piece of filth?

And standing there outside the gala I learn something vital about myself: when push comes to shove, I could care less about lofty ideals. It's me I love. It's me I want to protect.

Me.

I hustle back to the office for the burial gear. I roll Tim into the pit. I sprinkle on lime and cover him with dirt. I forge a letter in which he claims to be going to Mexico to clarify his relationship with God via silent meditation in a rugged desert setting.

"My friends," I write through tears in his childish scrawl, "you slave away for minimal rewards! Freedom can be yours if you open yourself to the eternal! Good health and happiness to you all. I'm truly sorry for any offense I may have given. Especially to you, Freeda, who deserved a better man than the swine I was. I am a new man now, and Freeda dear, I suggest counseling. Also: I have thought long and hard on this, and have decided to turn over the reins to Jeffrey, whom I have always wrongly maligned. I see now that he is a man of considerable gifts, and ask you all to defer to him as you would to me."

I leave the letter on Claude's chair and go out to sleep in my car. I dream of Tim wearing a white robe in a Mexican cantina. A mangy dog sits on his lap explaining the rules of the dead. No weeping. No pushing the other dead. Don't bore everyone with tales of how great you were. Tim smiles sweetly and rubs the dog behind the ears. He sees me and says no hard feelings and thanks for speeding him on to the realm of bliss.

I wake with a start. The sun comes up, driving sparrows before it, turning the corporate reflective windows wild with orange. I roll out of my car and brush my teeth with my finger.

My first day as a killer.

I walk to the pit in the light of fresh day, hoping it was all a dream. But no. There's our scuffling footprints. There's the mound of fresh dirt, under which lies Tim. I sit on a paint can in a patch of waving weeds and watch my colleagues arrive. I weep. I think sadly of the kindly bumbler I used to be, bleary-eyed in the morning, guiltless and looking forward to coffee.

When I finally go in, everyone's gathered stunned around the microwave.

"El Presidente," Claude says disgustedly.

"Sorry?" I say.

I make a big show of shaking my head in shock as I read and reread the note I wrote. I ask if this means I'm in charge. Claude says with that kind of conceptual grasp we're not exactly in for salad days. He asks Freeda if she had an inkling. She says she always knew Tim had certain unplumbed depths but this is ridiculous. Claude says he smells a rat. He says Tim never had a religious bone in his body and didn't speak a word of Spanish. My face gets red. Thank God Blamphin, that toady, pipes up.

"I say in terms of giving Jeffrey a chance, we should give Jeffrey a chance, inasmuch as Tim was a good manager but a kind of a mean guy," he says.

"Well put," Claude says cynically. "And I say this fattie knows something he's not telling."

I praise Tim to the skies and admit I could never fill his shoes. I demean my organizational skills and leadership abilities but vow to work hard for the good of all. Then I humbly propose a vote: Do I assume leadership or not? Claude says he'll honor a quorum, and then via show of hands I achieve a nice one.

I move my things into Tim's office. Because he'd always perceived me as a hefty milquetoast with no personal aspirations, he trusted me implicitly. So I'm able to access the corporate safe. I'm able to cater in prime rib and a trio of mustachioed violinists, who stroll from cubicle to cubicle hoping for tips. Claude's outraged. Standing on his chair, he demands to know whatever happened to the profit motive. Everyone ignores him while munching on my prime rib and enjoying my musicians. He says one can't run a corporation on good intentions and blatant naïveté. He pleads that the staff fire me and appoint him CEO. Finally Blamphin proposes I can him. Torson from Personnel seconds the motion. I shrug my shoulders and we vote, and Claude's axed. He kicks the watercooler. He gives me the finger. But out he goes, leaving us to our chocolate mousse and cocktails.

By nightfall the party's kicked into high gear. I bring in jugglers and a comedian and drinks, drinks, drinks. My staff swears their undying loyalty. We make drunken toasts to my health and theirs. I tell them we'll kill no more. I tell them we'll come clean with the appropriate agencies and pay all relevant fines. Henceforth we'll relocate the captured raccoons as we've always claimed to be doing. The company will be owned by us, the employees, who will come and go as we please. Beverages and snacks will be continually on hand. Insurance will be gratis. Day care will be available on-site.

Freeda brightens and sits on the arm of my chair.

Muzak will give way to personal stereos in each cubicle. We will support righteous charities, take troubled children under our collective wing, enjoy afternoons off when the sun is high and the air sweet with the smell of mown grass, treat one another as family, send one another fond regards on a newly installed electronic mail system, and, when one of us finally has to die, we will have the consolation of knowing that, aided by corporate largesse, our departed colleague has known his or her full measure of power, love, and beauty, and arm in arm we will all march to the graveyard, singing sad hymns.

Just then the cops break in, led by Claude, who's holding one of Tim's shoes.

"If you went to Mexico," he shouts triumphantly, "wouldn't you take your Porsche? Would you be so stupid as to turn your life's work over to this tub of lard? Things started to add up. I did some literal digging. And there I found my friend Tim, with a crushed rib cage that broke my heart, and a look of total surprise on his face."

"My Timmy," Freeda says, rising from my chair. "This disgusting pig killed my beautiful boy."

They cuff me and lead me away.

In court I tell the truth. The animal rights girl comes out of the woodwork and corroborates my story. The judge says he appreciates my honesty and the fact that I saved a life. He wonders why, having saved the life, I didn't simply release Tim and reap the laurels of my courage. I tell him I lost control. I tell him a lifetime of scorn boiled over. He says he empathizes completely. He says he had a weight problem himself when a lad.

Then he gives me fifty, as opposed to life without parole.

So now I know misery. I know the acute discomfort of a gray jail suit pieced together from two garments of normal size. I know the body odor of Vic, a Chicago kingpin who's claimed me for his own and compels me to wear a feminine hat with fruit on the brim for nightly interludes. Do my ex-colleagues write? No. Does Freeda? Ha. Have I achieved serenity? No. Have I transcended my horrid surroundings and thereby won the begrudging admiration of my fellow cons? No. They exult in hooting at me nude during group showers. They steal my allotted food portions. Do I have a meaningful hobby that makes the days fly by like minutes? No. I have a wild desire to smell the ocean. I have a sense that God is unfair and preferentially punishes his weak, his dumb, his fat, his lazy. I believe he takes more pleasure in his perfect creatures, and cheers them on like a brainless dad as they run roughshod over the rest of us. He gives us a need for love, and no way to get any. He gives us a desire to be liked, and personal attributes that make us utterly unlikable. Having placed his flawed and needy children in a world of exacting specifications, he deducts the difference between what we have and what we need from our hearts and our self-esteem and our mental health.

This is how I feel. These things seem to me true. But what's there to do but behave with dignity? Keep a nice cell. Be polite but firm when Vic asks me to shimmy while wearing the hat.

Say a kind word when I can to the legless man doing life, who's perennially on toilet duty. Join in at the top of my lungs when the geriatric murderer from Baton Rouge begins his nightly spiritual.

Maybe the God we see, the God who calls the daily shots, is merely a subGod. Maybe there's a God above this subGod, who's busy for a few Godminutes with something else, and will be right back, and when he gets back will take the subGod by the ear and say, "Now look. Look at that fat man. What did he ever do to you? Wasn't he humble enough? Didn't he endure enough abuse for a thousand men? Weren't the simplest tasks hard? Didn't you sense him craving affection? Were you unaware that his days unraveled as one long bad dream?" And maybe as the subGod slinks away, the true God will sweep me up in his arms, saying: My sincere apologies, a mistake has been made. Accept a new birth, as token of my esteem.

And I will emerge again from between the legs of my mother, a slighter and more beautiful baby, destined for a different life, in which I am masterful, sleek as a deer, a winner.

Big Ruthie Imagines Sex without Pain

She imagines it the way she tries to reconstruct dreams, really reconstruct. Or builds an image while she is praying. She imagines a blue castle somewhere on high, many steps, a private room, fur rug, long mattress, white stucco walls, tiny windows. She imagines leaving her body. It frightens her. If she leaves her body, leaves it cavorting on the bed/fur rug/kitchen table (all is possible when there is sex without pain)—she may not get it back. Her body may just get up and walk away, without her, wash itself, apply blusher mascara lipstick, draw up her clothes around it, take her purse and go out to dinner. Big Ruthie herself will be left on the ceiling, staring down at the indentations on the mattress and rug, wishing she could reach down and take a book from a shelf. She does not now nor has she ever owned a fur rug. But when Big Ruthie achieves sex without pain, she will have a fluffy fur rug. Maybe two. White, which she'll send to the cleaners, when needed.

She imagines sex without pain: an end to feeling Ruben tear at her on his way inside, scuffing his feet so harshly at her door, unwitting, can't help himself, poor husband of hers.

She thinks there must be a name for it. She has looked it up in various books and knows it is her fault. All she must do is relax. It was always this way, since the honeymoon. Of course the first months she told herself it was the newness. She is so big on the outside, so wide of hip, ample of waist, how could this be—a cosmic joke?—this one smallness where large, extra large would have smoothed out the wrinkles in her marriage bed? When all her clothes are size 18 plus elastic, why does this one part of her refuse to grow along with her? At first she thought, the membranes will stretch. Childbirth will widen. Heal and stretch, heal and stretch. But no. She has never healed, never quite healed. From anything. She carries all her scars from two childhood dog bites, from a particularly awful bee sting. I am marked, she thinks.

Ruben is the only lover she has ever had. "OK, God," Big Ruthie says, well into her thirty-fifth year, "I'm not asking for sex without ambivalence or sex without tiny splinters of anger/ resentment. I am not even asking, as per usual, for a new body, a trade-in allowance from my ever-larger and larger layers of light cream mounds. I am not asking you to withdraw my name-sake candy bar from the market, to wipe its red-and-white wrap-per from the face of the earth. I have grown used to the teasing. It's become second nature, in fact. And I am not asking you to cause my avoirdupois, my spare tire and trunk to melt in one great heavenly glide from my home to Yours. I am only asking for a slight adjustment. One that I cannot change by diet alone. As if I have ever changed any part or shape of my body through diet. For once I am not asking You to give me something that just looks nice. Make me, O Lord, more internally accommodating." Big Ruthie, turning thirty-five, prays. Alone, in bed.

She is afraid.

She is afraid she will lose herself, her body will siphon out into Ruben's, the way the ancient Egyptians removed the brains of their dead through the nose. Ruthie wants to carve out an inner largeness, yet fears she will become ghostlike, as see-through as a negligee, an amoeba, one of those floaters you get in your eye that's the size of an inch worm. A transparent cell. Mitosis, meiosis. She will be divided and conquered. She imagines her skin as nothing more than a bag, a vacuum-cleaner bag, col-lapsing when you turn off the control. No sound, no motion, no commotion, all the wind sucked out of her. Still. A fat polar bear lying on the rug. Hibernating without end. No one will be able to wake Big Ruthie or move her in order to vacuum. No one.

She mentioned it once, timidly, to the Ob/Gyn man. He patted her on the knee. Mumbled about lubrication. Maybe the pain didn't really exist, Big Ruthie thought. Maybe it was her imagination and this was the intensity of feeling they talked about. But it is pain. It combines with that other feeling so that she wants it and doesn't want it, can't push this word away from her brain: Invaded. My husband is invading me. He makes her feel rough and red down there. As if he's made of sandpaper. Even with the lubricant they bought. It makes her want to cry and sometimes she does, afterward, turning her head away. How could her Ceci and Ellen fit through there and not her Ruben?

Still Big Ruthie imagines sex without pain, imagines freedom: f—ing out of doors. In picnic groves. She imagines longing for it during the day, as she vacuums, sweeps, wipes dishes, changes diapers, slices cheese for sandwiches, bathes her daughters, reads them stories. She imagines it like a tune from the radio trapped in her mind. It will overtake her, this sex without pain, this wanting, this sweet insistence. A rope will pull her to bed. Beds. Fur rugs. Rooftops. Forests, tree houses. She imagines doing it without thinking. Her family does nothing without thinking, worrying, wringing, twisting hands, with a spit and glance over the shoulder at the evil eye. At Lilith, strangler of children, Adam's first wife, who wanted to be on top. Who wanted sex without pain. Whenever she wanted.

Sometimes Ruthie begins. She might tickle Ruben. She might hope: This time, this time, because I started it, we will share one pure, smooth sweep, one glide a note a tune a long song, as sweet as pleasant as a kiss. She thinks, if she can conquer this, get over this obstacle, she of two children, a house and a husband—if she Big Ruthie can find her way to this sex without pain—then Ruben would be able to rope her, he would be able to lasso her from the next room, from across the house. She would rely on him, and on sex, on sex without pain. Then any man would be able, with a nod of his head, a wink of his eye, to pull her to him. Ruthie and Anyman with a fur rug, without a fur rug. Big Ruthie will advertise herself: a woman who has sex without pain. She will become a woman in a doorway, a large woman blocking a large doorway, foot behind her, against the wall, a thrust to her head, a toss, a wafting of her cigarette. Big Ruthie will start to smoke, before, after, and during.

Nothing will stop her. She will be expert. Till she can do it in her sleep. With her capable hands, with her ever-so-flexible back, front, sides, mouth. With the mailman, roofer, plumber; she could become the plumber's assistant, he, hers. She will go at it. She will not be ladylike. She will be a bad girl. She will swing on a swing in a good-time bar. She will become a good-time girl, wearing garters that show, no girdle at all, black lace stockings rounded by her thighs and calves, brassy perfume that trails her down the street. People will know: That is Big Ruthie's scent. She will have a trademark, a signature.

Big Ruthie, the good-time girl.

Fleshy Ruthie, the good-time girl.

Bigtime Ruthie. Twobit Ruthie.

Ruthie knows that other people have sex without pain. Men, for instance. Ruben. She has watched his eyes squint in concentrated delight. She herself sometimes cries out, the way he does, but she knows his is a pure kind of white kind of pleasure, while hers is dark, gray, troubled. It hurts on the outside just as he begins and moments later when he moves inside her. This was Eve's curse—not cramps, not childbirth, but this; hurts as much as what—as the times Ruben doesn't shave and he kisses her and leaves her cheeks and chin pink and rough for days. But this is worse.

But if she could have sex without pain—sex without secrets—she will have sex without fear, and without fear of sex without pain.

Then the thought of no sex at all will make her afraid, more than she is now of sex with pain, more than she is afraid of losing her body, more than she is afraid of never losing it, never being light.

Ruben said once she was insatiable. This is because she squirmed and writhed, wanting to savor everything, all the moments that led to the act, she wanted to forestall the act of sex with pain. When she has sex without pain, she will go on forever, single-minded of purpose. One-track mind. She is afraid she will forget everything—will forget the multiplication table, the rule for i before e, to take vitamins, when to add bleach, how to can fruit, drive, run a PTA meeting using *Robert's Rules of Order*, bind newspapers for the Scouts' paper drives, change diapers, speak Yiddish, follow along in the Hebrew, sing the Adom Olam, make round ground balls of things: gefilte fish, matzo balls. Ruthie will become a performing trickster, a one-note gal, one-trick pony, performing this sex without pain, her back arching like a circus artist on a trapeze, a girl in a bar in the French Quarter. "You cannot contain yourself," Ruben will say, turning aside. She will feel as if she is overflowing the cups of her bra. Her body will fill the streets. People will say, "That Ruthie sure wants it."

She tries to avoid it. So does Ruben. They are sleepy. Or the children keep them awake, worrying. There is less and less time for it. When they travel and stay in hotels, the girls stay in the room with them, to save money for sightseeing. Ruben still kisses her, in the morning and when he comes home from work, after he removes his hat.

But if she and Ruben could have sex without pain—there would be no dinner for him waiting hot and ready at the table. Big Ruthie would ignore all her duties. She would become captive to it. Body twitching. Wet. Rivulets. She would no longer be in control. No longer in the driver's seat, but in back—necking, petting, dress up, flounces up, panties down or on the dash, devil-may-care, a hand on her—"Sorry, officer, we had just stopped to look for—" "We were on our way home, must have fallen asleep—"

Sex would become like chocolate fudge. Like lemon-meringue pie. Like pearls shimmering under a chandelier. Or

Van Gogh close enough to see the paint lines. Blue-gray clouds after a rainstorm. Loveliness. Would Big Ruthie ever sleep?

Big Ruthie's life will become a dream, a dream of those blue castles with long mattresses she will lie across, will f— in, far away, will never ever come back from, the place high on the improbable hill of sex without pain, the impossible land of sex without pain.

There in the castle she will find the Messiah himself. He too is insatiable. She will welcome him inside her. She will long for him, miss his rhythms when he departs her body. Up there in his castle, she will keep him from descending to do his duty for at least another forty years. In his land of sex without pain, she and he will tarry.

Waltzing the Cat

For as long as I can remember, my parents have eaten vicariously through the cat. Roast chicken, amaretto cheese spread, rum raisin ice cream: there is no end to the delicacies my parents bestow on Suzette. And Suzette, as a result, has developed in her declining years a shape that is at first glance a little horrifying. It isn't simply that she is big—and she *is* big, weighing in at twenty-nine pounds on the veterinarian's scale—but she is alarmingly out of proportion. Her tiny head, skinny tail, and dainty feet jut out from her grossly inflated torso like a circus clown's balloon creation, a nightmarish cartoon cat.

I remember choosing Suzette from a litter of mewing Pennsylvania barn cats, each one no bigger than the palm of my hand. I was sixteen then, and I zipped Suzette inside my ski jacket and drove back to the city with my brand-new license in the only car I ever really loved, my mother's blue Mustang convertible—the old kind—passed on to me and then sold, without my permission, when I went away to college.

At first Suzette was tiny and adorable, mostly white with black and brown spots more suited to a dog than to a cat, and a muddy-colored smudge on her cheek that my mother always called her coffee stain. But too many years of bacon grease and heavy cream have spread her spots across her immense and awkward body; her stomach hangs so low to the ground now that she can only waddle, throwing one hip at a time out and around her stomach, and dragging most of her weight forward by planting one of two rickety front paws.

Suzette has happily accepted her role as family repository for all fattening foods. She is, after all, a city cat who never did much exploring anyway, even when she was thin. She didn't really chase her tail even when she could have caught it. My parents are happy now to lift her to the places she used to like to get to under her own power: the sideboard in the dining room or the middle of their king-sized bed. Suzette has already disproved all the veterinarian's warnings about eating herself to death, about my parents killing her with kindness. This year, as I turn thirty-two, Suzette turns seventeen.

The cat and I were always friends until I left home and fell in love with men who raised dogs and smelled like foreign places. Now when I come home for a visit the cat eyes me a little suspiciously, territorial, like an only child.

I don't have any true memories of my parents touching each other. I have seen pictures of them the year before I was born when they look happy enough, look maybe like two people who could actually have sex, but in my lifetime I've never even seen them hug.

"Everything was perfect with your father and me before you were born," my mother has told me over and over, confusion in her voice but not blame. "I guess he was jealous or something," she says, "and then all the best parts of him went away. But it has all been worth it," she adds, her voice turning gay as she fixes the cat a plate of sour cream herring chopped up fine, "because of you."

When I was growing up there was never anything like rum raisin ice cream or amaretto cheese spread in the refrigerator. My mother has always eaten next to nothing: a small salad sprinkled with lemon juice, or a few wheat thins with her martini at the end of the day. (One of my childhood nightmares was of my mother starving herself to death, one bony hand extended like those Ethiopian children on late-night TV.) My father ate big lunches at work and made do at night with whatever there was. When I came home from school I was offered carrots and celery, cauliflower and radishes, and sometimes an orange as a special treat.

I have forgotten many things about my childhood, but I do remember how terrified my parents were that I would become overweight. I remember long tearful conversations with my mother about what my friends and teachers would say, what everyone in the world would say, behind my back if I got fat. I remember my father slapping my hand at a dinner table full of company (one of the few times we pretended to eat like normal people) when I got caught up in the conversation, forgot the rules, and reached for a warm roll. I remember my mother buying the family clothes slightly on the small side so we were always squeezing and tucking and holding our breaths. My mother said that feeling the constant pressure of our clothes would remind us to eat less.

What I know now is that I was never fat, that none of us was ever fat, and I have assembled years of photographs to prove it. The first thing I did when I went away to college was gain fifteen pounds that I have never been able to lose.

After college, when I left home for good, my father, in a gesture so unlike him that my mother attributed it to the onset of senility, began to listen with great regularity to the waltzes of Johann Strauss, and my mother, for reasons which are for me both unclear and all too obvious, started overfeeding the cat.

In my real life I live in California and volunteer twice a week at a homeless shelter, where I stir huge pots of muddy-colored stew and heap the plates with it, warm and steaming. My friend Leo stays over at my house every Saturday night and we watch movies until daylight and then we get up and work all day in my garden. I love watching the tiny sprouts emerge, love watching them develop. I even love weeding, pulling the encroaching vines and stubborn roots up and away from the strengthening plants, giving them extra water and air. I love cooking for Leo entire dinners of fresh vegetables, love the frenzy of the harvest in August and September when everything, it seems, must be eaten at once. I love taking the extra food to the shelter, and at least for a few months, putting the gloomy canned vegetables away.

What I love most of all is lying in bed on Sunday mornings thinking about the day in the garden and hearing Leo puttering around making coffee. It's never been romantic with Leo and I know it never will be, but still, on those mornings I feel a part of something. With the moon sliding behind the sunburnt hills, the sun up and already turning the tomatoes from green to red, the two of us get our hands dirty together, pulling out the dandelions, turning the rich dark soil.

Aside from the weight issue, which always gets us in trouble, my mother and I are very close. I told her the first time I smoked a cigarette, the first time I got drunk, the first time I got stoned, and at age sixteen when I lost my virginity to Ronny Kupeleski in the Howard Johnson's across the border in Phillipsburg, New Jersey, I told my mother in advance.

"It's just as well," my mother said, in what I regard now as one of her finest moments in parenting. "You don't really love him, but you think you do, and you may as well get it over with with someone who falls into that category."

It wasn't the last time I followed my mother's advice, and like most times, she turned out to be right on all counts about Ronny Kupeleski. And whatever I don't understand about my mother always gets filed away behind the one thing I do understand: my mother believes she has given up everything for me; she will always be my harshest critic, she will always be my biggest fan.

My father has had at least three major disappointments in his life that I know of. The first is that he didn't become a basketball star at Princeton; his mother was dying and he had to quit the team. The second is that he never made a million dollars. Or, since he *has* made a million dollars if you add several years together, I guess he means he never made a million dollars all at one time. And the third one is me, who he wanted to be blond, lithe, graceful, and a world-class tennis champion. Because I am none of these things and will never be a world-class sportsman, I have become instead a world-class sports fan, memorizing batting averages and box scores, penalties and procedures, and waiting for opportunities to make my father proud. Fourteen years after I left home sports is still the only thing my father and I have to talk about. We say, "Did you see that overtime between the Flyers and the Blackhawks?" or "How 'bout them Broncos to take the AFC this year," while my mother, anticipating the oncoming silence, hurries to pick up the phone.

My mother believes that her primary role in life has been to protect my father and me from each other: my rock music, failed romances, and teenage abortion; his cigarette smoke, addictive tendencies toward gambling, and occasional meaningless affairs. My mother has made herself a human air bag, a buffer zone so pliant and potent and comprehensive that neither my father nor I ever dare, or care, to cross it.

The older I get, the more I realize that my father perceives himself as someone who, somewhere along the line, got taken in by a real bad deal. I am not completely unlike him—his selfishness, and his inability to say anything nice—and I know that if it were ever just the two of us we might be surprised at how much we had to say to each other—that is, if we didn't do irreparable damage first. Still, it is too hard for me to imagine, after so many years of sports and silence, and he is ten years older than my mother. He will, in all likelihood, die first.

My parents, I have noticed in my last several visits, have run out of things to say to each other. They have apparently irritated and disappointed each other beyond the point where it is worth fighting about. If it weren't for the cat, they might not talk at all.

Sometimes they talk about the cat, more often they talk to the cat, and most often they talk *for* the cat, responding to their own gestures of culinary generosity with words of praise that they think Suzette, if she could speak, would say.

On a typical afternoon, my mother might, for example, drop everything to fry the cat an egg. She'll cook up some bacon, crumble the bacon into the egg, stir it up southwestern-style, and then start cooing to Suzette to come and eat it.

The cat, of course, is smarter than this and knows that if she ignores my mother's call my mother will bring the egg to her on the couch, perhaps having added a spot of heavy cream to make the dish more appetizing.

At this point my father will say, in a voice completely unlike his own, "She's already had the milky-wilky from my cereal and a little of the chicky-chick we brought from the restaurant."

"That was hours ago," my mother will say, although it hasn't been quite an hour, and she will rush to the cat and wedge the china plate between the cat's cheek and the sofa. My parents will hold their breath while Suzette raises her head just high enough to tongue the bacon chips out of the egg.

"We like the bak-ey wak-ey, don't we, honey," my father will say.

"Yes, yes, the bak-ey wak-ey is our fav-ey fav-ey," my mother will say.

I will watch them, and try to search my conscious and unconscious memory for any time in their lives when they spoke to me this way.

The more years I spend living on the other side of the country, the better my mother and I seem to get along. It is partly an act of compromise on both our parts: I don't get angry every time my mother buys me a pleated Ann Taylor skirt, and my mother doesn't get angry if I don't wear it. We had one bad fight several years ago Christmas Eve, when my mother got up in the middle of the night, snuck into my room and took a few tucks around the waist of a full hand-painted cotton skirt I loved, and then washed it in warm water so it shrank further.

"Why can't you just accept me the way I am?" I wailed, before I remembered that I was in the house where people didn't have negative emotions.

"It's only because I adore you, baby," my mother said, and I knew not only that this was true, but also that I adored my mother back, that we were two people who needed to be adored, and the fact that we adored each other was one of life's tiny miracles. We were saving two other people an awful lot of work.

When I am at home in California I don't communicate with my parents very much. I live a life they can't conceive of, a life that breaks every rule they believe about the world getting even. I have escaped from what my parents call reality by the narrowest of margins, and if I ever try to pull the two worlds together the impact will break me like a colored piñata, all my hope and humor spilling out.

One Saturday night, when Leo and I have stayed in the garden long after dark, planting tomatoes by the light of a three-quarter moon, I feel a tiny explosion in the core of my body, not pain exactly, or exactly joy, but a sudden melancholy relief.

"Something's happened," I say to Leo, though that's all I can tell him. He wipes the dirt off his hands and sits down next to me and we sit for a long time in the turned-up dirt before we go inside and get something to eat.

When the phone rings the next morning, so early that the machine picks it up before Leo—sleeping right beside it on the couch—can get to it, and I hear my father say my name once with something I've never heard before in his voice, something not quite grief but closer to terror, I know my mother is dead.

I hear Leo say, "She'll call you right back," hear him pause just a minute before coming into my bedroom, watch him take both of my hands and then a deep breath.

"Something bad?" I say, shaking my head like a TV victim, my voice already the unfamiliar pleading of a motherless child.

Later that day, I will learn that sometime in the night my mother woke up my father to ask him what it felt like when he was having his heart attack, and he described it to her in great detail, and she said, "That isn't like this," and he offered to take her to Emergency, and she refused.

But now, sitting in my bed with the sun pouring in the skylight and Leo holding my hands, I can only see my mother like a newscast from Somalia, cheeks sunken, eyes hollow, three fingers extended from one bony hand.

My mother was scheduled to go to the dentist that morning, and my father tried to wake her up several times, with several minutes in between—minutes in which the panic must have slowly mounted, realization finally seeping over him like a dark wave.

On the phone he says, "I keep asking the paramedics why they can't bring one of those machines in here." His voice loses itself in sobs. "I keep saying, why can't they do like they do on TV?"

"She didn't have any pain," I tell him, "and she didn't have any fear."

"And now they want to take her away," he says. "Should I let them take her away?"

"I'll be there as soon as I can get on a plane," I tell him. "Hang in there."

"There's a lady here who wants to talk to you, from the funeral home. I can't seem to answer her questions."

There is a loud shuffling and someone whose voice I have never heard before tells me, without emotion, how sorry she is for my loss.

"It was your mother's wish to be cremated," the voice goes on, "but we are having a little trouble engaging reality here, you know what I mean?"

"We?" I say.

"Your father can't decide whether to hold up on the cremation till you've had a chance to see the body. To tell you the truth, I don't think he's prepared for the fact of cremation at all."

"Prepared," I say.

"What it boils down to, you see, is a question of finances."

I fix my eyes on Leo, who is outside now. Bare-chested, he has started the lawn mower and is pushing it in ever-diminishing squares around the garden and in the center of the yard.

"If we don't cremate today, we'll have to embalm, which of course will wind up being a wasted embalming."

I count the baby cornstalks that have come up already: twenty-seven from forty seeds, a good ratio.

"On the other hand, you have only one chance to make the right decision."

"I don't think she would have wanted anyone to see her, even me," I say, maybe to myself, maybe out loud. I want only to get back in bed, wait for Leo to bring me my coffee and re-plan my day in the garden. I think about the radishes ready for dinner and the spinach that will bolt if I don't pick it in a few days.

"In this heat, though," the voice continues, "time is of the essence. The body has already begun to change color, and if we don't embalm today..."

"Does she look especially thin to you?" I ask, before I can stop myself.

I cannot leave, I think suddenly, without planting the rest of the tomatoes.

"Go ahead and cremate her," I say. "I can't be there until tomorrow."

"They're going to take her away," I tell my father. "It's going to be okay though. We have to do what she wanted."

"Are you coming?"

"Yes," I say, "soon. I love you," I say, trying the words out on my father for the first time since I was five.

There is a muffled choking, and then the line goes dead.

I hang up the phone and walk out to the middle of the yard. I say to Leo, "I think I am about to become valuable to my father."

After a lifetime of nervous visits to my parents' house, I walk into what is, I remind myself, now only my father's house, as nervous as I've ever been. I can hear Strauss, "The Emperor's Waltz," or is it "Delirium," streaming from my father's study.

The cat waddles up to me, yelling for food. No one ever comes to the house without bringing a treat to Suzette.

"I thought cats were supposed to run away when somebody dies," I say, to no one.

Run? Leo would say if he were here. *That?*

My father emerges from his study, looking more bewildered than anything else. We embrace the way people do who wear reading glasses around their necks, stiff and without really pressing.

"Look at all these things, Lucille," my father says when we separate, sweeping his hand around the living room, "all these things she did." And he is right, my mother is in the room without being there, her perfectly handmade flowered slipcovers, her airy taste in art, her giant, temperamental ferns.

"I told the minister you would speak at the service," my father says. "She would have wanted that. She would have wanted you to say something nice about her. She said you never did that in real life."

"That will be easy," I say.

"Of course it will," he says quietly. "She was the most wonderful woman in the world." He starts to sob again, lifetime-sized tears falling onto the cat who sits, patient as Buddha, at his feet.

———————

The night before the funeral, I dream that I am sitting with my mother and father in the living room. My mother is wearing my favorite dress, one that she has given away years before. The furniture is the more comfortable, older style of my childhood; my favorite toys are strewn around the room. It is as though everything in the dream has been arranged to make me feel secure. A basket full of garden vegetables adorns the table, untouched.

"I thought you were dead," I say to my mother.

"I am," my mother says, crossing her ankles and folding her hands in her lap, "but I'll stay around until you can stand to be without me, until I know the two of you are going to be all right." She smoothes her hair around her face and smiles. "Then I'll just fade away."

It is the first in a series of dreams that will be with me for years, my mother dissolving until she becomes as thin as a sheet of paper, until I cry out, "No, I'm not ready yet," and my mother solidifies, right before my eyes.

On the morning of the funeral, all I can think of is to cook, so I go to the market across the street for bacon and eggs and buttermilk biscuits, and come back and do the dishes that have already begun to accumulate.

"If you put the glasses in the dishwasher right side up, I discovered, they get all full of water," my father says.

I excuse myself, shut the bathroom door behind me, and burst into tears.

I fry bacon and eggs and bake biscuits and stir gravy as if my life depends on it. My father gives at least half of his breakfast to the cat, who is now apparently allowed to lie right on top of the dining-room table with her head on the edge of his plate.

We talk about the changes that will come to his life, about him getting a microwave, about a maid coming in once a week. I tell him I will come east for his birthday next month, invite him west for a visit next winter. We talk about the last trip the three of us took together to Florida. Did I remember, he wants to know, that it had rained, like magic, only in the evenings, did I remember how we had done the crossword puzzle, the three of us all together? And even though I don't remember, I tell him that I do. We talk about my mother, words coming out of my father's mouth that make me believe in heaven, I'm so desperate for my mother to hear. Finally, and only after we have talked about everything else, my father and I talk about sports.

Before the funeral is something the minister calls the "interment of the ashes." My father and I have our separate visions of what this word means. Mine involves a hand-thrown pot sitting next to a fountain; my father, still stuck on the burial idea, imagines a big marble tomb, opened for the service and cemented back up.

What actually happens is that the minister digs up a three-inch square of ivy in an inconspicuous corner of the church garden, digs a couple of inches of dirt beneath it, and sprinkles what amounts to little more than a heaping tablespoon of ashes into the hole. I can feel my father leaning over my shoulder as I too lean over to see into the hole. Whatever laws of physics I once knew cannot prepare me for the minuscule amount of ashes, a whole human being so light that she could be lifted and caught by the wind.

The sun breaks through the clouds then, and the minister smiles, in cahoots with his God's timing, and takes that opportunity to refill the hole with dirt, neatly replacing the ivy.

Later, inside the parish house, my father says to the minister, "So there's really no limit to the number of people who could be cremated and inter...ed," his voice falling around the word, "in that garden."

"Oh, I guess upwards of sixty, eighty thousand," the minister answers with a smile I cannot read.

My father has that bewildered look on his face again, the look of a man who never expected to have to feel sorry for all the things he didn't say. I pull gently on his hand and he lets me, and we walk hand in hand to the car.

After the reception, after all the well-wishers have gone home, my father turns on the Strauss again, this time "Tales from the Vienna Woods."

People have brought food, so much of it I think they are trying to make some kind of point. I sort through the dishes mechanically, deciding what to refrigerate, what to freeze.

It has begun raining, huge hard summer raindrops, soaking the ground and turning my mother, I realize almost happily, back to the earth, to ivy food, to dust. I watch my father amble around the living room, directionless for a while, watch a smile cross his lips, perhaps for the rain, and then fade.

"Listen to this sequence, Lucille," he tells me. "Is it possible that the music gets better than this in heaven?"

Something buzzes in my chest every time my father speaks to me in this new way, a little blast of energy that lightens me somehow, that buoys me up. It is a sensation, I realize, with only a touch of alarm, not unlike falling in love.

"She would have loved to have heard the things you said about her," my father says.

"Yeah," I say. "She would have loved to have heard what you said too."

"Maybe she did," he says, "from...somewhere."

"Maybe," I say.

"If there is a God..." he says, and I wait for him to finish, but he gets lost all of a sudden as the record changes to "The Acceleration Waltz."

"I love you so much," my father says suddenly, and I turn, surprised, to face him.

But it is the cat he has lifted high and heavy above his head, and he and the cat begin turning together to the trimetric throb of the music. He holds the cat's left paw in one hand, supporting her weight, all the fluffy rolls of her, with the other, nuzzling her coffee-stained nose to the beat of the music until she makes a gurgling noise in her throat and threatens to spit. He pulls his head away from her and continues to spin, faster and faster, the music gaining force, their circles bigger around my mother's flowered furniture, underneath my mother's brittle ferns.

"One two three, one two three, one two three," my father says as the waltz reaches its full crescendo. The cat seems to relax a little at the sound of his voice, and now she throws her head back into the spinning, as if agreeing to accept the weight of this new love that will from this day forward be thrust upon her.

I Want to Be Fat

I want to be fat,
I want a belly big enough to hold
A refrigerator stuffed with trout,
Big enough to house a husband with a beer gut,
A wife with a baby in her belly.

I want to be fat like a Volkswagen bug,
Candy-apple red, or cabbage green
With a burping engine and curving hood
Which opens to reveal my penis tucked
Safely between the crowbar and spare.

When I am fat,
Ladies sipping diet colas will whisper:
Look at him. My God how'd he get so big?
And beneath those questions they'll think,
I wonder if he still makes love?
I wonder what he looks like naked?

Love me skinny girls,
As you love jenny craig and vegetables,
Love me fat girls,
As you love insecurity and everything filling.
I'll let you kiss my triple chins,
I'll let you swim in the warmth of my embrace.

When I am fat
I'll scramble a dozen eggs each morning,
Brush my teeth after every meal
—this, of course, in the years

Before I am eight-hundred pounds,
Before I marry my mattress,
And lay all day swallowing
The light of tabloid TV.

I'll cry elephant tears
When *Cooking with Betty Crocker* is cancelled,
I'll curse flexing biker-shorts and ESPN,
And I'll never forget you, Fat Albert,
Your ass like heaving pistons of flesh,
Your stomach like a massive tit
Beneath your tight red shirt.

"You motherfuckers will have to give me
My own seat on the bus!"

I want to be the champion of excess,
The great American mouth with perfect snapping teeth,
I want fat children to send me letters
Of self-love and gratitude,
I want to swell thick with love and gratitude.

I want to be buried in an ocean of dirt,
This ocean of flesh, this heart
Like a fish flopping at the center of it;
This heart like a skinny man gasping
at center of it;
This heart. This heart. This heart

For the One Man Who Likes My Thighs

There was the expensive cream from France
that promised the dimples would vanish
if applied nightly to the problem spots.
Then, when that didn't work, Kiko, the masseuse
at Profile Health Spa, dug her thumbs
deep into my flesh as she explained
in quasi-scientific terms that her rough hands
could break up the toughest globules of cellulite.
I screamed, then bruised over, but nothing
else happened. When they healed, my legs still looked
like tapioca pudding. There was the rolling pin method
I tried as far back as seventh grade,
kneading my lumpy legs as though I was making bread.
Cottage Cheese Knees, Thunder Thighs—
I heard it all—under the guise of teasing,
under the leaky umbrella mistaken for affection.
I learned to choose long dresses
and dark woolen tights, clam diggers instead of short-shorts,
and, when I could get away with it, skirted bathing suits.
The nutritionist said that maybe Royal Jelly tablets
would break up the fat. I drank eight glasses
of water every day for a month. I ate nothing
but steak for a week. I had to take everyone's advice,
fearing that if I didn't, my thighs
would truly be all my own fault. Liposuction
cost too much. The foil sweat-it-out
shorts advertised in the back of *Redbook*
didn't work. Swimming, walking in place, leg lifts.

It's embarrassing, especially being a feminist.
I wondered if Andrea Dworkin had stopped worrying,
and how. If Gloria Steinem does aerobics,
claiming it's just for her own enjoyment.
Then I read in a self-help book:
if you learn to appreciate your thighs, they'll appreciate
you back. Though it wasn't romance at first sight,
I did try to thank my legs for carrying me up nine flights
the day when the elevator at work was out;
for their quick sprint that propelled me
through the closing doors of the subway
so that I wouldn't be late for a movie;
for supporting my nieces who straddled, one
on each thigh, their heads burrowing deep into my lap.
I think, in fact, that it was at that moment
of being an aunt I forgot for an instant
about my thigh dilemma and began, more fully,
as they say, enjoying my life. So when it happened later
that I fell in love, and as a bonus,
the man said he liked my thighs, I shouldn't have been
so thoroughly surprised. At first I was sure I'd misheard—
that he liked my eyes, that he had heard someone else sigh,
or that maybe he was having a craving for french fries.
And it wasn't very easy to nonchalantly say oh, thanks
after I'd made him repeat. I kept asking
if he was sure, then waiting for a punch
line of some mean-spirited thigh-related joke.
I ran my fingers over his calf, brown and firm,
with beautiful muscles waving down the back.
It made no sense the way love makes no sense.
Then it made all the sense in the world.

When Fat Girls Dream

When fat girls dream
it is not of pies filled with cream,
and chocolate so sweet it would
make their mothers cry.
Nor do they dream in wishes
for Marilyn Monroe's waist
and Lana Turner's legs—
hip bones, cheek bones, and short strapless dresses;
these would be easy,
the lottery wins of fat girls
that everyone would understand.

At night when round cheeks push eyes closed
and dimpled fingers tuck like prayer
under extra chins
their dreams are much smaller:
a dance with a man not blind drunk,
a folding chair that won't cringe,
one pair of non-stretch pants
and a mother/aunt/grandmother who doesn't say
"You could be such a pretty girl..."

They awaken with possibilities
that die in the bathroom mirror,
in the closet, in the refrigerator.
They wrap themselves up
in smiles and dark skirts

step out their door into the thin air of morning
and maybe
just maybe
into the arms of a man with Rubens' eyes.

Ballerina

Marlene has brought home half a German chocolate cake. It was unavoidable; she'd passed Bakery on her way to Produce and the cake was sliced in half, the filling oozing out against the cellophane. If it had been a plain chocolate cake or if its layering had been concealed she could have passed it by; she'd been dieting irreproachably for six days. But her mouth recalled the clash of mocha on coconut, the bittersweet resonance. And Svi liked German chocolate cake. "It's a crime to leave them out like that," she told the cashier, who smiled with the complicity of fat people.

Now she sits in her dashiki at the kitchen table carving minuscule slices. She takes a sample, the whittlings from the uneven edge, holding back, waiting for Svi. She works at a crossword and dreams she is dancing again: white tulle to her knees, tight satin bodice; she knows the dance by heart. Even sitting she feels the flex and extension of her muscles as she leaps, *jeté, jeté, pas de bourrée*. The applause is loud, and although she continues to nibble, she no longer tastes the cake.

She broke last week with the head of her dance ensemble. Joel Dennis Steiglitz, a little gnome of a man, dried up. Women to him are dance-machines. "You have become fat," he said. "Your partners can no longer lift you." He stood in his cream-colored tights, weight on the balls of both feet.

"But I've lost some," she told him. Her heart was beating loudly. She'd just finished a difficult routine, executing it well, thigh raised without a tremor. "I'm losing." In all the mirrors her reflection had appeared thinner but his eyes looked like little hard stones, and he said she could not return to class till she'd lost twenty pounds.

"Twenty pounds?! I'll be a stick!"

"I should have said thirty."

She doesn't like to think about it. "Marlene, you have some ability" was the only scrap she was thrown but it couldn't sustain her. Now she rephrases it: *Marlene, you have a great talent.* She makes it more respectful: *I'm honored to be working with you.* She adds a fatherly touch: *I'll do everything I can for you, I am behind you.* They work out special practice hours, which brings tears to her eyes, but still she isn't satisfied. "Steiglitz," she says, "you're a fourth-rate dancer. You move like an old chicken. Like a screen door flapping in the wind!" Breathing hard she makes a phone call.

"Janice, tell me the truth—in the last couple months have I gotten fatter or thinner?" She holds the phone to her ear with her shoulder, leans on both hands.

On the other end is silence, then a short laugh. "What's going on with you, Marlene?"

Marlene laughs too, dropping the phone. She scrambles for it. "I don't get to see you enough. Why don't you join us for dinner tonight?"

Janice says she's busy grading papers.

Marlene suggests she come when the papers are finished, remembering when they were best friends and traveled together in Europe and Israel. And the light in Israel, which was peach-colored, and how their skin glowed as they walked on the beach.

"Marlene," Janice says, "I love you. But Svi, you know, he makes me a little—"

Marlene hangs up. At the Institute for Personal Power where her friend goes once a week Janice has learned to make decisions that hurt people's feelings. With a dim quarter of her mind Marlene watches her hand move toward the cake, inexorably, helplessly. Until it dawns on her: an entire piece is gone! Her damn cat! "Mikki, how could you?!" His name is Mikhail

Baryshnikov and he comes to rub himself under her hand. He's a handsome cat, seal point Siamese with a slim, aristocratic head and pale blue eyes, but she loathes him because he craves petting like a container that can never be filled. She bats him away and he moves just out of reach, still purring, eyes drawn to the movements of her hand. "Bad!" she says, making smacking motions in the air. But the cake shows no sign of teeth marks. The sides descend cleanly to the cake dish.

She feels nauseated. The phone rings and she stares at it, sure it's Svi calling to say he has decided to go out for a beer after work with one of the people he installs hardwood floors with. Svi does exactly what he wants to do; it's what she hates about him, and what she loves— "Marlene Dolnick, please."

The unfamiliar male voice moves fast. She catches the name Zinner. A New York accent. Then: "Several months ago I observed one of your classes." She tries to remember how much she weighed then. "You were very good," Zinner is saying. "You have marvelous control. Your arabesque was superb."

Almost imperceptibly she straightens her back.

"I want to start a company along the lines of the New York City Ballet. New York has a surplus of dance troupes; Chicago has none, first rate, that is—"

She holds the receiver out from her ear, hearing the voice, small in the earpiece, "I'm auditioning this month. I'd like to see if you're as good as I remember."

She holds onto the receiver while Zinner's words settle in her mind like rain. "All this month," she says, almost whispering. "Is it okay if I come at the end of the month?"

"No problem."

Her voice gets a little stronger. "It's just that I'm involved with something right now. But a month should be enough time—"

"Fine, fine."

She scribbles down his number. She can't seem to steady her hand. The objects on her table look strange to her, especially in relation to each other: phone, cakebox, tangled white string. But as Zinner's invitation solidifies into memory she picks up Mikhail Baryshnikov and kisses him.

"Who needs Steiglitz, the conceited asshole! This guy Zinner thinks I'm good." She recalls his words of praise: marvelous. Superb. "And Svi loves me. And you do too, you gorgeous cat!" She punctuates her statement with passionate kisses and the cat begins to knead her arm with his claws. Generally when he pricks her she throws him hard across the room, but now she just disengages the nails. "I can do it," she tells him, rubbing the sensitive spot behind his whiskers. "I can drop twenty pounds in a month. No problem."

Standing in the middle of the kitchen with her shoulders soft, pelvis tucked, she raises her arms over her head. They bend slowly toward each other like fruit-heavy branches. This is not control exactly but a happy, luminous accord of mind and body, in which indulgence of any sort, any rasp in the harmony, is unimaginable. She could leap toward her partner and poise indefinitely high over his head, her hips snug in the cup of his palms, her back arcing toward itself like a cradle.

Marlene's apartment is quiet. It's early evening and the street sounds are muffled by distance and the falling snow. Marlene is filing her nails.

She is pleased with her day. She has washed the dishes of several dinners, boxed the cake so it won't dry out for Svi, and practiced all her bar exercises on a straight back chair. Tired now, she draws a fingertip along the edge of her thumbnail. The buzzer rings.

"At ohevet o-tee?"

Do you love me? It's what he shouts into the intercom every evening. She doesn't know whether he's insecure or too proud to come up insufficiently welcomed, but both she finds charming. *"Cain!"* she cries warmly in the Hebrew he has taught her. *"Ah-nee ohevet!"*

"*Mi at ohevet?*" The second question comes almost brusquely. "Who do you love, me or the guy behind of me? Me or the president of America?"

"You! Of course, you! You, you idiot!"

She waits for him to climb the four flights with the same flutter she feels before a performance. He has been staying at her apartment for the past six months but he keeps almost nothing there, a couple of books, an old zippered bag of toiletries, things he could stuff in a knapsack, and away. It's as if he's still in the army waiting to be called up, called away; each night she can't believe her luck that he has actually returned to her. Janice thinks he's using her for the free hotel but Janice is jealous. Her father doesn't like what he calls "the chip on his shoulder" ("at least he's Jewish," her mother says) but this "chip" is just what attracts her. She likes the language he speaks, so harsh and abrupt, no window of vulnerability between those rough-sawn logs of syllables. And the body he inhabits, those small muscles hardened by simple, necessary actions, a body he seems almost unconscious of, as if he's rejected its pleasures along with the possibility of pain. It's the body of people who live surrounded by their enemies, of the children of people who shuffled to their slaughter. He eats to "refuel," holding the apple or chicken leg with one hand, turning pages with the other; sometimes she wonders whether he loves anything besides his country. But in a weird way she likes that too. She wishes she were more like that, beyond sense-pleasure, her body the glowing projection of her spirit, her toe shoes soundless on the hardwood practice floor. A Bach two-part invention is on the stereo now and she begins to dance, wanting him to catch her in an arabesque, thigh and rib cage lifting from the torso.

"*Azeh yofee!*" He strides toward her, dropping his jacket onto the floor, touching her hair as if he's never seen anything so beautiful. She catches her breath, turns toward his fingers, exhaling quietly. He has a thick neck and a chest so wide her hands barely meet in back; he will protect her from punks on the street. In the areas that count with her he is good and kind: not once has he commented on her weight, while she in turn doesn't talk to him about the Palestinians. But he's already moving away from her, petting Baryshnikov, the cat purring so loudly she can hear him across the room.

"You're turning him on," she says, approaching. He's blowing in the cat's ear to make it twitch. "Honey, don't tease him."

The cat rolls on his back, claws up for battle, and Svi taps his nose with a Bic pen. The cat swipes at the pen, twice, again. She pulls the cat off his lap. "You're getting him all excited!"

"Sheet." Svi walks into the kitchen.

His accent softens the swear word, refines it, almost. She stands by the couch, allowing him to make a circuit and return to her. She finds him at the kitchen table reading the paper and eating a piece of her cake. He seems intact and oblivious and happy with himself. She puts a forgiving hand on his back.

He rubs his cheek against her shoulder. His beard is a black stubble, as sharp as the bristles of a nailbrush. Sometimes after making love her face and neck sting. But she has come to like the feeling, so definite; she likes his weight pressing her into the floor or the sofa. And his murmur *eh, Gingit,* affectionate Hebrew slang for redhead and bastard. She pulls at his newspaper.

"Cut it."

"Svi—"

"I must to read."

"You must to the sofa. We must to the sexual intercourse."

He does not respond to her humor. He is reading something on the editorial page about the Palestinian rioting. It's a letter to the editor: Philip Garth of Joliet thinks the Israeli prime minister is a thug. Svi's fist sits hard and white on the table amidst chocolate crumbs and shredded coconut.

"But see, Svi. It's hard to understand why all that—" she looks for a neutral word "—*force* was so necessary."

"You Americans. You are so stupid."

She does not know if he is angry with her or Philip Garth. She stands behind him waiting for a clue but he doesn't elaborate. "Do you mean Americans in general?" she asks bravely. "Or me in particular?"

"You know nothing for politics. You know nothing for Israel. Why do you speak?"

This has happened before. He has often criticized her fellow citizens for their ignorance of world politics. And she agrees; she has started listening to National Public Radio, the hour and a half of interviews and opinions. But her feelings are hurt. She thinks of their first night together: she asked him to shave, please, and he refused. He got red bumps, he said, if he shaved more than once every twenty-four hours. Janice thought it was outrageous. Now her face burns. She feels a surge of patriotism, of solidarity with all of apolitical America. "At least we don't shoot our protesters!"

"In Kent State," he says.

"That was unusual. Not normal."

"Ach, what is normal?"

He's flushed. His cheeks are red. She thinks she can see the red dots that will stand out and hurt if he shaves too often. "I'm sorry," she says. "It's not you. It's your country, your government. It isn't you."

"You are mistaken," he says, walking out of the room.

The weight of all she is mistaken about, that she must get straight in order to keep this man, lies heavy on one side of her brain, and she races after him. "No, no, no, no, no! You always do that. You always walk out when we have to talk!"

She grabs for the jacket he's putting on but he shakes her off. He seems furious. There are beads of sweat on his forehead and what might be tears in his eyes. She runs between him and the door, arms outspread. "You can't leave!" She's facing him, walking backwards. "I refuse to let you leave!" Her voice is commanding but she starts to cry.

"Aveenu malcainu!" He reaches for her, roughly at first, then more tenderly. "Shh, don't cry, don't cry." He kisses her forehead, he sinks down with her to the floor, rocking her. *"Eh, gingit."*

She lets him smooth her hair. She believes he loves her. She tells him about the call from Zinner. "I'm going to try for it," she says with some forcefulness. "I've got a month to practice. He says I'm good."

His response is muffled in the V of her robe. He is kissing her breasts. His face stings. She tries to ignore the sensation, but the skin burns all the way up her neck. She draws back, placing a gentle hand on his cheek. "Honey," she says, "I know you don't like to shave that often—"

He kisses her hard on the mouth. Her face hurts. She pictures her mouth, her breasts, pink and raw. "Will you shave, sweetheart? For me?"

He says something fast in Hebrew that she doesn't understand.

"Come on, Svi, please. Don't you think you're being a little selfish? I do. Really. You're being selfish."

"Mah zeh?"

She doesn't know what that means. Or care right now. She doesn't like his language, the sound of the words—so coarse, clumsy at showing love. *At ohevet otee?* May I see your license and registration? She pulls her arms and legs away from his arms and legs and seats herself on the couch. She sits up tall stroking her cat.

"What is this, Marlene? You are making a point?" He grabs her foot and shakes it once, again.

Later she will know she already knew this was dangerous ground. But the part of her in charge at the moment feels her foot trapped in his thick hand and kicks his hand away. She looks down at him from her perch on the couch, compassionate, almost. But he's yelling louder than the words in her mind, a blast of Hebrew like machine-gun fire, and her words fly up to the ceiling and shower down on her, and she needs stronger, more brutal words, and she holds up the cat between them. "You're a bully. Like your bullying country. That murders children. And buries them alive." Her voice isn't angry. It's sweet and oddly singsong, the voice of a child reading aloud from a book she doesn't need to understand. "I don't see. Why they buried them alive. Was there a point to that? How do you explain it?"

"Sheet you fat pig, I should hurt you!" He takes a step toward the couch, arm raised as if to crack her one, and she wards him off with the cat like a crucifix.

"See!" she cries in triumph. "What did I tell you?" Her eyes flash and her elation remains until the door slams.

"Svi?" Her voice is small in the empty apartment. Mikhail Baryshnikov has clawed her and stands bristling at the door.

"Svi!" She runs out and throws her voice, entreating, down the four flights. But through the echo she hears an engine whining, then sputtering into a gassy roar.

Robe hanging open, she holds onto the banister. Her head begins to fill like a washing machine, churning. Her eyes fill with tears. She walks to the kitchen. Across the street and four flights down, an empty parking spot is defined by the cars on either side and a grey-white rectangle of snow. The cakebox is open on the table beside Svi's plate and fork. The phone rings.

She opens the window, her arms to the cold dark air, and she wants to leap, one stupendous *grand jeté,* toward the spot Svi vacated. She wants to cram her mouth with coffee and chocolate, saliva cascading. She wants to answer the phone. It is still ringing.

She counts the rings: six, seven, eight. She hangs suspended above the cake, phone and window like a dancer in an arabesque, her two arms and her back and lofted leg in an arc so pure your eyes ache. Then she throws the cake in its box out the window. The cake plummets. The box turns end over end, then steadies itself, its top spread firm and graceful as a wing.

DONNA JARRELL

The Displaced Overweight Homemaker's Guide to Finding a Man

First, check around the house to see if you have one that can be repaired. Check the attic, the basement, the garage. Sometimes you'll find one at a neighbor's with another one, watching football and drinking beer, or cleaning his buddy's garage when his own is more cluttered. Never mind this. Seize him, regardless of his condition, and assess the damage. He will insist he works just fine—it's you that's malfunctioning. Don't believe him. Have him overhauled by a specialist. Replace his belts and shock absorbers. Align his front end. Express pleasure at any interest he develops in support groups, your favorite television shows, or the children's extracurricular activities. Do this once a year for at least five years. Finally, give up. D-i-v-o-r-c-e him. But don't take him to the cleaners. He's not a bad man. You are not a bitter woman.

Walk forty-five minutes a day and stop eating sugar. Lose thirty pounds, one-third of your goal, at record-breaking pace. Use the Internet to arrange blind dates with men who want nothing but sex and haven't had it for years, if ever. Watch them drool with desire. Shudder. Pretend this validates your sex appeal. Ignore the voice that tells you that the desire of these men is indiscriminate—they would have sex with any old cow, not just the ones branded, DISPLACED OVERWEIGHT HOMEMAKER (DOH). Have sex with a couple of these men, voluntarily; with a couple more, under pressure. Tell yourself it's okay. Tell yourself it's not okay. Tell yourself it doesn't matter now, these men are history, like your marriage. Never get into a car with anyone you don't know. Learn your lessons the hard way. Don't date for a while.

Regain the third of your goal. Hang size 18 clothes in back of closet; wash 24s. Continue your education. Formally. Get a degree. Maybe two. Work hard enough to fall asleep by nine P.M. on Friday nights to avoid your growing resentment and jealousy of anyone having a real life. Or a real date. Do laundry and take the kids to a movie on Saturday. Sunday, browse the newspaper personals. Wonder if these men are different than men on the Internet. Run your own ad. Make it clear you want more than sex. Sell your mind, not your body. Reject anyone who doesn't reject you—something must be wrong with this person. Write scathing editorials to no one in particular about the commodification of relationships.

Find out what's wrong with you and try to fix it—ask around: "The fat? The kids? The brains? All of the above?" Nod politely when your successfully wedded sister or mother tells you to stop letting men know how smart you are. Practice amazing grace when well-meaning friends remind you of your terrific personality and relatively few bad habits. Develop a new appreciation of your deeper qualities—you are personable and fun to be with. And don't forget, you are a good mother. Whatever happens, don't give up. The right man is out there. Remember you'll kiss a lot of frogs before one turns into a prince.

Encourage yourself in this quest by referring to conversations in response to your personal ads as research:

FROG: I smoke, is that a problem?

DOH: I don't smoke.

FROG: Would it help if I told you I wanted to quit?

DOH: (*Polite laugh. Awkward silence.*)

FROG: Your ad says full-figured. Exactly how full-figured are you?

DOH: I don't know.

FROG: You must know.

DOH: Trust me, I'm shrugging.

FROG: Tell me what size you wear. You know that, right?

DOH: Oh. That. Size I wear. Would it help if I told you I wanted to be thin?

This type of research will teach you to discern quality relationship potential from "other" potential. For example, this man will laugh, tell you you have balls, and invite you over for sex. Don't go. At least not immediately. He will call back later to confess to killing a squirrel as a teenager. Tell him that's not so bad, especially if the squirrel was a menace. Hang up quickly, bolt the doors. Order Caller ID.

After about eighteen months of fruitless searching, develop extensive personal problems so that finding a man loses its priority in your life, at least temporarily. Call the one man currently exchanging phone conversations with you when you know he is not home. Leave a message explaining your children are having lots of problems—it's bad timing for you. And besides you forgot to tell him one tiny thing: you're fat. He will leave you a message, thick with disbelief and disappointment. But you sound so thin.

The problems you're having with your children—you did not make these up. Though you, yourself, are cheerful and good-natured, you have not borne happy-go-lucky children. These children of yours are dark and brooding; sensitive and easily disturbed. Creative geniuses. Great thinkers who became obsessed with infinity and death at age eight. Brilliant artists who produced book-length comic books and clay animated videos at age ten.

This is what you tell yourself.

This is what the clinicians tell you—serious substance abuse and mental illness. And at such tender ages. Meds and hospitalization. IEPs[1] and rehabilitation. Delinquency and depression. You will be devastated, it's true, but remember, you are resilient, a survivor. You will smile into the accusing stares of mothers whose children are citizens of the month. You will hold

---

[1]Individual Education Plan

up nicely in the meetings with counselors and principals who only want the best for your child. At least you will hold up nicely on the outside. For a little while. And when your internal fragility seeps to the surface in the form of incomplete or incoherent sentences that have been invaded by uncontrollable tears, these professionals may actually offer you a hug. Feel free to accept. And on the bright side, remember that the self-doubt and overwhelming inadequacy you are now feeling will shortly result in a general sense of worthlessness and a drive to punish yourself that is sure to cure your longing for a man.

This absence of longing frees you to fulfill your duty to your family. Accept that your failed marriage and inadequate mothering has ruined your children. Remarry your ex-husband at the Justice of the Peace, but cross your fingers behind your back when you repeat, "till death do us part." (Do they want you to murder the man to finally escape him?) Reconstruct your nuclear family. Buy a house in an affluent suburb so your children will have the special education services they need.

Make a list of the *personal* benefits of this reconciliation. Insurance. Familiar sex. Use self-talk and rationalization to boost your morale: your new husband measures no better on the scale of disrepair than he did when he was your old husband, but he will feel better because he can now be ordered on a broad continuum of men in disrepair, or worse. With any luck, he will have acquired a fresh appreciation of you as well.

After six months of futile attempts to reconstruct a "real" marriage, take separate bedrooms, coming together every week or two, then three, then six, for sex without kissing. Threaten violence to the inner voice that reminds you that prostitutes don't kiss their clients. Do all you can just keeping up with the appointments. The family therapists and the case managers, the guidance counselors and the psychiatrists. Be grateful that the Chief of Child Psychiatry at a clinic providing "world-class care" is following the mental health of your children. You:

Follow her directions. Make sure the children get their meds. Keep them clean and sober. Whatever the price.

From time to time, remember you have a new husband. So what if he's the same one you dumped a few years back. See a movie together. Do holidays at the in-laws'. Share a mortgage and a bank account. At night, close your bedroom door. Don't turn off the light. Remember your other life, the one where you were a den mother and taught your scout to be prepared. There may be a middle-of-the-night emergency with one of your depressed, addicted children. Unlock your jaw and breathe. Spread out in your half-empty bed with lots of room to get comfortable and nobody to be kept awake by your delicate little snore.

How bad could it really be?

Do this for a year. Do it for two. Do it until the situation has stabilized, and destabilized. Do it until you are haunted by the recurring image of your hands, cut off of your arms, poised on a three-legged table with ruffled pink cloth cover. Until you are haunted by the image of a public de-breasting of yourself and believe the little voice in your head who suggests this is what upright citizens probably did to bad mothers in seventeenth-century New England.

In a more rational moment, decide that despite your best efforts, all your mother-housewife energy isn't making *this* nuclear family do what it's supposed to do: fix the children. Suspect there might be a problem with the father-breadwinner energy. Suspect you might do better on your own. Suspect you might have a nervous breakdown if you stay. Rehearse the Serenity Prayer for a few months. Make plans to bail. Jump ship with any child who will come. Leave behind the one who won't. It is a matter of survival. Move to a new city where your grief will be strongest on Tuesdays, the day you took the one left behind to drum lessons.

In time, a surprisingly short time, your longing for a man will resurface. But you are a woman with a history now, a truckload of baggage. No one will have you—and why should they? Don't answer this. The damage could be irreparable. And don't ask around. The time has come to seek the assistance of a personal professional. Despite your concern, she will not ask you about your man-worthiness. Instead, she will encourage you to talk about your ill children. About your alcoholic father. Your raging mother. Your complacent ex. She will ask you to talk about yourself. To study your relationship patterns. Uncover subconscious motivations. Articulate your ambivalence. You want a relationship. You don't want a relationship.

Cooperate. When you tell her about the images of dismemberment, she will affirm leaving, again, was an appropriate choice. She will not yell at you when you displace your desire and your anti-desire for a man by renting a new apartment you don't like very much by the park you like a lot.

After some hard work, you will begin to feel a little like a human being again. A woman again. Despite Dr. Spock and the implied perfectibility of children with adequate mothers, you will forgive yourself. You forgive everyone else. This is the kind of person you are. Now that you are able to remember you are a person.

On weekends, drive two hours two times to exchange children with the ex. Even in winter, even in snow. Some weekends you will have to yourself. Take long walks in the park. Notice the men and their dogs. Smile. Long for the sun. Long for a man. Remember the clichés about love in the springtime.

Find yourself laughing pleasantly when a nice man's not-so-nice dog slobbers all over your arm. This earns you a coffee date. If his dog pees on your shoes, you are entitled to dinner. Dog lovers do not necessarily make good lovers, or good dates. Change populations. Visit bookstores. Practice flirting with intellectuals. Wear glasses and tie up your hair. Lounge in a chair with a philosophy book and practice looking severe. Don't slouch. Pretend you're bashful, awkward at conversation, but eager to try. When this doesn't capture his attention, trip him.

Explore the international community. Be choosy, but flexible. He must be intelligent, but can come from any culture that appreciates women with flesh. For instance, Middle Eastern. Act demure and encourage him to lavish you with his praise: your nose is perfect, your knees are perfect, your body is only a little too perfect. Your face does not even look fat! And those nipples of yours, they're just a tad on the small size.

Accept that men of this culture, as a rule, will not appreciate your fervent love of independence and general bossiness despite their admiration of your passionate nature. You will be rated good material for a second wife. You will consider this option but not admit this to anyone. Attempt, if you must, to persuade him you are good first-wife material, which he won't believe because you are divorced. Despite your sane sensibility, cling to this relationship where your external beauty is finally and fully appreciated. End it with a loud fight in a public parking lot. Wish him the worst for the future. Scold yourself for being a bad sport, but keep the scolding brief.

Discover you find Spanish men sexier than Middle Eastern men. Meet one at a party. Let him try to teach you salsa dancing. Fail miserably, but this time be a good sport. Talk to him in a corner and tell him how noble he is, a postdoc working on a pharmaceutical cure for cancer. Invite him for a drink the next week. In between, roll his name, with all its *n*s and *r*s and oh-so-long vowels, over your tongue as if it's an exquisite lingual delicacy. Meet him on the Tuesday following, sip wine, and talk for hours. Despite his delight in conversing with you, his appreciation for your intellect and keen insight into human nature, see through him to understand his interest in you is not far-reaching, not beyond sex on his sofa in front of his new television set. Pass him on the streets months later with a perky blonde that could be a skinny you. Give him a sad smile when he stops to say something but is tugged past you by his companion.

Next try a German fellow. Don't try for long. He will be

nice and funny but will confess an antipathy for his mother that makes you uncomfortable.

Revert to men from your immediate locale. Assess each one you encounter for relationship potential: ring? approximate age? approximate IQ? sense of humor? good teeth? clean nails? If you're close enough, pit odor. Don't eliminate anyone: the postal clerk, the library clerk, the man sitting in the car next to you at the red light. Don't believe the ruled-out possibilities, aka men rejecting you, who take time, like a thoughtful editor, to give you polite feedback, and say, preferably over e-mail, you're a very special person; you might find a man if you'd stop looking so hard.

Stop looking so hard. Turn off man radar. Do not check for rings. Do not flirt. Do not ask about anyone's relationship status. Do not inquire about age. Do this for six months, or until you notice your active search has mutated into dark fantasies involving live married men who want to leave their wives to pursue their love of you, and in doing so, drag you center stage into a messy, distasteful domestic crisis, which you think you and your conscience are ill equipped to handle. However, by the time you avoid the coercion of friends to join a single-parents group—citing your preference for compartmentalizing your life—and go to a D & S group[2] and hear stories of betrayed wives, you are shocked to find yourself so lonely you can turn from their pain and eye most anyone's husband with lust and longing and an "every-woman-for-herself" attitude.

Leave this group for a singles' group. Try to find one with men. This will be a challenge, but you are up for it. Or so you think. Empathize with men who steer clear of singles' groups. You may be large and lonely, but you're not, as your children would phrase it, a loser. Give up on singles' groups.

---

[2]Divorced & Separated

Relent. Give single-parent groups a try. Here you can mingle with men who have similar interests—children. Aside from compartmentalization, you have this problem: your own children have been so difficult, you have no interest in the children of others. This is a lie; don't tell the truth—you care about others too much. Wish these single parents well, and run, run, as fast as you can, before you are swallowed whole by your historically dominant role, which begins with the letter C[3].

Join a card club, a book club, any special interest group that might attract men. Learn to contra dance and paint miniature Revolutionary War figurines. Be pleasantly surprised when you discover an unexplained male interest in venues where available men are actually present. Focus on men without children. Men who have time to focus on you.

Enjoy this male interest. Enjoy the respite from motherhood. Enjoy the jealousy of skinny friends: "Every time I look at you, you have a cute man at your side!" Share their bafflement. Say it's a fluke—it probably won't last. Say you don't care. No one will believe you. They will say you're being glib to hide your true feelings. Say, "What's wrong with hiding my true feelings?" Call yourself a plush mama and eat fat-full ice cream in their skinny presence. Lick. Lick.

---

[3]Caregiver

Weight Bearing

Opening the door to a fat person
Is like drowning, sometimes you think you can't stand it,

What are all those immense, painfully thick slabs

Of skin built up to hold out
Or in?

Poured into himself like concrete,
Like a candle big as an elephant that has gone out,

Sweat beads on the forehead
Of the young Kiowa sitting in my office,

With hair so black you'd think it came from a box,
In shirts fragrant with Tide,

With sides drooping all over my tiny chair
Like a grand piano in soft sculpture

He lets kids climb on him like puppies.

The murmur of his soft voice
Surrounds all sides of the subject like honey,

But if he is a messenger what has he got to say?

Wind passes its rough hand over the keyboard,
Then sighs.

In the vast folds of his body

First there is the hissing of warm breath,
Then there is all that flesh pressing against its own belt buckle.

How does he manage to sit, stand, breathe?
But he does, he tells me he's not had a drop to drink for
    months

And I believe him: self pity in liquid form
Is poison he doesn't need.

Besides, he has his own pupils to think of.

Back home on the reservation
The river is beginning to dry up.

The old stories disappear: whose grandmother
First spoke with Harvest Woman,

Whose uncle thought he could trick Coyote...

Next door a gang of white sociologists discusses the matter
    loudly
Quarreling like magpies.

But who has time nowadays to listen?

The traffic ticket for speeding, the pain
Visiting his parents in a Home,

These things sink into the ground like blood,
Like antelope oil into earth

That has absorbed too much.

Expanding into the room like a balloon
Hotter and hotter, it is about to burst

And the young man knows it, he tries to say something,
Anything, at the center of himself he is starving.

He thinks he is a wild leaf snapping against the sky
And then folding, when there is no breeze

What food should he take to soothe him?

Heavy with lard, with the children heaped up on his back
He bows to suffering like a gentleman.

Out there on the mesa he is a lone cottonwood
Muttering to itself in the wind.

Anxious as a smoke signal looking left right left right
Finally there is no comforting the dry purplish lips

That shape words out of the air like waterless clouds
Scouring the land for sustenance.

Tobias Wolff

Hunters in the Snow

Tub had been waiting for an hour in the falling snow. He paced the sidewalk to keep warm and stuck his head out over the curb whenever he saw lights approaching. One driver stopped for him but before Tub could wave the man on he saw the rifle on Tub's back and hit the gas. The tires spun on the ice.

The fall of snow thickened. Tub stood below the overhang of a building. Across the road the clouds whitened just above the rooftops, and the street lights went out. He shifted the rifle strap to his other shoulder. The whiteness seeped up the sky.

A truck slid around the corner, horn blaring, rear end sashaying. Tub moved to the sidewalk and held up his hand. The truck jumped the curb and kept coming, half on the street and half on the sidewalk. It wasn't slowing down at all. Tub stood for a moment, still holding up his hand, then jumped back. His rifle slipped off his shoulder and clattered on the ice, a sandwich fell out of his pocket. He ran for the steps of the building. Another sandwich and a package of cookies tumbled onto the new snow. He made the steps and looked back.

The truck had stopped several feet beyond where Tub had been standing. He picked up his sandwiches and his cookies and slung the rifle and went up to the driver's window. The driver was bent against the steering wheel, slapping his knees and drumming his feet on the floorboards. He looked like a cartoon of a person laughing, except that his eyes watched the man on the seat beside him. "You ought to see yourself," the driver said. "He looks just like a beach ball with a hat on, doesn't he? Doesn't he, Frank?"

The man beside him smiled and looked off.

"You almost ran me down," Tub said. "You could've killed me."

"Come on, Tub," said the man beside the driver. "Be mellow. Kenny was just messing around." He opened the door and slid over to the middle of the seat.

Tub took the bolt out of his rifle and climbed in beside him. "I waited an hour," he said. "If you meant ten o'clock why didn't you say ten o'clock?"

"Tub, you haven't done anything but complain since we got here," said the man in the middle. "If you want to piss and moan all day you might as well go home and bitch at your kids. Take your pick." When Tub didn't say anything he turned to the driver. "Okay, Kenny, let's hit the road."

Some juvenile delinquents had heaved a brick through the windshield on the driver's side, so the cold and snow tunneled right into the cab. The heater didn't work. They covered themselves with a couple of blankets Kenny had brought along and pulled down the muffs on their caps. Tub tried to keep his hands warm by rubbing them under the blanket but Frank made him stop.

They left Spokane and drove deep into the country, running along black lines of fences. The snow let up, but still there was no edge to the land where it met the sky. Nothing moved in the chalky fields. The cold bleached their faces and made the stubble stand out on their cheeks and along their upper lips. They stopped twice for coffee before they got to the woods where Kenny wanted to hunt.

Tub was for trying someplace different; two years in a row they'd been up and down this land and hadn't seen a thing. Frank didn't care one way or the other, he just wanted to get out of the goddamned truck. "Feel that," Frank said, slamming the door. He spread his feet and closed his eyes and leaned his head way back and breathed deeply. "Tune in on that energy."

"Another thing," Kenny said. "This is open land. Most of the land around here is posted."

"I'm cold," Tub said.

Frank breathed out. "Stop bitching, Tub. Get centered."

"I wasn't bitching."

"Centered," Kenny said. "Next thing you'll be wearing a nightgown, Frank. Selling flowers out at the airport."

"Kenny," Frank said, "you talk too much."

"Okay," Kenny said. "I won't say a word. Like I won't say anything about a certain babysitter."

"What babysitter?" Tub asked.

"That's between us," Frank said, looking at Kenny. "That's confidential. You keep your mouth shut."

Kenny laughed.

"You're asking for it," Frank said.

"Asking for what?"

"You'll see."

"Hey," Tub said, "are we hunting or what?"

They started off across the field. Tub had trouble getting through the fences. Frank and Kenny could have helped him; they could have lifted up on the top wire and stepped on the bottom wire, but they didn't. They stood and watched him. There were a lot of fences and Tub was puffing when they reached the woods.

They hunted for over two hours and saw no deer, no tracks, no sign. Finally they stopped by the creek to eat. Kenny had several slices of pizza and a couple of candy bars: Frank had a sandwich, an apple, two carrots, and a square of chocolate; Tub ate one hard-boiled egg and a stick of celery.

"You ask me how I want to die today," Kenny said, "I'll tell you burn me at the stake." He turned to Tub. "You still on that diet?" He winked at Frank.

"What do you think? You think I like hard-boiled eggs?"

"All I can say is, it's the first diet I ever heard of where you gained weight from it."

"Who said I gained weight?"

"Oh, pardon me. I take it back. You're just wasting away before my very eyes. Isn't he, Frank?"

Frank had his fingers fanned out, tips against the bark of the stump where he'd laid his food. His knuckles were hairy. He wore a heavy wedding band and on his right pinky another gold ring with a flat face and an "F" in what looked like diamonds. He turned the ring this way and that. "Tub," he said, "you haven't seen your own balls in ten years."

Kenny doubled over laughing. He took off his hat and slapped his leg with it.

"What am I supposed to do?" Tub said. "It's my glands."

They left the woods and hunted along the creek. Frank and Kenny worked one bank and Tub worked the other, moving upstream. The snow was light but the drifts were deep and hard to move through. Wherever Tub looked the surface was smooth, undisturbed, and after a time he lost interest. He stopped looking for tracks and just tried to keep up with Frank and Kenny on the other side. A moment came when he realized he hadn't seen them in a long time. The breeze was moving from him to them; when it stilled he could sometimes hear Kenny laughing but that was all. He quickened his pace, breasting hard into the drifts, fighting away the snow with his knees and elbows. He heard his heart and felt the flush on his face but he never once stopped.

Tub caught up with Frank and Kenny at a bend of the creek. They were standing on a log that stretched from their bank to his. Ice had backed up behind the log. Frozen reeds stuck out, barely nodding when the air moved.

"See anything?" Frank asked.

Tub shook his head.

There wasn't much daylight left and they decided to head back toward the road. Frank and Kenny crossed the log and they started downstream, using the trail Tub had broken. Before they had gone very far Kenny stopped. "Look at that," he said, and pointed to some tracks going from the creek back into the woods. Tub's footprints crossed right over them. There on the bank, plain as day, were several mounds of deer sign. "What do you think that is, Tub?" Kenny licked at it. "Walnuts on vanilla icing?"

"I guess I didn't notice."

Kenny looked at Frank.

"I was lost."

"You were lost. Big deal."

They followed the tracks into the woods. The deer had gone over a fence half buried in drifting snow. A no hunting sign was nailed to the top of one of the posts. Frank laughed and said the son of a bitch could read. Kenny wanted to go after him but Frank said no way, the people out here didn't mess around. He thought maybe the farmer who owned the land would let them use it if they asked. Kenny wasn't so sure. Anyway, he figured that by the time they walked to the truck and drove up the road and doubled back it would be almost dark.

"Relax," Frank said. "You can't hurry nature. If we're meant to get that deer, we'll get it. If we're not, we won't."

They started back toward the truck. This part of the woods was mainly pine. The snow was shaded and had a glaze on it. It held up Kenny and Frank but Tub kept falling through. As he kicked forward, the edge of the crust bruised his shins. Kenny and Frank pulled ahead of him, to where he couldn't even hear their voices any more. He sat down on a stump and wiped his face. He ate both the sandwiches and half the cookies, taking his own sweet time. It was dead quiet.

When Tub crossed the last fence into the road the truck started moving. Tub had to run for it and just managed to grab hold of the tailgate and hoist himself into the bed. He lay there, panting. Kenny looked out the rear window and grinned. Tub crawled into the lee of the cab to get out of the freezing wind. He pulled his earflaps low and pushed his chin into the collar of his coat. Someone rapped on the window but Tub would not turn around.

He and Frank waited outside while Kenny went into the farmhouse to ask permission. The house was old and paint was curling off the sides. The smoke streamed westward off the top of the chimney, fanning away into a thin gray plume. Above the ridge of the hills another ridge of blue clouds was rising.

"You've got a short memory," Tub said.

"What?" Frank said. He had been staring off.

"I used to stick up for you."

"Okay, so you used to stick up for me. What's eating you?"

"You shouldn't have just left me back there like that."

"You're a grown-up, Tub. You can take care of yourself. Anyway, if you think you're the only person with problems I can tell you that you're not."

"Is something bothering you, Frank?"

Frank kicked at a branch poking out of the snow. "Never mind," he said.

"What did Kenny mean about the babysitter?"

"Kenny talks too much," Frank said. "You just mind your own business."

Kenny came out of the farmhouse and gave the thumbs-up and they began walking back toward the woods. As they passed the barn a large black hound with a grizzled snout ran out and barked at them. Every time he barked he slid backwards a bit, like a cannon recoiling. Kenny got down on all fours and snarled and barked back at him, and the dog slunk away into the barn, looking over his shoulder and peeing a little as he went.

"That's an old-timer," Frank said. "A real graybeard. Fifteen years if he's a day."

"Too old," Kenny said.

Past the barn they cut off through the fields. The land was unfenced and the crust was freezing up thick and they made good time. They kept to the edge of the field until they picked up the tracks again and followed them into the woods, farther and farther back toward the hills. The trees started to blur with the shadows and the wind rose and needled their faces with the crystals it swept off the glaze. Finally they lost the tracks.

Kenny swore and threw down his hat. "This is the worst day of hunting I ever had, bar none." He picked up his hat and brushed off the snow. "This will be the first season since I was fifteen I haven't got my deer."

"It isn't the deer," Frank said. "It's the hunting. There are all these forces out here and you just have to go with them."

"You go with them," Kenny said. "I came out here to get me a deer, not listen to a bunch of hippie bullshit. And if it hadn't been for dimples here I would have, too."

"That's enough," Frank said.

"And you—you're so busy thinking about that little jailbait of yours you wouldn't know a deer if you saw one."

"Drop dead," Frank said, and turned away.

Kenny and Tub followed him back across the fields. When they were coming up to the barn Kenny stopped and pointed. "I hate that post," he said. He raised his rifle and fired. It sounded like a dry branch cracking. The post splintered along its right side, up towards the top. "There," Kenny said. "It's dead."

"Knock it off," Frank said, walking ahead.

Kenny looked at Tub. He smiled. "I hate that tree," he said, and fired again. Tub hurried to catch up with Frank. He started to speak but just then the dog ran out of the barn and barked at them. "Easy, boy," Frank said.

"I hate that dog." Kenny was behind them.

"That's enough," Frank said. "You put that gun down."

Kenny fired. The bullet went in between the dog's eyes. He sank right down into the snow, his legs splayed out on each side, his yellow eyes open and staring. Except for the blood he looked like a small bearskin rug. The blood ran down the dog's muzzle into the snow.

They all looked at the dog lying there.

"What did he ever do to you?" Tub asked. "He was just barking."

Kenny turned to Tub. "I hate you."

Tub shot from the waist. Kenny jerked backward against the fence and buckled to his knees. He folded his hands across his stomach. "Look," he said. His hands were covered with blood. In the dusk his blood was more blue than red. It seemed to belong to the shadows. It didn't seem out of place. Kenny eased himself onto his back. He sighed several times, deeply. "You shot me," he said.

"I had to," Tub said. He knelt beside Kenny. "Oh God," he said. "Frank. Frank."

Frank hadn't moved since Kenny killed the dog.

"Frank!" Tub shouted.

"I was just kidding around," Kenny said. "It was a joke. Oh!" he said, and arched his back suddenly. "Oh!" he said again, and dug his heels into the snow and pushed himself along on his head for several feet. Then he stopped and lay there, rocking back and forth on his heels and head like a wrestler doing warm-up exercises.

Frank roused himself. "Kenny," he said. He bent down and put his gloved hand on Kenny's brow. "You shot him," he said to Tub.

"He made me," Tub said.

"No no no," Kenny said.

Tub was weeping from the eyes and nostrils. His whole face was wet. Frank closed his eyes, then looked down at Kenny again. "Where does it hurt?"

"Everywhere," Kenny said, "just everywhere."

"Oh God," Tub said.

"I mean where did it go in?" Frank said.

"Here." Kenny pointed at the wound in his stomach. It was welling slowly with blood.

"You're lucky," Frank said. "It's on the left side. It missed your appendix. If it had hit your appendix you'd really be in the soup." He turned and threw up onto the snow, holding his sides as if to keep warm.

"Are you all right?" Tub said.

"There's some aspirin in the truck," Kenny said.

"I'm all right," Frank said.

"We'd better call an ambulance," Tub said.

"Jesus," Frank said. "What are we going to say?"

"Exactly what happened," Tub said. "He was going to shoot me but I shot him first."

"No sir!" Kenny said. "I wasn't either!"

Frank patted Kenny on the arm. "Easy does it, partner." He stood. "Let's go."

Tub picked up Kenny's rifle as they walked down toward the farmhouse. "No sense leaving this around," he said. "Kenny might get ideas."

"I can tell you one thing," Frank said. "You've really done it this time. This definitely takes the cake."

They had to knock on the door twice before it was opened by a thin man with lank hair. The room behind him was filled with smoke. He squinted at them. "You get anything?" he asked.

"No," Frank said.

"I knew you wouldn't. That's what I told the other fellow."

"We've had an accident."

The man looked past Frank and Tub into the gloom. "Shoot your friend, did you?"

Frank nodded.

"I did," Tub said.

"I suppose you want to use the phone."

"If it's okay."

The man in the door looked behind him, then stepped back. Frank and Tub followed him into the house. There was a woman sitting by the stove in the middle of the room. The stove was smoking badly. She looked up and then down again at the

242

child asleep in her lap. Her face was white and damp; strands of hair were pasted across her forehead. Tub warmed his hands over the stove while Frank went into the kitchen to call. The man who had let them in stood at the window, his hands in his pockets.

"My friend shot your dog," Tub said.

The man nodded without turning around. "I should have done it myself. I just couldn't."

"He loved that dog so much," the woman said. The child squirmed and she rocked it.

"You asked him to?" Tub said. "You asked him to shoot your dog?"

"He was old and sick. Couldn't chew his food any more. I would have done it myself but I don't have a gun."

"You couldn't have anyway," the woman said. "Never in a million years."

The man shrugged.

Frank came out of the kitchen. "We'll have to take him ourselves. The nearest hospital is fifty miles from here and all their ambulances are out anyway."

The woman knew a shortcut but the directions were complicated and Tub had to write them down. The man told them where they could find some boards to carry Kenny on. He didn't have a flashlight but he said he would leave the porch light on.

It was dark outside. The clouds were low and heavy-looking and the wind blew in shrill gusts. There was a screen loose on the house and it banged slowly and then quickly as the wind rose again. They could hear it all the way to the barn. Frank went for the boards while Tub looked for Kenny, who was not where they had left him. Tub found him farther up the drive, lying on his stomach. "You okay?" Tub said.

"It hurts."

"Frank says it missed your appendix."

"I already had my appendix out."

"All right," Frank said, coming up to them. "We'll have you in a nice warm bed before you can say Jack Robinson." He put the two boards on Kenny's right side.

"Just as long as I don't have one of those male nurses," Kenny said.

"Ha ha," Frank said. "That's the spirit. Get ready, set, *over you go*," and he rolled Kenny onto the boards. Kenny screamed and kicked his legs in the air. When he quieted down Frank and Tub lifted the boards and carried him down the drive. Tub had the back end, and with the snow blowing in his face he had trouble with his footing. Also he was tired and the man inside had forgotten to turn the porch light on. Just past the house Tub slipped and threw out his hands to catch himself. The boards fell and Kenny tumbled out and rolled to the bottom of the drive, yelling all the way. He came to rest against the right front wheel of the truck.

"You fat moron," Frank said. "You aren't good for diddly."

Tub grabbed Frank by the collar and backed him hard up against the fence. Frank tried to pull his hands away but Tub shook him and snapped his head back and forth and finally Frank gave up.

"What do you know about fat," Tub said. "What do you know about glands." As he spoke he kept shaking Frank. "What do you know about me."

"All right," Frank said.

"No more," Tub said.

"All right."

"No more talking to me like that. No more watching. No more laughing."

"Okay, Tub. I promise."

Tub let go of Frank and leaned his forehead against the fence. His arms hung straight at his sides.

"I'm sorry, Tub." Frank touched him on the shoulder. "I'll be down at the truck."

Tub stood by the fence for a while and then got the rifles off the porch. Frank had rolled Kenny back onto the boards and they lifted him into the bed of the truck. Frank spread the seat blankets over him. "Warm enough?" he asked.

Kenny nodded.

"Okay. Now how does reverse work on this thing?"

"All the way to the left and up." Kenny sat up as Frank started forward to the cab. "Frank!"

"What?"

"If it sticks don't force it."

The truck started right away. "One thing," Frank said, "you've got to hand it to the Japanese. A very ancient, very spiritual culture and they can still make a hell of a truck." He glanced over at Tub. "Look, I'm sorry. I didn't know you felt that way, honest to God I didn't. You should have said something."

"I did."

"When? Name one time."

"A couple of hours ago."

"I guess I wasn't paying attention."

"That's true, Frank," Tub said. "You don't pay attention very much."

"Tub," Frank said, "what happened back there, I should have been more sympathetic. I realize that. You were going through a lot. I just want you to know it wasn't your fault. He was asking for it."

"You think so?"

"Absolutely. It was him or you. I would have done the same thing in your shoes, no question."

The wind was blowing into their faces. The snow was a moving white wall in front of their lights; it swirled into the cab through the hole in the windshield and settled on them. Tub clapped his hands and shifted around to stay warm, but it didn't work.

"I'm going to have to stop," Frank said. "I can't feel my fingers."

Up ahead they saw some lights off the road. It was a

tavern. Outside in the parking lot there were several jeeps and trucks. A couple of them had deer strapped across their hoods. Frank parked and they went back to Kenny. "How you doing, partner," Frank said.

"I'm cold."

"Well, don't feel like the Lone Ranger. It's worse inside, take my word for it. You should get that windshield fixed."

"Look," Tub said, "he threw the blankets off." They were lying in a heap against the tailgate.

"Now look, Kenny," Frank said, "it's no use whining about being cold if you're not going to try and keep warm. You've got to do your share." He spread the blankets over Kenny and tucked them in at the corners.

"They blew off."

"Hold on to them then."

"Why are we stopping, Frank?"

"Because if me and Tub don't get warmed up we're going to freeze solid and then where will you be?" He punched Kenny lightly in the arm. "So just hold your horses."

The bar was full of men in colored jackets, mostly orange. The waitress brought coffee. "Just what the doctor ordered," Frank said, cradling the steaming cup in his hand. His skin was bone white. "Tub, I've been thinking. What you said about me not paying attention, that's true."

"It's okay."

"No. I really had that coming. I guess I've just been a little too interested in old number one. I've had a lot on my mind. Not that that's any excuse."

"Forget it, Frank. I sort of lost my temper back there. I guess we're all a little on edge."

Frank shook his head. "It isn't just that."

"You want to talk about it?"

"Just between us, Tub?"

"Sure, Frank. Just between us."

"Tub, I think I'm going to be leaving Nancy."

"Oh, Frank. Oh, Frank." Tub sat back and shook his head.

Frank reached out and laid his hand on Tub's arm. "Tub, have you ever been really in love?"

"Well—"

"I mean *really* in love." He squeezed Tub's wrist. "With your whole being."

"I don't know. When you put it like that, I don't know."

"You haven't then. Nothing against you, but you'd know it if you had." Frank let go of Tub's arm. "This isn't just some bit of fluff I'm talking about."

"Who is she, Frank?"

Frank paused. He looked into his empty cup. "Roxanne Brewer."

"Cliff Brewer's kid? The babysitter?"

"You can't just put people into categories like that, Tub. That's why the whole system is wrong. And that's why this country is going to hell in a rowboat."

"But she can't be more than—" Tub shook his head.

"Fifteen. She'll be sixteen in May." Frank smiled. "May fourth, three twenty-seven p.m. Hell, Tub, a hundred years ago she'd have been an old maid by that age. Juliet was only thirteen."

"Juliet? Juliet Miller? Jesus, Frank, she doesn't even have breasts. She doesn't even wear a top to her bathing suit. She's still collecting frogs."

"Not Juliet Miller. The real Juliet. Tub, don't you see how you're dividing people up into categories? He's an executive, she's a secretary, he's a truck driver, she's fifteen years old. Tub, this so-called babysitter, this so-called fifteen-year-old has more in her little finger than most of us have in our entire bodies. I can tell you this little lady is something special."

Tub nodded. "I know the kids like her."

"She's opened up whole worlds to me that I never knew were there."

"What does Nancy think about all of this?"

"She doesn't know."

"You haven't told her?"

"Not yet. It's not so easy. She's been damned good to me all these years. Then there's the kids to consider." The brightness in Frank's eyes trembled and he wiped quickly at them with the back of his hand. "I guess you think I'm a complete bastard."

"No, Frank. I don't think that."

"Well, you *ought* to."

"Frank, when you've got a friend it means you've always got someone on your side, no matter what. That's the way I feel about it, anyway."

"You mean that, Tub?"

"Sure I do."

Frank smiled. "You don't know how good it feels to hear you say that."

Kenny had tried to get out of the truck but he hadn't made it. He was jack-knifed over the tailgate, his head hanging above the bumper. They lifted him back into the bed and covered him again. He was sweating and his teeth chattered. "It hurts, Frank."

"It wouldn't hurt so much if you just stayed put. Now we're going to the hospital. Got that? Say it—I'm going to the hospital."

"I'm going to the hospital."

"Again."

"I'm going to the hospital."

"Now just keep saying that to yourself and before you know it we'll be there."

After they had gone a few miles Tub turned to Frank. "I just pulled a real boner," he said.

"What's that?"

"I left the directions on the table back there."

"That's okay. I remember them pretty well."

The snowfall lightened and the clouds began to roll back

off the fields, but it was no warmer and after a time both Frank and Tub were bitten through and shaking. Frank almost didn't make it around a curve, and they decided to stop at the next roadhouse.

There was an automatic hand-dryer in the bathroom and they took turns standing in front of it, opening their jackets and shirts and letting the jet of hot air breathe across their faces and chests.

"You know," Tub said, "what you told me back there, I appreciate it. Trusting me."

Frank opened and closed his fingers in front of the nozzle. "The way I look at it, Tub, no man is an island. You've got to trust someone."

"Frank—"

Frank waited.

"When I said that about my glands, that wasn't true. The truth is I just shovel it in."

"Well, Tub—"

"Day and night, Frank. In the shower. On the freeway." He turned and let the air play over his back. "I've even got stuff in the paper towel machine at work."

"There's nothing wrong with your glands at all?" Frank had taken his boots and socks off. He held first his right, then his left foot up to the nozzle.

"No. There never was."

"Does Alice know?" The machine went off and Frank started lacing up his boots.

"Nobody knows. That's the worst of it, Frank. Not the being fat, I never got any big kick out of being thin, but the lying. Having to lead a double life like a spy or a hit man. This sounds strange but I feel sorry for those guys, I really do. I know what they go through. Always having to think about what you say and do. Always feeling like people are watching you, trying to catch you at something. Never able to just be yourself. Like when I make a big deal about only having an orange for breakfast and then scarf all the way to work. Oreos, Mars Bars, Twinkies. Sugar Babies. Snickers." Tub glanced at Frank and looked quickly away. "Pretty disgusting, isn't it?"

"Tub. Tub." Frank shook his head. "Come on." He took Tub's arm and led him into the restaurant half of the bar. "My friend is hungry," he told the waitress. "Bring four orders of pancakes, plenty of butter and syrup."

"Frank—"

"Sit down."

When the dishes came Frank carved out slabs of butter and just laid them on the pancakes. Then he emptied the bottle of syrup, moving it back and forth over the plates. He leaned forward on his elbows and rested his chin in one hand. "Go on, Tub."

Tub ate several mouthfuls, then started to wipe his lips. Frank took the napkin away from him. "No wiping," he said. Tub kept at it. The syrup covered his chin; it dripped to a point like a goatee. "Weigh in, Tub," Frank said, pushing another fork across the table. "Get down to business." Tub took the fork in his left hand and lowered his head and started really chowing down. "Clean your plate," Frank said when the pancakes were gone, and Tub lifted each of the four plates and licked it clean. He sat back, trying to catch his breath.

"Beautiful," Frank said. "Are you full?"

"I'm full," Tub said. "I've never been so full."

Kenny's blankets were bunched up against the tailgate again.

"They must have blown off," Tub said.

"They're not doing him any good," Frank said. "We might as well get some use out of them."

Kenny mumbled. Tub bent over him. "What? Speak up."

"I'm going to the hospital," Kenny said.

"Attaboy," Frank said.

The blankets helped. The wind still got their faces and Frank's hands but it was much better. The fresh snow on the road and the trees sparkled under the beam of the headlight. Squares of light from farmhouse windows fell onto the blue snow in the fields.

"Frank," Tub said after a time, "you know that farmer? He told Kenny to kill the dog."

"You're kidding!" Frank leaned forward, considering. "That Kenny. What a card." He laughed and so did Tub. Tub smiled out the back window. Kenny lay with his arms folded over his stomach, moving his lips at the stars. Right overhead was the Big Dipper, and behind, hanging between Kenny's toes in the direction of the hospital, was the North Star, Pole Star, Help to Sailors. As the truck twisted through the gentle hills the star went back and forth between Kenny's boots, staying always in his sight. "I'm going to the hospital," Kenny said. But he was wrong. They had taken a different turn a long way back.

The Fat Lady Travels

On any train
she is the occupant
of either seat—
no hopes for a handsome stranger,
no petty arguments
as to who
will get the window
or the aisle.
She gets them both.

When she dreams,
she is never the goddess
turning men to pigs.
She is the pig.
She is the one gross eye
of the Cyclops
fending off the spears
of her disgrace.

She is all of Brobdingnag.

Her green dress blowzes
in the halcyon wind.
She is turgid water
flooding the station,
home for leviathans.

What she should lose
would be enough

to make the sister
she never had,

and how thin
the both of them would be
gliding on fine-point skates
across some fragile pond

and, oh, it holding!

RAWDON TOMLINSON

Fat People at the Amusement Park

They are laughing like the rest of us,
amused at being here
among bright lights and whirling things

laughing, despite their particular knowledge
of gravity, which is why they ride
the fastest and highest rides,

a release from the demands of earth
between bouts with blue cotton candy,
stuffed bears and peanuts—

we watch them bounce along the midway
with their rosy-cheeked smiles and jouncing
asses, chattering as though they'd entered

the kingdom, they step into the cars
of the tilt-a-whirl, and take off
into a scream of weightlessness.

Disappearing

When he starts in, I don't look anymore, I know what it looks like, what he looks like, tobacco on his teeth. I just lie in the deep sheets and shut my eyes. I make noises that make it go faster and when he's done he's as far from me as he gets. He could be dead he's so far away.

Lettie says leave then stupid but who would want me. Three hundred pounds anyway but I never check. Skin like tapioca pudding, I wouldn't show anyone. A man.

So we go to the pool at the junior high, swimming lessons. First it's blow bubbles and breathe, blow and breathe. Awful, hot nosefuls of chlorine. My eyes stinging red and patches on my skin. I look worse. We'll get caps and goggles and earplugs and body cream Lettie says. It's better.

There are girls there, what bodies. Looking at me and Lettie out the side of their eyes. Gold hair, skin like milk, chlorine or no.

They thought when I first lowered into the pool, that fat one parting the Red Sea. I didn't care. Something happened when I floated. Good said the little instructor. A little redhead in an emerald suit, no stomach, a depression almost, and white wet skin. Good she said you float just great. Now we're getting somewhere. The whistle around her neck blinded my eyes. And the water under the fluorescent lights. I got scared and couldn't float again. The bottom of the pool was scarred, drops of gray shadow rippling. Without the water I would crack open my head, my dry flesh would sound like a splash on the tiles.

At home I ate a cake and a bottle of milk. No wonder you look like that he said. How can you stand yourself. You're no

Cary Grant I told him and he laughed and laughed until I threw up.

When this happens I want to throw up again and again until my heart flops out wet and writhing on the kitchen floor. Then he would know I have one and it moves.

So I went back. And floated again. My arms came around and the groan of the water made the tight blondes smirk but I heard Good that's the crawl that's it in fragments from the redhead when I lifted my face. Through the earplugs I heard her skinny voice. She was happy that I was floating and moving too.

Lettie stopped the lessons and read to me things out of magazines. You have to swim a lot to lose weight. You have to stop eating too. Forget cake and ice cream. Doritos are out. I'm not doing it for that I told her but she wouldn't believe me. She couldn't imagine.

Looking down that shaft of water I know I won't fall. The water shimmers and eases up and down, the heft of me doesn't matter I float anyway.

He says it makes no difference I look the same. But I'm not the same. I can hold myself up in deep water. I can move my arms and feet and the water goes behind me, the wall comes closer. I can look down twelve feet to a cold slab of tile and not be afraid. It makes a difference I tell him. Better believe it mister.

Then this other part happens. Other men interest me. I look at them, real ones, not the ones on TV that's something else entirely. These are real. The one with the white milkweed hair who delivers the mail. The meter man from the light company, heavy thick feet in boots. A smile. Teeth. I drop something out of the cart in the supermarket to see who will pick it up. Sometimes a man. One had yellow short hair and called me ma'am. Young. Thin legs and an accent. One was older. Looked me in the eyes. Heavy, but not like me. My eyes are nice. I color the lids. In the pool it runs off in blue tears. When I come out my face is naked.

The lessons are over, I'm certified. A little certificate signed by the redhead. She says I can swim and I can. I'd do better with her body, thin calves hard as granite.

I get a lane to myself, no one shares. The blondes ignore me now that I don't splash the water, know how to lower myself silently. And when I swim I cut the water cleanly.

For one hour every day I am thin, thin as water, transparent, invisible, steam or smoke.

The redhead is gone, they put her at a different pool and I miss the glare of the whistle dangling between her emerald breasts. Lettie won't come over at all now that she is fatter than me. You're so uppity she says. All this talk about water and who do you think you are.

He says I'm looking all right, so at night it is worse but sometimes now when he starts in I say no. On Sundays the pool is closed I can't say no. I haven't been invisible. Even on days when I don't say no it's all right, he's better.

One night he says it won't last, what about the freezer full of low-cal dinners and that machine in the basement. I'm not doing it for that and he doesn't believe me either. But this time there is another part. There are other men in the water I tell him. Fish he says. Fish in the sea. Good luck.

Ma you've lost says my daughter-in-law, the one who didn't want me in the wedding pictures. One with the whole family, she couldn't help that. I learned how to swim I tell her. You should try it, it might help your ugly disposition.

They closed the pool for two weeks and I went crazy. Repairing the tiles. I went there anyway, drove by in the car. I drank water all day.

Then they opened again and I went every day sometimes four times until the green paint and new stripes looked familiar as a face. At first the water was heavy as blood but I kept on until it was thinner and thinner, just enough to hold me up. That was when I stopped with the goggles and cap and plugs, things that kept the water out of me.

There was a time I went the day before a holiday and no one was there. It was echoey silence just me and the soundless empty pool and a lifeguard behind the glass. I lowered myself so slow it hurt every muscle but not a blip of water not a ripple not one sound and I was under in that other quiet, so quiet some tears got out, I saw their blue trail swirling.

The redhead is back and nods, she has seen me somewhere. I tell her I took lessons and she still doesn't remember.

This has gone too far he says I'm putting you in the hospital. He calls them at the pool and they pay no attention. He doesn't touch me and I smile into my pillow, a secret smile in my own square of the dark.

Oh my God Lettie says what the hell are you doing what the hell do you think you're doing. I'm disappearing I tell her and what can you do about it not a blessed thing.

For a long time in the middle of it people looked at me. Men. And I thought about it. Believe it, I thought. And now they don't look at me again. And it's better.

I'm almost there. Almost water.

The redhead taught me how to dive, how to tuck my head and vanish like a needle into skin, and every time it happens, my feet leaving the board, I think, this will be the time.

Fat

I am sitting over coffee and cigarettes at my friend Rita's and I am telling her about it.

Here is what I tell her.

It is late of a slow Wednesday when Herb seats the fat man at my station.

This fat man is the fattest person I have ever seen, though he is neat-appearing and well dressed enough. Everything about him is big. But it is the fingers I remember best. When I stop at the table near his to see to the old couple, I first notice the fingers. They look three times the size of a normal person's fingers—long, thick, creamy fingers.

I see to my other tables, a party of four businessmen, very demanding, another party of four, three men and a woman, and this old couple. Leander has poured the fat man's water, and I give the fat man plenty of time to make up his mind before going over.

Good evening, I say. May I serve you? I say.

Rita, he was big, I mean big.

Good evening, he says. Hello. Yes, he says. I think we're ready to order now, he says.

He has this way of speaking—strange, don't you know. And he makes a little puffing sound every so often.

I think we will begin with a Caesar salad, he says. And then a bowl of soup with some extra bread and butter, if you please. The lamb chops, I believe, he says. And baked potato with sour cream. We'll see about dessert later. Thank you very much, he says, and hands me the menu.

God, Rita, but those were fingers.

I hurry away to the kitchen and turn in the order to Rudy, who takes it with a face. You know Rudy. Rudy is that way when he works.

As I come out of the kitchen, Margo—I've told you about Margo? The one who chases Rudy? Margo says to me, Who's your fat friend? He's really a fatty.

Now that's part of it. I think that is really part of it.

I make the Caesar salad there at his table, him watching my every move, meanwhile buttering pieces of bread and laying them off to one side, all the time making this puffing noise. Anyway, I am so keyed up or something, I knock over his glass of water.

I'm so sorry, I say. It always happens when you get into a hurry. I'm very sorry, I say. Are you all right? I say. I'll get the boy to clean up right away, I say.

It's nothing, he says. It's all right, he says, and he puffs. Don't worry about it, we don't mind, he says. He smiles and waves as I go off to get Leander, and when I come back to serve the salad, I see the fat man has eaten all his bread and butter.

A little later, when I bring him more bread, he has finished his salad. You know the size of those Caesar salads?

You're very kind, he says. This bread is marvelous, he says.

Thank you, I say.

Well, it is very good, he says, and we mean that. We don't often enjoy bread like this, he says.

Where are you from? I ask him. I don't believe I've seen you before, I say.

He's not the kind of person you'd forget, Rita puts in with a snicker.

Denver, he says.

I don't say anything more on the subject, though I am curious.

Your soup will be along in a few minutes, sir, I say, and I go off to put the finishing touches to my party of four business-men, very demanding.

When I serve his soup, I see the bread has disappeared again. He is just putting the last piece of bread into his mouth.

Believe me, he says, we don't eat like this all the time, he says. And puffs. You'll have to excuse me, he says.

Don't think a thing about it, please, I say. I like to see a man eat and enjoy himself, I say.

I don't know, he says. I guess that's what you'd call it. And puffs. He arranges the napkin. Then he picks up his spoon.

God, he's fat! says Leander.

He can't help it, I say, so shut up.

I put down another basket of bread and more butter. How was the soup? I say.

Thank you. Good, he says. Very good, he says. He wipes his lips and dabs his chin. Do you think it's warm in here, or is it just me? he says.

No, it is warm in here, I say.

Maybe we'll take off our coat, he says.

Go right ahead, I say. A person has to be comfortable, I say.

That's true, he says, that is very, very true, he says.

But I see a little later that he is still wearing his coat.

My large parties are gone now and also the old couple. The place is emptying out. By the time I serve the fat man his chops and baked potato, along with more bread and butter, he is the only one left.

I drop lots of sour cream onto his potato. I sprinkle bacon and chives over his sour cream. I bring him more bread and butter.

Is everything all right? I say.

Fine, he says, and he puffs. Excellent, thank you, he says, and puffs again.

Enjoy your dinner, I say. I raise the lid of his sugar bowl and look in. He nods and keeps looking at me until I move away.

I know now I was after something. But I don't know what.

How is old tub-of-guts doing? He's going to run your legs off, says Harriet. You know Harriet.

For dessert, I say to the fat man, there is the Green Lantern Special, which is a pudding cake with sauce, or there is cheesecake or vanilla ice cream or pineapple sherbet.

We're not making you late, are we? he says, puffing and looking concerned.

Not at all, I say. Of course not, I say. Take your time, I say. I'll bring you more coffee while you make up your mind.

We'll be honest with you, he says. And he moves in the seat. We would like the Special, but we may have a dish of vanilla ice cream as well. With just a drop of chocolate syrup, if you please. We told you we were hungry, he says.

I go off to the kitchen to see after his dessert myself, and Rudy says, Harriet says you got a fat man from the circus out there. That true?

Rudy has his apron and hat off now, if you see what I mean.

Rudy, he is fat, I say, but that is not the whole story.

Rudy just laughs.

Sounds to me like she's sweet on fat-stuff, he says.

Better watch out, Rudy, says Joanne, who just that minute comes into the kitchen.

I'm getting jealous, Rudy says to Joanne.

I put the Special in front of the fat man and a big bowl of vanilla ice cream with chocolate syrup to the side.

Thank you, he says.

You are very welcome, I say—and a feeling comes over me.

Believe it or not, he says, we have not always eaten like this.

Me, I eat and I eat and I can't gain, I say. I'd like to gain, I say.

No, he says. If we had our choice, no. But there is no choice.

Then he picks up his spoon and eats.

What else? Rita says, lighting one of my cigarettes and pulling her chair closer to the table. This story's getting interesting now, Rita says.

That's it. Nothing else. He eats his desserts, and then he leaves and then we go home, Rudy and me.

Some fatty, Rudy says, stretching like he does when he's tired. Then he just laughs and goes back to watching the TV.

I put the water on to boil for tea and take a shower. I put my hand on my middle and wonder what would happen if I had children and one of them turned out to look like that, so fat.

I pour the water in the pot, arrange the cups, the sugar bowl, carton of half and half, and take the tray in to Rudy. As if he's been thinking about it, Rudy says, I knew a fat guy once, a couple of fat guys, really fat guys, when I was a kid. They were tubbies, my God. I don't remember their names. Fat, that's the only name this one kid had. We called him Fat, the kid who lived next door to me. He was a neighbor. The other kid came along later. His name was Wobbly. Everybody called him Wobbly except the teachers. Wobbly and Fat. Wish I had their pictures, Rudy says.

I can't think of anything to say, so we drink our tea and pretty soon I get up to go to bed. Rudy gets up too, turns off the TV, locks the front door, and begins his unbuttoning.

I get into bed and move clear over to the edge and lie there on my stomach. But right away, as soon as he turns off the light and gets into bed, Rudy begins. I turn on my back and relax some, though it is against my will. But here is the thing. When he gets on me, I suddenly feel I am fat. I feel I am terrifically fat, so fat that Rudy is a tiny thing and hardly there at all.

That's a funny story, Rita says, but I can see she doesn't know what to make of it.

I feel depressed. But I won't go into it with her. I've already told her too much.

She sits there waiting, her dainty fingers poking her hair.

Waiting for what? I'd like to know.

It is August.

My life is going to change. I feel it.

Permissions Acknowledgments

Contributors

Dorothy Allison has published two novels, *Bastard Out of Carolina*—a National Book Award finalist in 1992—and *Cavedweller*. She has also published a memoir, *Two or Three Things I Know For Sure*; an anthology of essays, *Skin: Talking about Sex, Class and Literature*; and a collection of poems, *The Women Who Hate Me*.

Frederick Busch has published twenty-one books of fiction, including *The Mutual Friend, Girls, The Night Inspector, Don't Tell Anyone*, and his most recent novel, *A Memory of War*. He has also authored a number of books on writing: *Letters to a Fiction Writer, A Dangerous Profession*, and *When People Publish*.

Peter Carey has twice received the Booker Prize, once for *Oscar and Lucinda* and again for *True History of the Kelly Gang*. His other honors include the Commonwealth Prize and the Miles Franklin Award.

Raymond Carver (1938–1988) was the author of ten books of short stories and poetry, including: *Where I'm Calling From*; *Cathedral*; *Will You Please Be Quiet, Please?*; *What We Talk about When We Talk about Love*; *Fires*; *Where Water Comes Together with Other Water*; and *Ultramarine*. Carver was the recipient of many writing awards including a Guggenheim Memorial Fellowship, a National Endowment for the Arts Fellowship, and the Mildred and Harold Strauss Livings stipend, and he was named to the American Academy of Arts and Letters.

Jack Coulehan teaches and practices medicine at the State University of New York at Stony Brook. His poems and essays appear frequently in medical and literary magazines. His books include *The Medical Interview: Mastering Skills for Clinical Practice, The Heavenly Ladder,* and a collection of poems, and he is the co-editor of *Blood & Bone: Poems by Physicians.*

Rebecca Curtis's short fiction has appeared in the *New Yorker, Harper's, Fence,* the *Gettysburg Review,* and several other distinguished journals. She teaches creative writing at the University of Kansas.

Junot Díaz was born in Santo Domingo, Dominican Republic. He is a graduate of Rutgers University and received his M.F.A. from Cornell University. He is the author of *Drown,* a collection of short stories, and his fiction has appeared in *Story,* the *New Yorker,* the *Paris Review,* and has been reprinted in *Best American Short Stories.*

Andre Dubus (1936–1999) was the author of nine works of fiction, including *Dancing After Hours* and *Adultery and Other Choices.* He also published two collections of essays: *Broken Vessels* and *Meditations from a Moveable Chair.* He received the PEN/Malamud Award, the Rea Award for excellence in short fiction, the Jean Stein Award from the American Academy of Arts and Letters, and fellowships from both the Guggenheim and MacArthur foundations.

Denise Duhamel is the author of numerous books and chapbooks of poetry; her most recent is *Queen for a Day: Selected and New Poems.* She was a winner of a National Endowment for the Arts Fellowship and her work has appeared in a number of anthologies, including several volumes of *The Best American Poetry.* Duhamel teaches creative writing and literature at Florida International University.

Stephen Dunn is the author of eleven collections of poetry and is a professor of creative writing at Richard Stockton College of New Jersey. He was awarded the 2000 Pulitzer Prize for Poetry for *Different Hours.*

Patricia Goedicke has published more than twelve collections of poetry, including *As Earth Begins to End, Invisible Horses, Paul Bunyan's Bearskin,* and *The Tongues We Speak.* She has received the Rockefeller Foundation Residency at its Villa Serbelloni, a National Endowment for the Arts Fellowship, a Pushcart Prize, the William Carlos Williams Prize, the 1987 Caroline Kizer Prize, the Hohenberg Award, and the 1992 Edward Stanley Award from *Prairie Schooner.*

J. L. Haddaway's poem "When Fat Girls Dream" originally appeared in *Hiram Poetry Review,* and was later reprinted in the anthology *The Tyranny of the Normal.*

Terrance Hayes, author of *Hip Logic* and *Muscular Music,* has received a Red Brick Review Award, a Whiting Writers Award, and a Kate Tufts Discovery Award for his poetry. He received his M.F.A. from the University of Pittsburgh and is an assistant professor of English at Carnegie Mellon University.

Conrad Hilberry, Professor Emeritus at Kalamazoo College, has published five volumes of poems and four chapbooks, including *Player Piano* and *Taking Notes on Nature's Wild Inventions,* the 1990 winner of the Iowa Prize. Hilberry has been a recipient of fellowships from the National Endowment for the Arts, the Chapelbrook Foundation, the MacDowell Colony, the Virginia Center for the Creative Arts, and the Breadloaf Writers' Conference.

Pam Houston is the author of two collections of linked short stories, *Cowboys are My Weakness* and *Waltzing the Cat,* and a collection of autobiographical essays, *A Little More about Me.* Houston also edited *Women on Hunting: Essays, Fiction, and Poetry,* and wrote the text for *Men Before Ten A.M.,* a book of photographs by the French photographer Veronique Vial. She is an associate professor in the writing program at University of California Davis.

Donna Jarrell, the co-editor of *What Are You Looking At?,* earned a B.A. in psychology and creative writing at Case Western Reserve

University and an M.F.A. in creative writing at Ohio State University. Her fiction has won the Kennedy Prize and has appeared in the anthology, *The Answer My Friend: Stories by the People Who Sell Them.*

Allison Joseph is the author of *What Keeps Us Here, Soul Train, In Every Seam,* and *Imitation of Life.* A fifth volume of poetry, *Worldly Pleasures,* won the Word Press Poetry Contest, and is forthcoming in 2004. Joseph lives in Carbondale, Illinois, where she teaches at Southern Illinois University.

Jill McCorkle has written five novels: *The Cheer Leader, Tending to Virginia, Ferris Beach,* and *Carolina Moon,* and two collections of short stories, *Final Vinyl Days* and *Crash Diet,* which won the New England Booksellers Award for Fiction in 1993. Her short fiction and articles have been published in both literary and popular magazines, including the *Atlantic Monthly, Cosmopolitan,* and *Ladies' Home Journal.*

Erin McGraw is the author of *Lies of the Saints* and *Bodies at Sea.* A new collection of stories, *Appearance of Scandal,* is forthcoming in 2004. Her stories and essays have appeared in the *Atlantic Monthly, Story,* the *Gettysburg Review,* the *Southern Review,* and other magazines. She teaches at Ohio State University.

Wesley McNair is the author of five collections of poetry, the last four of which have been published by David R. Godine. He is also the author of *Mapping the Heart,* a volume of essays on place and poetry. He has been the recipient of many awards, including two National Endowment of the Arts fellowships, the Eunice Tietjens Prize from *Poetry* magazine, and grants from the Fulbright and Guggenheim foundations.

Katherine Riegel received her M.F.A. from the University of Iowa Writers' Workshop. Her poetry and essays have appeared in numerous publications, including the *Chicago Tribune, Crazyhorse,* the *Gettysburg Review,* and *Hayden's Ferry Review.*

Vern Rutsala has published nine books, four chapbooks, and more than seven hundred poems in literary reviews and anthologies. He has won numerous prizes, including a Pushcart Prize, as well as fellowships from the Guggenheim Foundation and the National Endowment for the Arts. He received the Juniper Prize for his book *Little Known Sports*. He is a professor of English at Lewis & Clark College.

George Saunders has published two collections of stories, *Pastoralia* and *CivilWarLand in Bad Decline,* and a children's story, *The Very Persistent Gappers of Frip*. His fiction has appeared in the *New Yorker, Harper's, Story,* and many other publications. He won the National Magazine Award in 1994 for his story "The 400-Pound CEO."

Cathy Smith-Bowers is the author of two full-length volumes of poetry: *The Love that Ended Yesterday in Texas* and *Traveling in Time of Danger*. Her poems have appeared in nearly forty journals, including the *Atlantic Monthly* and the *Southern Review*.

Sharon Solwitz is the author of *Blood and Milk* and *Bloody Mary*. Her short stories, published in such magazines as *TriQuarterly, Mademoiselle,* and *Ploughshares,* have won numerous awards, including the Pushcart Prize, the Katherine Anne Porter Prize, and grants from the Illinois Arts Council. She teaches fiction at Purdue University in Lafayette, Indiana.

Rhoda B. Stamell's stories have appeared in the *Boston Review* and the *Kenyon Review*. She has attended artists' colonies at Mac-Dowell, Ragdale, Virginia Center for the Creative Arts, Vermont Studio Center, and the Writers' Colony at Dairy Hollow. She was a resident at the Helen Wurlitzer Foundation in Taos, New Mexico, and is working on a novel called *The Art of Ruin,* set in Detroit.

Rawdon Tomlinson's first full-length book of poetry, *Deep Red,* was published by the University of Central Florida's Contemporary Poets series in 1995. He lives in Denver and teaches at Arapaho Community College.

S. L. Wisenberg is the author of an essay collection, *Holocaust Girls: History, Memory & Other Obsessions,* and a short-story collection, *The Sweetheart Is In.* She is the creative nonfiction editor of *Another Chicago Magazine* and teaches in the Chicago area.

Tobias Wolff's books include *Old School, The Barracks Thief,* two memoirs, *This Boy's Life* and *In Pharaoh's Army*; and three collections of short stories, *In the Garden of the North American Martyrs, Back in the World,* and most recently, *The Night in Question.* His work appears regularly in the *New Yorker,* the *Atlantic, Harper's,* and other magazines.

Monica Wood is the author of the novels *My Only Story, Secret Language,* and *Ernie's Ark.* Her short stories have been widely published and have appeared in many fiction anthologies.